NICAEA

THE RISE OF THE
IMPERIAL CHURCH

NICAEA

THE RISE OF THE IMPERIAL CHURCH

BY

WILLIAM SPEIR

All rights reserved.
Published 2017 by Progressive Rising Phoenix Press, LLC
www.progressiverisingphoenix.com

ISBN: 978-1-946329-05-9

*

Printed in the U.S.A.

Cover Artwork by René Aigner, Munich, Germany
(http://www.rene-aigner.de). Used by permission of the artist.
© Copyright 2016 René Aigner.

Book and Cover design by William Speir
Visit: http://www.williamspeir.com

Acknowledgments

I want to thank all of my loyal readers, without whom I would not enjoy the creative process of writing.

Thanks to Amanda Thrasher and Jannifer Powelson at Progressive Rising Phoenix Press for believing in my books.

Special thanks goes to my editors, critiquers, and beta readers for their valuable edits.

Deepest gratitude goes to my wife for giving me the freedom of pursuing my passion. She is truly the love of my life. I am also grateful for my family, without whom there would be no words worth writing.

To Betty Jacobs for teaching me that real history is a complex set of cause-and-effect relationships, not just cold dead facts.
To Dr. Stephen O. Glosecki for teaching me comparative religion between classes at UAB.
To Nancy Fischer for helping me understand the historical context of the passages in the King James Version of the Bible and for first explaining about the Council of Nicaea.
To Jean S. Hebenstreit for showing me The Way.

The four of you have had a profound impact on my life, and I miss you all very much.

AUTHOR'S NOTES

Arias of Baucalis is a fascinating historical figure. In all of my research, no one other than Judas Iscariot has been so vilified as has Arias. He has been called the anti-Christ and a heretic, possession of his writings was punishable by death, and he was considered to be so dangerous that he was exiled from the Roman Empire and then assassinated when the Emperor allowed him to return.

What was Arias' crime? Why did he deserve such harsh treatment by historians over the centuries? He disagreed with other priests and bishops on key points of theology – points that the Roman Emperor wanted to become part of the theology of the churches.

Arias and his supporters stood up against an attempt to usurp church doctrine and transform the churches into a tool of statecraft, rather than allow them to remain institutions of salvation. In the end, Arias couldn't withstand the might of the bishops in league with the Emperor. Because Arias lost the fight, and winners write the history books, Arias' viewpoints have been altered and ridiculed by theologians and historians.

This book looks at Arias in a different light. Was he a good man whose principles didn't allow him to go along with the Emperor and his supporters? Was he a sincere follower of the words and works of Jesus – a priest who wanted to preserve what he felt was the true religion of Christ? I believe that he was.

I have attempted to peel back the dogma and look at the central characters in the Arian controversy as real people, not as pious historical caricatures created by historians to delude the masses. I hope that I've been successful.

William Speir
June 2016

A Note on the Organization of the Early Churches:

The early Christian churches didn't have the same structure as today's religions. The early Christian churches, collectively, were a loose association of congregations that banded together for mutual interests and mutual protection (most congregations were under the constant threat of exposure and persecution at the hands of Rome and her provinces). The structure of the churches was based on service (serving the congregations, serving the acolytes, serving the priests, serving the bishops), not command or control. There was no "ruling" body (Pope, College of Cardinals, Apostolic Council, etc.).

Each church had a priest (or multiple priests if the congregation was large enough) and acolytes who were studying to become priests. Bishops were responsible for all churches in a specific geographic area, and they appointed priests and worked to ensure a level of consistency in the doctrine preached in the churches under their oversight. Five bishops (the bishops of Alexandria, Antioch, Constantinople/Byzantium, Jerusalem, and Rome) were the Patriarchs of the churches, and these senior theologians were responsible for appointing bishops, appointing their own successors, and settling theological disputes between the churches that the bishops couldn't handle. Patriarchs and bishops had influence over the churches, but no absolute authority.

A Note on Scriptural Quotations and References:

The scriptural quotes and references used throughout this book are from the King James Version of the Holy Bible. Punctuation and capitalization used in quotes from this version of the Bible are preserved as is. While not a perfect translation of the original source material, it is the one Bible version that, in my opinion, has the least slant toward any one religious doctrine.

A Note on Locations:

The names of many cities mentioned throughout the book are the names they had during the time of Emperor Constantine I's reign over the Roman Empire. The following gives their modern names:

Historic Name:	Modern Name:
Alexandria, Egypt	Alexandria, Egypt
Antioch, Greece	Antakya, Turkey
Arelate, Gaul	Arles, France
Barcino, Hispania	Barcelona, Spain
Baucalis, Egypt	Alexandria, Egypt
Byzantium (Constantinople)	Istanbul, Turkey
Carthago (Carthage)	Tunis, Tunisia
Córdoba, Hispania	Córdoba, Spain
Ephesus, Greece	Selçuk, Turkey
Gades, Hispania	Cádiz, Spain
Illyricum	Split, Croatia
Jerusalem, Judea	Jerusalem, Israel
Nicaea, Greece	İznik, Turkey
Ptolemais, Egypt	Al Manshah, Egypt
Rome	Rome, Italy
Thessalonika, Greece	Thessaloniki, Greece

INTRODUCTION

The history of the early Christian Church is often misunderstood. Many believe that the Church, its structure, and its doctrines were ordained by the Apostles under the leadership of Peter (Simon Bar-Jona) as the heir to Jesus' mission on earth. Nothing could be further from the truth.

For centuries after the crucifixion of Jesus, the Followers of The Way (as the early Christians called themselves) continued performing the healing works of Jesus and his disciples. They lived their lives, following the teaching of Jesus and the Apostles, while trying to avoid persecution and death at the hands of the Romans. They had only their faith to sustain them. Many were martyred for their beliefs.

To the Romans, Christians (a derogatory term that the Romans used for the Followers of The Way) were an infestation that needed to be wiped out. Because of the peaceful nature of the Followers of The Way, they were easily captured. The captives provided great sport in the arena as they were tortured, burned alive, or fed to hungry lions – all while being watched by the Romans, who shouted at their captives to call upon their God and save themselves.

Over time, many of the Followers of The Way either stopped performing healing works to avoid calling attention to themselves, or they found the discipline required to perform the healing works of Jesus too hard. They lost the ability to do the works of Jesus, and they were unable to teach others to do these works. Soon, the works of Jesus moved from practice to memory to legend. These Followers began to doubt that the healing works and other miracles had been performed by anyone other than Jesus and his Apostles. In their attempts to understand Jesus' ability to perform miracles, they reasoned that Jesus' abilities came not from an ability that lies within each true believer, but from an exclusively divine source. This conclusion evolved into a belief that Jesus must have been divine himself. This was the birth of the great schism between the early churches.

The faithful Followers of The Way continued performing the works of Jesus during this time, but an ever-growing number of the early Christians (as they now openly referred to themselves) followed only the words of Jesus – misinterpreted and misunderstood by the belief that Jesus was God on earth. The two factions within the early churches couldn't reach an agreement between the original theology of the churches and the new, revised theology being embraced by more and more Christians.

By the early 4th Century AD, two figures emerged as the champions of the two factions. Alexander of Alexandria, a believer in the divinity of Jesus, was the Bishop of Alexandria, making him one of the five Patriarchs of the churches along with the Bishops of Antioch, Constantinople, Jerusalem, and Rome. Arias, a priest from the church at Baucalis near Alexandria who had been considered for the position of Bishop of Alexandria, was a staunch believer in The Way. The two men argued constantly over which theology was correct, but both were unmovable from their beliefs.

Then, in the first half of the 4th Century AD, a number of things happened that would change the face of Christianity forever. Constantine I, the Emperor of the Roman Empire, successfully defeated his political rivals (by open warfare and by guile and treachery) and consolidated the rule of the Eastern and Western Empires under himself. His lifelong friend and confidant, Hosius of Córdoba (a Christian Bishop in Hispania), urged Constantine to end the persecution of Christians. In 313 AD, Constantine issued the Edict of Milan, allowing Christians to worship openly throughout the empire.

Constantine, then the absolute ruler of the Roman Empire, knew that his legions alone couldn't hold the empire together indefinitely. The legions' roles were to defend the empire from its enemies and to conquer new lands. Constantine wanted a way to unite the hearts and minds of his citizens, so he turned to his old friend Hosius for help. Hosius suggested making Christianity the state religion of the empire and using the churches to unite the citizens. Constantine agreed and directed Hosius to make it happen.

Only one thing stood in the way of Hosius' plan for the churches: the intractability of the two theological factions under Arias and Alexander. After a number of failed attempts to induce the two factions to reach common ground, Constantine grew restless. He needed a united Church to help him hold the empire together, and he needed it soon. So, in 325 AD, he invited the Christian Bishops to gather at his palace in Nicaea to decide once and for all what the one official theology of the churches would be.

This is the story of the men at the center of the controversy that led to the first Council of Nicaea, the debates between those who believed in The Way and those who believed in the divinity of Jesus, and the rise of a new Imperial Church created to serve the needs of the Roman Empire.

CHAPTER 1

As he entered his chamber, Arias immediately knew what the scroll on his chair was even before he saw the all-too-familiar wax seal in the center. *What does Alexander want this time?*

Arias glanced out the window on the far side of his chamber and noticed the messenger standing in the shade of a date palm tree. *He's waiting for my reply. Alexander's demands must be urgent if he wants my response sent back immediately.*

Arias picked up the scroll and sat in the chair, running a finger along the seal of the Patriarch of Alexandria stamped into the wax. The theological disagreement between Arias and Alexander had been going on for years, but recently, the tone of Alexander's epistles had become more like edicts rather than part of an ongoing discussion, and Arias wondered if it were still possible for the two men to engage in a polite, rational discussion of their differences.

Alexander was the Bishop of Alexandria, Egypt, making him one of the five Patriarchs of the churches devoted to Jesus Christ. Arias had been considered for the post, but he was passed over in favor of Alexander. Arias retained his post as the priest of the church in Baucalis, near where the Apostle Mark had been martyred, but his relationship with his superior grew more strained by the day.

Arias broke the seal on the scroll and unrolled the letter, feeling the rough texture of the paper in his hands and smelling the smoky scent of the charcoal pencil used to write the words. He immediately recognized the handwriting of Athanasius, Alexander's scribe and chief assistant. As he read Alexander's epistle, Arias wondered how someone could become one of the five Patriarchs with such a distorted view of theology.

Brother Arias,

It has come to my attention that you have once again ignored my instructions to alter your preaching and bring your public views on theology in line with what has been approved. Never forget that you serve your congregation at my pleasure. If you wish to retain your post, you will obey my instructions.

I am aware of your reservations regarding the Divine Trinity, but the Trinity is part of the accepted doctrine of the churches. Your position that the Father, the Son, and the Holy Spirit are separate and distinct entities is not in keeping with the doctrine approved by the Patriarchs of the churches. Further, your position that there is no scriptural basis for the concept of the Trinity is heresy and will not be tolerated.

You are commanded to obey my instructions, or you risk disciplinary action. My messenger has been told to wait for your response.

Alexander, Bishop
Patriarch of Alexandria

Arias leaned back in his chair and ran a hand through his shoulder-length, silver streaked hair. *This again! The Patriarchs have forgotten what the healing ministry of Jesus was all about. For centuries, the faithful Followers of The Way have healed the sick, raised the dead, and cast out disorders of the mind according to the teachings of our Master. These are not miracles performed only by a divine entity and his closest followers. These are natural occurrences that can be performed by anyone who studies the words and works of our Master. But because the Patriarchs have forgotten how to heal, they assume that the power to heal is divine and therefore that Jesus must have been a divine entity in order to wield that power. Their new theology is little better than pagan superstition.*

Arias glanced at window across the room and watched the messenger waiting outside. When the messenger turned toward the window, Arias recognized him – Athanasius. *Alexander sent his chief lackey to deliver the message and take back my reply. There's more going on here than I'm aware of.*

A soft knocking on his chamber door pulled his attention away from the window. "Enter," he said. Botherik, Arias' Goth servant, entered the chamber carrying a tall flagon of liquid.

"Refreshments, sir?" Botherik asked softly.

"Yes, thank you," Arias replied. As Botherik retrieved a cup from the table in the corner of the room and filled it with the liquid from the flagon, Arias asked, "Have you offered anything to our guest outside?"

"No, sir," Botherik replied, handing Arias the filled cup. "I wasn't sure if such courtesies were to be extended to *him*."

Arias hid a smile. Athanasius was well-known in Baucalis and disliked by all who served with Arias there. He had publically challenged Arias several times on behalf of Alexander, and his zeal for antagonizing Arias and his followers was a frequent topic of conversation.

"We must continue to practice charity toward those who need it," Arias reminded his servant. "Those who are impolite and speak with little or no respect have the greatest need for our compassion and good deeds. We cannot allow their manners to alter our duty to mankind as taught to us by our Master. Jesus taught us to love our enemies, bless them that curse us, do good to them that hate us, and pray for them which despitefully use us, and persecute us. And while I don't consider Athanasius an *enemy*, his demeanor toward us certainly cries out for our love. Please take him refreshments, and tell him that I'll have my reply to Alexander ready as soon as I'm able."

"Yes, Arias." Botherik nodded and left the chamber.

Arias stared at Athanasius, still standing in the shade one of the date palms that lined the courtyard outside Arias' chamber. Athanasius was a tall man with a pleasant face and curly dark hair. His features made him look Greek.

A moment later, Arias smiled when he saw Botherik bring Athanasius a cup and a plate of fruit. *We must never allow those who antagonize us to change who we are. Those who are the hardest to love are the ones we must love the most. And if it requires extra effort on our part to love them, it's because their need is greatest. This is an opportunity to demonstrate the love that* our Master showed to his persecutors. *If Jesus could forgive those who crucified him, I can certainly show forgiveness and love to Athanasius and Alexander.*

Arias put down the scroll on his desk and walked across the room to a cupboard where he kept his writing supplies. He selected a pencil and a blank scroll before returning to his chair. The chamber was not a large room – certainly smaller than the sanctuary where he preached his sermons to the faithful Followers of The Way but large enough to serve as Arias' bedroom, office, and a classroom for instructing his acolytes. The floor was made of stone tiles, covered in rugs, and the walls were ornately carved and painted wood – a gift from a long-forgotten patron to one of Arias' predecessors in gratitude for being healed of consumption through The Way. There were two windows – one faced the courtyard, and the other, on the adjacent wall, overlooked a small garden. The chamber was comfortable, but Arias preferred being in the company of the faithful – preaching, healing, and helping others learn The Way.

He sipped from his cup and then began writing his latest reply to his superior in Alexandria.

Brother Alexander,

I have received your latest epistle, and while your instructions are quite clear, I must once again decline to obey. I implore you to cease your support for this revisionist theology that can serve no purpose but to lead mankind farther and farther from The Way as given to us by our Master.

Since you specifically mention the Trinity, I will attempt to confine my reply to that theological issue. I am aware that the concept of a Divine Trinity is the latest doctrine change approved by the Patriarchs. However, there is no difference between the five Patriarchs declaring a man to be a god and the Roman Senate declaring that Julius, Augustus, and Livia were gods. Man cannot create God, and by declaring that the Father and the Son are the same entity – in direct contradiction to the gospels where Jesus denied that he was God and drew clear distinctions between himself and his Father – you and the other Patriarchs are attempting to do just that.

The writings of the prophets and the apostles, as well as the gospels, give us the names for God. Yahweh and Jehovah were the tribal name for the Hebrew God of Abraham. Adonai is the name used by some of the prophets as their concept of God grew to embrace the idea of one God over all of creation, not just the god of the Jews. Elohim is the name of God first introduced by the third prophet Isaiah as the God who created the heavens, earth, and man in his image and likeness. Now you and the other Patriarchs are attempting to add the name of Jesus of Nazareth, or Joshua Bar-Joseph, to the list of the names for God. But you are not prophets, and you are not apostles, so where does your authority come from to declare that our Master is a god?

Arias leaned back and closed his eyes, thinking about how he wanted to word the next part of the letter. Then he took a sip from the cup and started writing again.

For years, I have endured listening to you and other bishops and priests misinterpret the scriptures. Jesus' statement that "I and my father are one" is NOT stating that the Father and the Son are one entity, but that the Father and the Son are of one mind – acting in concert with each other, yet distinct and separate persons. Our Master's failure to deny that he is God on earth to the priests is also mistakenly seen as proof that he is, indeed God. As one of your acolytes put it, "Jesus is God, but he didn't want anyone to know that he is God, so he denied that he is God to some and refused to answer the question to others. This is proof that he IS God because his denial is what you'd expect from the true God in disguise on earth." What utter rubbish! For every verse of scripture you point to that lends evidence to your position that Jesus is God, I can point to twenty others that show the opposite.

Even you must acknowledge our Master's assertion: "I am the way, the truth, and the life." I also believe that you preach the infallibility of God. But if Jesus lied to his disciples and the priests about being God, then he is a liar. How can a liar be infallible? If our Master were willing to admit that he was the Messiah and the Son of God, why would he deny being God if he were, in fact, God? If Jesus lied about his divinity, what else did he lie about? And if he were God, how could he die on the cross? You cannot have it both ways. Either God is infallible or he is a liar. If he is infallible, then Jesus is NOT God; if he is a liar, then he is fallible, the gospels are false, and our faith is also false.

Botherik quietly entered the chamber, trying not to disturb Arias. The servant placed a plate of food on a small table beside Arias' desk and then withdrew quickly, closing the door gently behind him. Arias continued writing.

The concept of the Divine Trinity being three facets of a single entity is supported neither by scripture nor by rational thought. For more than two hundred years, the church here in Baucalis has faithfully followed The Way as taught by our Master. The Way has existed for nearly three hundred years – ever since our Master walked on this earth – and it has been practiced since the early disciples first began spreading the word by preaching the gospel beyond the borders of the Judean Province. I will not abandon The Way in favor of this new revisionist theology that you and the other Patriarchs are insisting upon, because you have no authority to misinterpret scripture, based on your own misunderstanding, and call it our new doctrine. I will continue to preach what I have always preached, and I will continue to demonstrate The Way as I have always demonstrated it, no matter how you and the other Patriarchs choose to change the theology of the churches. There have been many Patriarchs in the past, and there will be many more in the future, but The Way is always The Way, and I will not deviate from the words and works of our Master simply to suit your demands.

Arias, Priest Presbyter
Church of Baucalis

Arias put down his pencil and re-read the letter. Satisfied, he rolled the scroll and tied a ribbon around it to keep it closed. Then he stood. Looking through the window, he saw Athanasius sitting on the ground with his back against the date palm tree. *Time for him to return to Alexander.*

Arias left the chamber and exited the building through the archway that led to the small garden. When he reached the courtyard, Athanasius saw him and got to his feet.

"Peace to you, Brother Athanasius," Arias said formally as he approached the man. "Does Alexander have no other messengers that he can use for such errands?"

"Peace to you as well, Arias," Athanasius replied with a curt nod. "I do Alexander's bidding, as should you." Seeing the scroll in Arias' hand, Athanasius added. "Is that your reply to Alexander's letter?"

Arias nodded and handed the scroll to Athanasius. Arias was of lean build, and Athanasius appeared to be more athletic. Athanasius used his different in size to appear intimidating, which only amused Arias.

Athanasius placed the scroll in the leather pouch that hung from a strap around his neck. "Will you end this contention with the Patriarchs and finally give in to their demands?" he asked.

Arias smiled thinly. "I am a faithful Follower of The Way, Athanasius. I won't deny my faith, no matter what threats are made against me. The Apostle Peter denied being a disciple of Jesus out of fear of what the Judeans would do to him. I'm not afraid of what the Patriarchs will do to me. When it's my time to stand before God and answer for my life, I don't intend to be counted with Peter. My intention is to be counted with John, the Obedient Apostle. I obey our Master, Jesus; and in matters of theology, I acknowledge no other authority."

"Peter is the rock upon which our churches are built," Athanasius reminded Arias.

"Peter's declaration of Jesus as the son of God is the rock upon which our churches are built," Arias corrected him, "not Peter the man. Our Master would never build his church on the shoulders of a man who had denied him three times in the days leading up to the crucifixion. No structure could survive a foundation that weak."

"You're a fool, Arias," Athanasius said, bending down to pick up the empty cup and plate. "You have no concept of what's happening within the other churches. It's not wise to stand against the Patriarchs."

"If the three Hebrew boys survived being thrown into the fiery furnace and the Apostle John survived being boiled in a pot of oil through their faith in and reliance upon God, surely I can survive the superstitious ignorance and animosity of my fellow priests in the same way."

Athanasius shook his head and handed the empty cup and plate to Arias. "There's no reasoning with you, is there, Arias?"

"Reasoning is possible between two reasonable people, Athanasius. My position is reasonable because it's the same position held to by the priests of this church since its founding. Your position has no such foundation, so which of us is being reasonable?"

"There's more going on here than a simple theological disagreement, Arias." Athanasius turned to leave. "You may find that losing your church here is the least of the fates that await you if you don't curb your tongue and start preaching as instructed by the Patriarchs. The heresy that you and your supporters are preaching and teaching will not be tolerated. Keep that in mind."

"Oh, I promise to keep that in mind, *Brother* Athanasius," Arias said as the young man strode out of the courtyard to his waiting horse. Arias stood motionless as Athanasius mounted and rode off. The wind caught the cloud of dust kicked up by the horse's hooves and blew it away from the courtyard.

Arias turned and saw Andrew, Barnabas, and Euric waiting for him across the courtyard on the edge of the garden. He walked over to his three acolytes, who bowed to him as he approached.

"Was that Athanasius?" Andrew asked.

Arias nodded.

"What did *he* want?" Barnabas asked as they followed Arias through the garden. Both Andrew and Barnabas were Greek, but they had lived in Egypt since they were children.

"What he always wants," Euric said with his heavy accent. His straw-colored hair fluttered in the breeze. "He's Alexander's lackey and takes pleasure acting like the voice of the Bishop."

Like Botherik, Euric was a Goth. Two years earlier, Euric had written to Arias, asking for an opportunity to learn from the priest. When Arias accepted Euric as an acolyte, the young Goth left his home and traveled south.

"Be kind, Euric," Arias said, amused. "Always be kind to others. Your rewards come not from those you help but from heaven. If you fail to help others – even to show them kindness when they're not present – then you forfeit heaven's rewards. Love is the way. Never forget that."

"Yes, Arias," Euric said.

"But what *did* he want?" Barnabas repeated.

"To demand that I preach the Divine Trinity instead of The Way, and to make threats of what will happen to me if I don't," Arias replied as he led his acolytes to his chamber.

"The same as the last time he was here?" Andrew asked.

Arias nodded. "And the time before that, and the time before that."

"And what will you do?" Euric asked.

"I'll be a faithful Follower of The Way," Arias replied, sitting down and gesturing for his three acolytes to sit on the bench facing his desk.

Arias spent the next two hours teaching his acolytes in The Way, emphasizing the healing ministry of Jesus and the Apostles. Botherik entered the chamber once the acolytes had left. He removed the remnants of the food that he had brought in earlier, and when he saw Arias take fresh scrolls from the cupboard, he lit several candles to provide extra light.

Late that afternoon, as the sunset filled the chamber with shades of red and orange, Arias sat at his desk, busy writing letters to the Bishops who still faithfully followed The Way and stood with Arias against the attempts to revise the gospels. *Athanasius is right. There's more going on here than a simple disagreement over theology. Alexander has never been tolerant of my views, but he's never threatened me before. Perhaps the others have heard something. We need to be watchful. For over two hundred years, we were hunted down by the Romans. In the 20 years since the*

Edict of Milan allowed us to worship openly, the doctrine of the churches has been altered, leading us away from the true faith. If The Way is going to survive, we need to know who's behind these alterations and why it's happening.

He finished the last letter and tied the scroll closed. He looked at the small stack of scrolls on the edge of his desk. The names of the other recipients were visible on the outside of each scroll: Zphyrius, Dathes, Secundus of Ptolemais, Theonus of Marmarica, Eusebius of Nicomedia, Maris of Chalcedon, Theognus of Nicaea, Paulinus of Tyrus, Actius of Lydda, and Menophantus of Ephesus.

Arias wrote the name of the recipient on the outside of the last scroll – Hosius of Hispania – and placed the scroll on top of the other scrolls.

I'll have Euric take these letters to the harbor and arrange for messengers to deliver them. He's a resourceful lad; I wouldn't be surprised if he found a way to have Hosius' letter carried by Imperial Courier. Hopefully I'll hear from Hosius before the next epistle from Alexander arrives. He's always given good advice about how to deal with Alexander. I don't know what I'd do without his support and friendship.

Arias summoned Euric and gave him the letters and money to pay for the messengers. After Euric had left the chamber with his instructions, Arias sat down, blew out the candle on his desk, and looked out the window facing the courtyard, watching the colors of the sky change as the sun set in the west.

The sun sat low on the horizon by the time Athanasius was finally escorted into Alexander's chamber. It was a short distance from the church of Baucalis to Alexandria, and Athanasius had returned with Arias' reply several hours earlier. But Alexander had been tied up in meetings all afternoon and couldn't be disturbed. Athanasius waited outside Alexander's chamber until the bishop was ready to receive him.

Once inside, Athanasius handed Alexander the scroll from Arias. "Arias' reply, sir."

Alexander looked up at Athanasius. "Were you received well?"

"Yes, but I don't think that your letter was."

Alexander snorted in disgust and untied the scroll. The bishop was a robust man who was several years older than Arias and Athanasius, but his skin was pale and burned easily in the sun. He read the letter while Athanasius waited motionless on the other side of the desk.

After he finished reading Arias' letter, Alexander slammed the scroll onto his desk. "What arrogance! What defiance! Does he alone think he's the final word on the truth? I give him instructions, and he digs his heels in even deeper. He presumes to lecture me on theology when I'm his superior, a bishop, and one of the five Patriarchs of the churches! Who does he think he is?"

Alexander's pale face grew red with anger. After a few moments, he calmed down. "Do you still have a copy of the original letter that I sent to Arias?" he asked.

Athanasius nodded. He walked over to a cupboard against the wall, pulled out a scroll from one of the slots, and brought it back to Alexander.

"Good," Alexander said, taking the scroll from Athanasius. "I need to send it and this reply to Hosius in Hispania. I need his counsel on how to handle this situation. Go arrange for a messenger while I write a quick letter to Hosius. I want this on its way before morning."

"Allow me to take the messages to Hosius," Athanasius offered.

"You have other duties," Alexander reminded his chief priest.

"I know, but do you want to entrust something this important to a simple messenger? Besides, I can give Hosius a first-hand account of my conversation with Arias.

Alexander stared at Athanasius, thinking about the young man's suggestion.

"And what if Hosius isn't at his church in Córdoba?" Athanasius continued. "A simple messenger would either wait for Hosius to return, or he'd come back here with the messages undelivered. I could go and find Hosius; I know where to look."

Alexander nodded. "Very well. Gather what supplies and clothing you'll need, and be back here quickly."

"Yes, sir," Athanasius said happily as he left the chamber.

Alexander wrote a quick note to Hosius. He then put the note, the copy of the letter he had sent to Arias, and Arias' reply, into a leather pouch. He looped a piece of leather through the opening of the pouch and knotted it to keep the pouch sealed until it reached Hosius.

Athanasius returned a few moments later. Alexander handed the pouch to Athanasius, along with payment and money to cover expenses for the journey from Alexandria to Hispania. "Find Hosius, and return as soon as you're able." Alexander instructed.

Athanasius bowed and left the chamber, closing the door behind him.

Alexander stared at the empty dish on his desk. *What am I going to do about Arias? I hope Hosius can guide me through this. Arias and his followers are few in numbers but strong in their faith. The last thing we need is for a mere priest to become a beacon for the discontented. We need unity if the churches are going to grow and take their rightful place in the world. This disagreement is doing nothing but giving our enemies fuel to pour on our funeral pyre. It must end.*

Alexander shook his head. *Don't Arias and his followers understand that their heresy will condemn them in the afterlife? By denying that Jesus is God, they condemn themselves to damnation. Is that what they want?*

Alexander stood and walked across the room to the window. He looked out over the city as the torches cast their light along the streets under the starlit sky above. *Hosius will know what to do. He always does.*

CHAPTER 2

Emperor Constantine was now the undisputed ruler of the entire Roman Empire. His legions had defeated the superior forces of Licinius, the last remaining challenger to the Imperial Throne, and had broken the defenses around Byzantium. Unlike the other challengers to the Imperial Throne – Galerius, Maximinus, and Maxentius – Licinius had surrendered his legions, and Constantine spared the life of his former rival. Then the Emperor and his legions marched triumphantly into Byzantium.

Constantine looked out over the conquered city from the window of his temporary palace. The smell of smoke drifted from the southern quarter of the city, where the fighting had been the most intense. Most of the fires were out, but some buildings near the harbor still sat smoldering in the late morning breeze. *I love this city - even more than I love Rome. Now that it's mine, I'm going to rebuild it into the most glorious city in the empire – in the world! It will be the jewel of my reign; I'll make it my capital city. And I'll rename it to a name befitting its role as my capital: Constantinople.*

Constantine heard soldiers marching. Looking down to the street below, he saw that another one of his legions had arrived to strengthen the city garrison. Constantine returned the salute of the senior officer. *Licinius managed to raise an army larger than mine, but only because he left the empire's eastern border completely unguarded. I'll have to move quickly to restore order. I can't afford rebellion or invasion in my eastern provinces.*

Constantine watched the legion march out of sight through the wisps of smoke that floated over the street. *My legionnaires are the best in the world, but the empire's too large to be held by legions alone. I need my legions to fight wars and protect my borders, not to police the provinces in case of rebellion. I need another way to keep the citizens in line. I need the church that Hosius promised me. I don't believe in his god, but there's nothing new about using religion as a tool of statecraft – it's been done since the dawn of time. My legions can break armies, but religion is better suited to unite the hearts and minds of the people.*

The wind shifted, blowing smoke into Constantine's eyes. The Emperor turned away from the window and gestured for one of the ever-present servants to hand him a cup of wine. As he sipped it, he remembered when the legion he had just seen marching past his palace had opposed him in battle. It was twelve years earlier when he had fought against Maxentius near Milvian Bridge on the Tiber River. *They had me outnumbered five to one on that day. I knew that I couldn't win unless I had a way to shake their confidence. That's when I decided to march into battle carrying crosses. Maxentius and his legions knew immediately what it meant; no quarter would be given. I even had my legionnaires paint crosses on their shields. Maxentius' legions thought that I planned to crucify them all, and their spirit broke. Maxentius died trying to get away. And when I spared the lives of his surviving legionnaires, I turned enemies into loyal soldiers willing to follow me anywhere.*

Constantine's smile turned into a sneer as he took another sip of wine. *Later, my old friend Hosius came to me and begged me to let him tell everyone that I'd had a vision of the Christ on the eve of battle – that the crosses were to honor my newfound faith, rather than to serve as a threat to my enemies. Then he convinced me to allow Christians to worship openly and freely throughout Rome and the provinces. And in return, he promised that I'd get a church that I could use to help me control the empire.*

Well, I did my part, but where is my imperial church? Where is this religion that will serve my needs by controlling the people in ways that my legions can't? Hosius can't even get his churches to agree upon a single theology. How can they convert the empire to one religion when they can't agree on what that religion is? I'm tired of waiting. Hosius may be my oldest friend, but I'm Emperor. It's time for him to keep his end of the bargain.

Constantine shouted for the Captain of the Guard.

"You sent for me, My Emperor?" Imperial Guard Captain Titus Horatius Corvinus asked a few moments later when he arrived.

"Yes. Titus. Send two ships to Córdoba in Hispania and fetch Hosius, the Christian Bishop there. I need to see him. Bring him here."

"Yes, My Emperor," Titus acknowledged. He saluted and then left Constantine's chamber to carry out his orders.

I want my church, and I don't care what Hosius has to do to get it for me.

It was still several hours before dawn, and Athanasius couldn't believe the activity going on all around him. He knew that Alexandria was one of the busiest ports in the southern provinces of the Roman Empire, but ships were being unloaded and loaded by torchlight at breakneck speed.

For two days straight, Athanasius had been waiting outside of the Imperial Harbor Official's office to find out if there were any ships heading west that were still taking on passengers. He knew that there were no ships that could make the voyage all the way from Alexandria to Gades on the southwest coast of Hispania, so he searched for a ship heading to Carthago. From there, he could get a ship heading for Barcino in eastern Hispania. It would be easy to find a ship in Barcino that would take him to Gades. If all went well, he'd be in Córdoba in seventeen days… if only he could find passage on a ship heading from Alexandria to Carthago.

Athanasius was so busy watching the activity on the docks that he didn't hear his name being called. The Chief Assistant to the Imperial Harbor Official raised his lantern and touched Athanasius' shoulder to get his attention. "Athanasius? I've found you passage on a galley bound for Carthago. It's loading now and will be sailing soon. Follow me."

Athanasius grabbed the bag carrying his garments and supplies, checked to make sure that Alexander's letters were still around his neck, and followed the harbor official into the crowd of dockworkers, merchants, and people also seeking passage on outbound ships.

When they reached the merchant galley heading for Carthago, the harbor official had to shout to be heard over the noise of ships being loaded and unloaded. He introduced Athanasius to the ship's captain before disappearing back into the crowd. Athanasius paid the fare, and the captain escorted him to a small sleeping compartment near the rear of the ship. The compartment was just large enough to hold a cot and a bench, but Athanasius didn't mind. *I'm just glad to finally be on my way.* He dropped his bag onto the floor and lay down on the cot, falling asleep immediately.

When he awoke, Athanasius heard the sound of oars rhythmically hitting the water. *We must be at sea. I wonder how long we've been rowing west.*

A short while later, he went up on the deck and watched the shore slip past in the distance. From the angle of the sun, he decided that it must be near mid-day. There were few clouds in the sky, and the breeze felt good against his face.

Sailors were busy working all around him, and Athanasius stayed out of their way. He heard a drum beat coming from beneath the deck, and he watched the oars moving to its cadence.

He looked around the deck and noticed a few other passengers also trying to stay out of the way of the busy sailors. Toward the front of the ship, the cook was preparing the midday meal. Feeling hungry, he made his way forward to see what kind of food the cook was serving.

The meal consisted of salted fish, a mix of leeks and beans, a small wedge of cheese, and a hunk of bread with a distinctive barley taste. Athanasius ate it gratefully. Then he returned to his compartment to meditate.

It took nine days to reach Carthago, and other than a rain shower on the fifth day, the weather had been perfect throughout the entire voyage. The galley entered Carthago's harbor late in the afternoon. Hundreds of ships were anchored in the harbor, making it difficult to navigate through them. The smells of the harbor were pungent with spices and the sweat of the dockworkers. Athanasius disembarked as soon as the galley had been tied to the dock, and he immediately headed for the Imperial Harbor Official's office to find passage on a ship heading for Barcino.

It only took a day to find a galley bound for Barcino that still had room for a passenger. The trade route between Carthago and Barcino was one of the busiest, and Athanasius managed to book passage on a much larger ship than the one from Alexandria. His compartment was the same size as the one on the ship from Alexandria, and the food was no better, but the voyage only lasted a couple of days, so Athanasius didn't mind at all.

When he arrived in Barcino on the third morning of the voyage from Carthago, he quickly managed to arrange passage on a ship for Gades that would be leaving the next day before dawn.

It had been a long time since Athanasius had seen the southern coast of Hispania, and he spent most of the voyage on deck watching the coastline. *I remember Hosius explaining the history of southern Hispania when I was a boy, and I remember my first view of this coastline when he took me with him to Rome for the first time. I met Emperor Constantine on that trip. That was the first time that Hosius explained to me his plans for the churches. He was my first teacher, and I miss seeing him every day. I know that the reasons he sent me to serve Alexander are important, and even though I still serve Hosius, I'd rather be serving him in Córdoba.*

Three days later at mid-day, the galley rowed into the harbor at Gades. Athanasius could hardly contain his excitement to be back in the city again. The smells and sounds assaulted his senses, triggering happy memories from his youth. As much as he wanted to spend time walking along its all-too-familiar streets, he had messages to deliver to Córdoba. He walked past two Roman warships that were taking on supplies as he headed for the city. Once he had left the harbor area, he began looking for ground transportation to Hosius' church.

As Athanasius walked through the crowded streets at the base of the hill east of the harbor, he recognized the pucker from an old scar near the left ear of a man walking away from him. The man turned, and Athanasius saw his face. "Sebastian!" he called out.

The short, balding young man turned and noticed Athanasius. "Athanasius!" he called back, making his way through the crowd to his old friend. Hosius' acolyte and chief scribe grasped Athanasius by the wrists. "It's good to see you, my friend. What brings you to Gades?"

Athanasius held up the leather pouch hanging around his neck. "I have messages from Alexander to Hosius. I was about to hire a chariot or ox-cart to take me to Córdoba. Perhaps we can ride there together?"

Sebastian shook his head. "It's good that you arrived today. Hosius isn't in Córdoba; he's here in Gades. He received a summons to Byzantium by the Emperor. We leave in the morning."

"Then I'm glad that I arrived just in time," Athanasius said, surprised. "Can you take me to him? I have instructions to wait for his reply before returning to Alexandria."

"Sounds important," Sebastian noted. "Follow me. We're staying at an inn two streets over.

As they walked to the inn, Athanasius asked, "Why did the Emperor summon Hosius?"

"I have no idea," Sebastian replied. "Do you think Hosius tells me such things? All I know is that the Emperor sent two warships and some of his personal guards to make sure that Hosius comes as quickly as possible." Dropping his voice to a whisper, he added, "But I can guess what the summons is about."

Athanasius leaned forward, and Sebastian continued. "It's the Imperial Church. Constantine's impatient for a religion that he can use to control the people of the empire."

Athanasius nodded. *Hosius is playing a dangerous game with the churches and the Emperor, and I've had my part to play in that game. Hosius instructed me to make things worse between Alexander and Arias, and I've done my best to do that. When I'm serving as Alexander's scribe, I always make a copy of each letter to Arias for Alexander to keep. How would he react if he discovered that his copies don't match the letters that Arias actually receives? Would he forgive me, send me back to Hispania, or banish me from the churches altogether? One thing is for certain: he'd never trust me again. And now the Emperor is growing impatient. I wonder why Hosius wanted me to keep Alexander and Arias unable to reach an agreement.* "Emperors are dangerous to cross," Athanasius said aloud. "I wonder if Hosius has figured out how to get the churches to agree to the new theology."

"I don't know," Sebastian said. "But he'd better figure it out before we reach Byzantium."

They reached the inn a few moments later, and Athanasius saw an imperial guard blocking the entrance.

"Don't worry," Sebastian said to Athanasius as they approached the guard.

"State your business," the guard said to Athanasius.

"Athanasius, I'd like you to meet Imperial Guard Lucius Artorius Gemellus. Lucius, this is Athanasius. He has messages for Hosius from the Patriarch of Alexandria."

Lucius nodded curtly and allowed Athanasius and Sebastian to enter the inn.

The inn was a two story building along a narrow road that ran from the harbor to the base of the hills east of the city. Athanasius followed Sebastian through the large common room to a corridor that ran to the back of the inn. Sebastian knocked on the last door on the right.

The door opened, and Athanasius recognized Titurius, another one of Hosius' trusted acolytes. His close-cropped black hair and hawk-nose made the tall acolyte look sinister, but he was man with a tremendous love for life. "Athanasius! Welcome to Gades! Come in, come in. We had no idea you were coming."

"Thank you, Titurius." Athanasius and Sebastian entered the long room covered in rugs and thick wooden furniture.

Athanasius saw Hosius sitting next to the window at the far end of the room, reading a letter. The bishop had sandy hair and Celtic features, making him look more like a barbarian tribesmen that a Roman citizen. Hosius looked up when Athanasius entered the room and jumped to his feet, causing the pile of letters in his lap to fall onto the floor.

"Athanasius! You're a welcome sight. What brings you here?"

Athanasius and Hosius embraced. Athanasius then removed the leather pouch from around his neck and handed it to Hosius. "I have messages from Alexander. He's instructed me to wait for your reply."

Hosius took the pouch and smiled. Reaching down to pick up the letters he had dropped, he said, "I expected as much. I received Arias' letter three days ago – delivered by an imperial courier."

"I've heard that Arias' servant is clever, but I had no idea he was connected to the imperial couriers," Athanasius said. "It took me seventeen days to get here. The courier made good time!"

Hosius gestured for Athanasius to sit down in another chair near the window. Sebastian poured a cup of wine for Athanasius and refilled Hosius' cup. He and Titurius withdrew across the room so Athanasius and Hosius could speak in private.

"I hear that you've been summoned to Byzantium," Athanasius said as Hosius opened the leather pouch.

"Yes, Emperor Constantine wants to see me," Hosius said casually as he removed the contents of the pouch.

Athanasius sat quietly as Hosius read Alexander's letters and the reply from Arias. Hosius shook his head several times but didn't say anything until he had read each letter twice.

Hosius looked up at Athanasius, smiling. "May I assume that the letter here from Alexander to Arias is not the same letter that Arias received?"

Athanasius grinned and nodded.

"You've done well, Athanasius. I think it's safe to say that neither Alexander nor Arias will ever be able to reach agreement on points of theology."

"That much is certain," Athanasius agreed. "But won't that make the Emperor angry? I hear that he's impatient for the Imperial Church to be handed over to him."

Hosius glanced across the room at his acolytes. "Sebastian talks too much." Looking back to Athanasius, he continued, "But you're right. Constantine wants his church, and he wants it soon."

"But instead of getting the two theological factions led by Alexander and Arias to come to an agreement, we've been making things worse between them."

Hosius smiled. "Exactly."

"I don't understand. Why?" Athanasius asked.

"Because I need the Emperor to step in and personally resolve the disagreement. What's more, I need the churches to practically *beg* the Emperor to step in. That way the Imperial Church can be crafted as Constantine wants it with the full blessing of the Patriarchs and the churches."

Athanasius nodded. "So your plan is to make Constantine the head of the Imperial Church?"

"The *secular* head of the Imperial Church, yes."

"And who will be the spiritual head of the Imperial Church?"

Hosius waved his hand in the air. "Who knows? For now it will be the Patriarchs, but who knows what the future will bring?"

Athanasius sipped his wine. "What message do you want me to take back to Alexander?"

Hosius thought about this for a moment. "I'm not sure. I need to craft a reply for Arias as well, and what I tell them depends on how my meetings go with the Emperor. You should come with me to Byzantium. I'll meet with Constantine, and then I'll craft a reply for you to take back. It's a twenty day voyage from here to Byzantium, and then it's only a nine day voyage from there to Alexandria. You'll be home in just over a month. Surely Alexander can spare you for that long."

Athanasius' excitement at the prospect of traveling again with Hosius filled his mind with memories of his first voyage to Rome. *I'd like to know Hosius' plans for how the Imperial Church will do what the Emperor needs it to do. Besides, I've never been to Byzantium before, and I've always wanted to go.*

Before Athanasius could respond, Hosius called to his two acolytes across the room. "Tell Lucius that there will be another passenger on the voyage. And then find somewhere for Athanasius to sleep. It's a long journey to Byzantium, and we leave before dawn.

CHAPTER 3

Arias sat at his desk, reading his well-worn copy of the Gospel of John. It was his favorite text – the only one of the gospels written by an apostle of Jesus. Arias believed that its eyewitness account of Jesus' ministry on earth had greater clarity than the other gospels.

As he read, several verses stood out to him.

"God is a spirit; and they that worship him must worship him in spirit and in truth,"

"Verily, verily, I say unto you, The Son can do nothing of himself, but what he seeth the Father do: for what things soever he doeth, these also doeth the Son likewise."

"I can of mine own self do nothing: as I hear, I judge: and my judgment is just; because I seek not mine own will, but the will of the Father which hath sent me."

"A new commandment I give unto you, That ye love one another; as I have loved you, that ye also love one another. By this shall all men know that ye are my disciples, if ye have love one to another."

"Verily, verily, I say unto you, He that believeth on me, the works that I do shall he do also; and greater works than these shall he do; because I go unto my Father."

"This is my commandment, That ye love one another, as I have loved you. Greater love hath no man than this, that a man lay down his life for his friends."

"If the world hate you, ye know that it hated me before it hated you."

Arias put down the scroll and meditated on the meanings of the passages he had read. It was more than an hour before he opened his eyes and looked around his chamber, feeling the peace of God surrounding and filling him. He felt at one with all living things. *If only all men could feel as I feel right now.*

He noticed a stack of letters on the edge of his desk. *My letter should have reached Hosius by now. I look forward to his reply. I'll never see Alexander as an enemy, but sometimes I wonder if Alexander views me in the same way that the Pharisees viewed our Master.*

As he thought about his disagreements with Alexander, a rapid knocking on his door interrupted him. "Enter."

His acolyte Andrew entered the chamber. "Arias, come quick. A boy has been hit by a chariot. The physician told his parents that he doesn't have long to live."

Arias leapt to his feet and followed Andrew into the town.

When they reached the house of the child, Arias turned to Andrew. "When we go inside, I want you to take the parents and anyone else who's there outside so I can be alone with the lad."

"Yes, Arias," Andrew responded.

Arias entered the house. The front room was empty. Arias announced himself but heard no response. Arias crossed the front room, looking for any signs of the house's occupants. He heard a woman crying, and he and Andrew followed the sound to a room at the rear of the house. When he reached the room, he saw several people standing or kneeling around the boy's bed. The lad was pale and the bedding blood-soaked.

Andrew ushered everyone out of the room as Arias approached the lad and sat down on the edge of the bed. Andrew returned a few moments later and stood in the doorway so no one could enter.

Arias closed his eyes and bowed his head in silent communion with God. After a short while, he placed a hand on the lad's chest. At first, nothing happened. Then the child began to moan – softly at first, and then louder. Arias never moved his hand from the lad's chest. The color returned to the child's face. A moment later, his eyes opened.

"What happened to me?" the lad asked, looking confused.

"Nothing, my boy," Arias answered kindly, removing his hand from the boy's chest and helping him sit up. "You are made in God's image, and no accident can change that fact."

Arias turned toward Andrew, who called for the parents. When the parents entered the room, they were astonished to see their son sitting up and smiling.

"Your son is fine," Arias said, getting to his feet.

"How can we thank you, Arias?" the lad's father asked as the mother hugged her son. Tears of gratitude were evident on the father's cheeks.

"No need," Arias replied softly. Then he added, "But tell no one what has happened here. The healing of your son is a gift from God, and it's God who deserves your thanks."

The father nodded and then joined his wife next to their son. Arias motioned to Andrew, and the two men left the house to return to the church.

As they walked away from the house, Andrew asked, "Why didn't you want the father to say anything about what happened?"

"Because healings like this are no longer commonplace. I don't want anyone looking at the child differently, nor do I want the parents ridiculed by those who don't believe in the power of God to heal the sick and injured. And there is no need to keep talking about the accident. The boy is healed, and talking about what may or may not have happened will not make the healing any more or less real. Besides, I don't want anyone saying that the healing came about because of me. I didn't *do* anything special. I knew that the boy was perfect, as God created him, and that no supposed accident could ever change that. I helped the child see the truth, and the truth set him free."

"I don't understand," Andrew said.

"Then I'll explain it to you," Arias said, kindly. "Do you remember reading the first part of the book of Genesis?"

"Yes."

"What does it say about the creation of man?"

"That God created man in his own image, in the image of God created he him; male and female created he them. And God blessed them. And God saw everything that he had made, and, behold, it was very good."

"That's right. Now in the Gospel of John, it says that 'God is a spirit.' If God is a spirit, then his image and likeness must also be spiritual, right?"

"Yes."

"That's the true nature of man: he is spiritual, and he is the image and likeness of God. The image and likeness of God can't have something that God can't have, can it?"

"No," Andrew replied.

"And if God is a spirit, and He's all-powerful, then He can't have an accident, can He?"

"No."

"So then how can man, who is spiritual and is the image and likeness of God, have an accident?"

"I don't know," Andrew said.

"He can't," Arias stated. "If God made man in his image and likeness, and God cannot have an accident, then man cannot have an accident either. And if man is spiritual because he is the image and likeness of spirit, then no earthly condition can have any effect on man as God's creation, can he?"

"I guess not," Andrew replied slowly.

"Man – man's true being – is the image and likeness of God. That's what the scriptures tell us. No matter what the situation appears to be, it doesn't change the true nature of man. Jesus didn't heal by accepting the situation and then trying to change it; he healed by never acknowledging or accepting the situation in the first place. He saw man as God sees man – perfect, indestructible, and spiritual – the image and likeness of God. And once Jesus had that perfect view of man clearly in his thoughts, all that remained was to have the patient see himself in the same way. The healing takes place in thought, and its manifestation in the body follows."

"So all healing takes place in our thinking?" Andrew asked.

"Yes!" Arias replied. "Once you've cast out all thoughts about the patient other than his absolute perfection as a spiritual child of God, you can heal the patient by having the patient see themselves as you see them – as God sees them. You're not trying to change the body as a result of a disease or accident; you're seeing that no disease or accident can have any effect on a child of

God. If God can't experience it, then neither can man. That's the standpoint for all healings."

"Can you heal an enemy?" Andrew asked.

"Of course, as soon as you stop seeing him as an enemy. If he's a child of God and everything God made is good, can he also be an enemy?"

"No," Andrew replied. Then he asked, "Is that how you're able to remain so calm when Alexander attacks you and your beliefs?"

"Yes. I never stop seeing him as a beloved child of God. If I ever saw him as anything else, then *I'd* be the one needing healing because *I'd* be in error."

"What about raising the dead?" Andrew asked.

"It's the same thing," Arias replied. "Think of Lazarus. His family and friends thought that he had been dead for days, and yet Jesus raised him from the dead. Jesus told his followers that Lazarus was sleeping and that he was going to wake him up. Jesus never saw Lazarus as a dead man that needed to be restored to life; he saw Lazarus as a child of God over whom death had no power. Jesus came to earth to show us how to overcome death, to prove that it is powerless, and to prove that life is eternal. He raised the dead, and he raised himself from the dead. What greater proof is there that man is indestructible in God's kingdom? As long as we see that, as long as we understand that, then no earthly condition can have power over us or over anyone else. This is the truth that heals every ill, accident, or situation."

"It sounds too easy," Andrew noted.

"I know," Arias said. "It may sound easy, but it requires great discipline. Some aren't able, or are simply unwilling, to be that disciplined. That's why so many of the churches have abandoned their healing missions and why they now attack those of us who still practice healing as our Master taught us."

The two men continued walking back to the church in silence. As they passed by the marketplace in the center of town, Arias thought back to what he had just taught Andrew. *Why is it that the Patriarchs don't appreciate the simplicity of healing through the power of God as our Master taught us? Why is it that they no longer believe healing is possible, that the healing works of The Way were only practiced by Jesus and the Apostles? Jesus said: "He that believeth on me, the works that I do shall he do also; and greater works than these shall he do; because I go unto my Father." Why can't the Patriarchs and their bishops acknowledge this? I hope Hosius can give me guidance. If the churches turn their back on our healing mission, then what remains of true faith and our duty to our Master? What will we become without the words and works of our Master as the cornerstone of our religion?*

Athanasius woke early the next morning, feeling excited about the journey ahead. Unable to sleep any longer, he rose quietly and dressed, trying not to wake Sebastian and Titurius, who were asleep in the same room. Athanasius made sure that all his belongings were in his bag, and then he left the room.

As he closed the door behind him, he saw lights coming from underneath Hosius' door. He walked across the hall and knocked softly in case Hosius was still asleep.

"Come in," he heard Hosius shout.

Athanasius opened the door and stepped inside. "I hope I'm not disturbing you. I saw light under your door and wanted to see if you needed anything."

Hosius smiled. "Just your company, Athanasius," he said, gesturing for the young man to sit beside him at the table in the center of the room. Hosius filled an empty cup with water from a small flagon in the center of the table and placed it in front of Athanasius. Then he pushed a dish of fruit and dried venison closer to the young priest.

"You'd better eat something. We'll be heading for the harbor within the hour."

Just as Hosius said that, Athanasius heard banging on the doors in the hallway. "Everyone wake up," the voice of the Imperial Guard Lucius Artorius Gemellus shouted. "We leave in half an hour. Anyone not ready will be left behind."

There was a knock on Hosius' door, and Lucius walked in before Hosius could respond. "Oh, good. You're up," the Imperial Guard said. "You can't be left behind."

"I'll be ready to leave when you need me to be," Hosius stated pleasantly.

"I'll come fetch you when it's time," Lucius said, closing the door. Athanasius heard the Guard's footsteps heading back toward the common room.

"Isn't that nice of him?" Hosius asked blandly after Lucius had left.

Athanasius laughed. "He's just doing his job."

"I know," Hosius admitted. "This isn't my first imperial summons, although I admit that Constantine has never before sent so many guards to make sure that I obeyed."

A moment later, Sebastian and Titurius entered the room to finish packing Hosius' traveling chests. Once the chests were packed, they carried them to the common room for the guards to load onto the ox-carts waiting outside.

When Lucius returned, the Imperial Guard escorted Hosius through the inn to the ox-carts, followed by Athanasius, Sebastian, and Titurius. They climbed into the carts, and soon the caravan of ox-carts headed down the narrow street to the harbor.

Even though it was more than an hour until sunrise, the air was already warm and humid. Athanasius gripped the cart railings tightly as the carts bumped and swayed. The wheels of the ox-carts rattled down the brick-paved street, and the buildings on either side of the street echoed and amplified the sound. *It's a wonder everyone in the city isn't awake already from the racket.*

The two warships that Athanasius had passed the day before were illuminated with torchlight. The sailors, wearing the uniforms of the Imperial Navy, quickly unloaded the ox-carts and escorted the passengers to their compartments. Hosius was given one of the cabins reserved for high-ranking officials, but Athanasius's compartment, one deck below Hosius', was barely larger than the ones provided to him on his journey from Alexandria.

Athanasius placed his bag on the cot and returned to the deck. He had seen sailors operate merchant galleys before, but he'd never seen sailors of the Imperial Navy in action.

Light on the eastern horizon was just beginning to appear as the warships rowed out of the harbor and turned southeast. The sky looked like fire burning in the distance, which grew as the sun climbed higher. Athanasius chewed on a piece of dried boar meat as the galley cut through the water like a knife. *No merchant ship I've ever been on sails this smoothly.*

According to the captain of the warship, it would take 20 days to reach Byzantium. The galleys would be making several stops along the way for supplies: Barcino in eastern Hispania, Arelate in Gaul, Rome, and Thessalonika in Greece. Athanasius was particularly interested in seeing Thessalonika since the Apostle Paul had written epistles to the churches there, but he doubted that the Captain would give him time to explore the city. *The Emperor's summons is more important than the curiosity of a simple priest.*

Athanasius remained on deck until Gades had disappeared behind them and the sun was fully visible above the horizon. Then he returned to his compartment to meditate until summoned to Hosius' cabin.

CHAPTER 4

Athanasius awoke to knocking on the door of his compartment. "Who is it?" he called.

"Sebastian," was the reply. "Hosius wants you."

Athanasius rose and stretched his legs; they were stiff from falling asleep while kneeling in meditation. "Coming," he said.

Sebastian led Athanasius up the narrow stairs to Hosius' cabin. The two men entered, and Athanasius saw Titurius and Hosius seated in the far corner. Titurius stood, and he and Sebastian left the cabin and closed the door behind them. Athanasius noticed that Hosius was using his travel chests as seats and a table.

"Come in, Athanasius," Hosius said, motioning for Athanasius to sit on the chest vacated by Titurius.

Hosius poured a cup of wine from a stoppered jug and handed it to Athanasius. The young priest accepted the cup and took a sip. It was a fruity-tasting wine – the kind popular in southern Hispania – and the aroma reminded Athanasius of how much he missed Gades. He took another sip and looked at Hosius.

"The first part of our plan has been a success," Hosius began. "We've created a divide between the churches that cannot be resolved through polite conversations between the two factions. I knew when I made my bargain with Constantine that I could never deliver all of the churches to him with a unified theology. The devout Followers of The Way would never give up their beliefs for the simpler doctrine of the Divine Trinity, and they'd never allow themselves to be used as tools of statecraft for the empire."

"So you're still planning to propose a council of bishops to establish one unified theology?" Athanasius asked.

Hosius nodded. "Yes. It's the only way to force the dissenting faction members to either join with the rest of us or be banished from the churches and the protections of the empire."

"Then what?" Athanasius asked.

Hosius smiled. "That's the right question! If the council is successful, then it will end with a single unified doctrine for all Christian churches. But Christianity is still a loose collection of churches spread out all over the empire – and outside the empire as well. With one theology comes the need for a central church to control the other churches – like the main trunk of a tree giving life to each of its branches. Each church cannot continue to have its own identity and ways of doing things. We need one identity, common orders of service and ceremonies, standardized prayers and blessings... in short, we need one common set of rules for the churches and for the governing of the churches. These rules must give Constantine and his successors a church that stands as an equal beside the Imperial Throne, the Senate, the legions, and the bureaucracy for governing the empire."

"That's the role you see for the church?"

"It's what Constantine wants," Hosius replied. "And it's what we need. Think about it. The Emperor is the embodiment of the empire's purpose. The Senate establishes laws that govern the empire. The legions keep the empire secure. The bureaucracy maintains the civil services that keep the machinery of the empire's government working. But who controls the hearts and minds of the people? There are dozens of religions worshipped across the empire. If we establish a single Imperial Church preaching one doctrine that all men must worship, then *we* are the ones who control the hearts and minds of the people!"

"But how is that a tool for the empire to use?" Athanasius asked, feeling confused. "It sounds like the church will be the true power of the empire, and the emperor will just be a figurehead."

"I knew you were my brightest student," Hosius said with a wide grin on his aging face. "You've discovered *my* vision for the church. But it could take generations before that vision is realized. Until then, our immediate problems are creating a church that does what Constantine needs for it to do and getting Constantine to agree with the level of authority that the church needs to have to carry out its mission on his behalf."

"I see an even more immediate problem, Hosius," Athanasius said.

"What?"

"You keep talking about control – that the church will control the people. But how will that happen? Our priests don't have any authority over their congregations. They lead the congregations in prayer and in the study of the gospels, but they are servants of the congregations, just as Jesus commanded his disciples to be. I see how a unified theology can guide people toward a common understanding of the prophets, the gospels, and the epistles, but each individual communes directly with God and won't be manipulated as easily as you're suggesting."

"I've been wrestling with that," Hosius admitted. "But I don't have an answer yet. Do *you* have any ideas?"

The two men sat in silence for a long time as Athanasius thought about the problem. Hosius waited patiently for the young priest to respond.

Finally, Athanasius replied. "I keep coming back to the Roman Legions. When you were first describing the unification of the churches under a single church, I thought about how the legions are organized. I saw the priests as legionnaires, the bishops as centurions, and the Patriarchs as the generals. But to make the church work as you envision, it's the *people* who'd be the legionnaires, the priests would be the centurions, the bishops would be the tribunes, and the Patriarchs would be the generals. The supreme head of the church would be the Emperor."

Hosius nodded. "An interesting analogy. Go on."

"The priests would have to command the congregations with the same authority that a centurion has over his legionnaires. Priests would reward good behaviors and punish bad behaviors to keep their congregations in line. If Christianity is truly about the salvation of man, as preached by the apostles, then salvation must come from the priests and not from individual communion with God. Just like a legion's chain of command, the priests will intercede between their congregations and God as God's representatives on earth. Through the priests, the church will grant forgiveness of sins, grant salvation, define what behaviors are acceptable, and condemn those who disobey the church's commands. We will essentially be altering Jesus' edict that 'No

32

man cometh to the Father, but by me,' into 'No man cometh to the Father, but by my church.' It's the only way we can make the people *obey* the church, as far as I can tell."

"I like where you're going," Hosius said, "but how can we give the church the authority to intercede between God and man?"

"Well," Athanasius began, "you and I acknowledge that Jesus established Peter as the head of the church, right?"

Hosius nodded, and Athanasius continued. "In Matthew, right after the passage where Jesus declares that Peter is the rock upon which he will build his church, he says, 'And I will give unto thee the keys of the kingdom of heaven: and whatsoever thou shalt bind on earth shall be bound in heaven: and whatsoever thou shalt loose on earth shall be loosed in heaven.' Now I know how Arias and his followers read this passage. They believe that Jesus was admonishing his apostles to free people from mental and physical bondage on earth, that the bondage freed on earth will remain freed in heaven, and that the bondage not freed on earth will still need to be freed in the afterlife. But what if it means something else? What if Jesus is giving his church divine authority? What if Jesus is saying that he'll have bound in heaven whatever the church binds on earth, and that he'll have loosed in heaven whatever the church looses on earth? If *that* was his meaning, then the church has the authority to do anything it wants, and heaven will have to approve!"

"Arias and his followers will accuse you of blasphemy," Hosius noted. "And they don't accept that Jesus made Peter the head of the church. They believe that it was Peter's declaration of Jesus being the Son of God that is the foundation of the church."

"I know. Arias and I had that discussion shortly before I sailed from Alexandria. But if the new church adopts my interpretation of this passage, then anyone standing against us will be the one guilty of blasphemy."

Hosius leaned back with a pleased look on his face. Then he said, "What you're describing is quite a departure from the way that the priests currently serve their congregations. How would we transform the churches to be more like the legions with the priests in command of the congregations? There would be pushback from some bishops and priests, not to mention some of the congregations."

"Based on what?" Athanasius asked.

"Based on their understanding and interpretation of the gospels and the epistles," Hosius replied. "This is something I've been thinking about for some time – especially regarding the Divine Trinity and the arguments against it by Arias and his followers. If we want to ensure that there is no doubt as to what the scriptures are saying, then we may need to *clarify* the scriptures."

"You mean alter them?" Athanasius asked.

"I wouldn't use that word," Hosius replied. "But we may need to create an *official* version of the gospels and epistles – one that will replace all of the existing versions and be worded so that there is no misunderstanding among the priests about what the passages mean. The theological decisions made by the council of bishops would be included in the official version."

"And what about the congregations?" Athanasius asked.

"What about them? They don't need to read the scriptures. They'll have the priests to teach them all that they need to know. But back to my question: how do we transform the churches to be more like the legions, over the objections of any bishops and priests?"

Athanasius drained his cup, and Hosius refilled it too full. The wine sloshed over the rim as the warship swayed, and the young priest quickly drank it down while thinking about Hosius' question. Finally, he sat up with a smile on his face.

"I think that you've already given us what we need to force the transformation," he said happily.

"What are you talking about?" Hosius asked.

"Arias! Specifically, the conflict between Alexander and Arias, between the Divine Trinity and the Followers of The Way. If the council of bishops is successful and Arias and his supporters are defeated, then there's still the risk of Arias' philosophies remaining ingrained in many of the congregations, not to mention many of the priests and bishops. If the council votes that Arias' philosophies are no longer acceptable, then it would be prudent to implement safeguards against them resurfacing, wouldn't it? We might not be able to make the complete transformation quickly, but we can implement parts of it immediately, and then add the rest of the parts slowly so that the transformation of the churches happens gradually. We'll also need to educate the priests in the new theology and official scriptures, and we can educate them on the new rules and the reasons for the transformation at the same time."

"And the pushback from the congregations?" Hosius asked.

"If Christianity becomes the state religion for the empire and all other religions are abolished, then pushback from the congregations won't matter. They won't have a choice but to comply with the new theology and the new authority of the church."

Hosius smiled and nodding enthusiastically. "And this is why I wanted you to accompany me to Byzantium. I've been so focused on the theological questions that I couldn't see the way to make everything else work as Constantine expects."

"Will the council of bishops be considering the other things that the Emperor wants in addition to the theological questions?"

"No," Hosius replied. "Only the Patriarchs will be privy to the other plans for the church. Once they're in agreement with the plans, they'll help convince the bishops and priests."

Athanasius nodded. "If you'd share with me all that Constantine wants, perhaps I can help you figure out how to make it work with the new theology," he offered.

"I was hoping you'd say that."

Athanasius was exhausted when he returned to his compartment late that night. As he lay down on his cot, he suddenly thought of something that Arias had said to him. *"My position is reasonable because it is the same position held to by the priests of this church since its founding. Your position has no such foundation, so which of us is being reasonable?"*

Why did I think of that? Am I doubting what Hosius and I are doing? Was Arias right?

Athanasius stared at the ceiling of his compartment. *Hosius has spent most of his life securing the free worship of Christianity in the empire, and now he's even managed to convince the Emperor to make it the state religion. Christians are no longer being persecuted for their beliefs. Isn't that what's important? No more martyrs, no more fear. And all that we have to do to secure the safety of all Christians is to give the Emperor what he wants.*

Arias is a purist. He'd rather die that change his beliefs. But this is the real world, and compromise is required if we're going to survive. *All that Hosius and I are doing is unifying the doctrine of the churches, which needs to happen anyway, and establishing a few additional functions to be performed by the churches on behalf of the empire. We're ensuring that the churches will flourish for as long as Rome herself stands – perhaps longer!*

Athanasius smiled. *Even Jesus told his followers to render unto Caesar that which is Caesar's. He paid his taxes, and God gave him the coin with which to do it. If Jesus knew that obedience to the empire was required to live freely within its borders, then why can't Arias understand that? Hosius and I aren't recommending changes to the churches for ourselves; we're recommending changes to ensure the survival of the churches. If we don't, and Christianity loses its imperial protections, who will be left to worship Jesus and serve God's church? If we're all martyred, who will keep the gospels and epistles alive in the hearts of men? What Hosius and I are doing is small compared to what will happen if we don't please the Emperor.*

Arias doesn't understand, and he never will. He represents the past. Hosius and I represent the future, and we'll be the ones remembered for saving the churches and setting our religion on the path to everlasting glory. That's what reasonable men do.

Athanasius's confidence in what he and Hosius were doing was restored. He closed his eyes and drifted off to sleep to the swaying of the warship.

The two warships docked in Barcino two days later. Sebastian and Titurius went ashore to get more blank scrolls and pencils for Hosius. Athanasius barely noticed that the galley was no longer moving. He and Hosius remained cloistered the entire time the ships were in Barcino, working on detail after detail of how the new Imperial Church would function.

The two warships left Barcino the next morning, and they arrived in Arelate two days later. Once again, Athanasius and Hosius remained on board, working all day and through most of the night.

The day before the warships arrived in Rome, Athanasius and Hosius were discussing ideas through most of the night. Shortly before sunrise, Athanasius said, "I think that one of the most valuable imperial services the church can provide is information. The priests will know what's going on in the areas around their churches, and they can report back anything that the imperial government might need to know. We'll need permission to use the Imperial Courier Service to send this information so it can arrive quickly, unless we want to someday set up our own courier service. But there's another kind of information that should prove useful to the Emperor."

"What's that?" Hosius asked.

"The kind of information that can be used against political rivals."

"I don't understand. How will our priests become privy to information like that?"

"There are three passages in the gospels and the epistles that I keep coming back to. The passage in the gospels is in Matthew, where Jesus says that 'I am not come to call the righteous, but sinners to repentance.' In the epistle of James, it says, 'And the prayer of faith shall save the sick, and the Lord shall raise him up; and if he have committed sins, they shall be forgiven him. Confess your faults one to another, and pray one for another, that ye may be healed. The effectual fervent prayer of a righteous man availeth much.' And in the first epistle of John, it says, 'If we say that we have no sin, we deceive ourselves, and the truth is not in us. If we confess our sins, he is faithful and just to forgive us our sins, and to cleanse us from all unrighteousness.' I think that the answer might be in these three passages."

"Go on," Hosius said, still not clear on what Athanasius was proposing.

"According to the first epistle of John, all men are sinners. Matthew says that Jesus came to call the sinners to repentance. Both James and John mention that confessing sins is the first step in the removal of sin. So what if we make the confession of sins a duty of every Christian – part of the way they reach salvation through the church? Each Christian must confess his sins on a regular basis to earn and retain God's favor, the priest will test him by giving him some sort of task to be sure that he is truly repenting from his sins, and then the priest can forgive the sin in the name of God. The church has called the sinner to repentance, and the priest now knows the secrets of every Christian in the congregation. The more that the members of the congregation confess, the more the priest learns. Information that's of value to the Emperor can be passed along. We can also have the priest assign tasks that benefit either the Emperor, the empire, or the church as part of achieving forgiveness and salvation. *That's* how the church can control the congregations, and by extension, the empire!"

"Wouldn't there have to be some expectation of privacy between the person confessing and the priest?" Hosius asked. "Would people be willing to confess their sins if they learned that their confessions were being used against them?"

"The information would never leave the church," Athanasius replied. "It would just be provided up the chain of command within the church."

"To the Emperor…" Hosius began.

"Who is the secular head of the church," Athanasius finished.

Hosius laughed. "It's brilliant! The people will think that they're attaining salvation for this life and for the afterlife, but they're actually giving the church what it needs to control them on behalf of the empire. And the priests become the eyes and ears of the empire and the church."

"In places where we have churches," Athanasius added. "But we might want to think about how to get the same information in territories where there are no churches."

"Territories outside of the empire? Couldn't we just build new churches in those territories?" Hosius asked.

"Yes, but it would take time to build churches in those territories and in territories of the empire that have not yet been converted to Christianity. Just as governments send spies into foreign lands, we may have to do the same by sending missionaries to lands where the church has no influence."

Alexander climbed the stairs to his chamber. The wall sconces at the top of the stairs illuminated the way through the darkness of the early evening.

Alexander reached the top of the stairs and turned the corner to enter his chamber. Wine and food were waiting for him on his desk. He closed the door, sat down, and poured himself a cup of wine.

Athanasius has been gone for over three weeks. If he found Hosius quickly, he should be back here in two weeks with Hosius' reply to my letter. I'm anxious to read what he suggests that I do. I don't want to strip Arias of his post, but I can't have his open defiance disrupt the other churches in this region. Something must be done.

Alexander took a sip of the wine. *I wonder if I should visit Arias at his church and try to resolve our differences directly. My letters aren't working, and he's always defensive when I summon him here. Perhaps if I go there, he'll feel comfortable enough to reason with me. Maybe that's what I should have done in the first place.*

Alexander thought about this, and then he thought about the last letter he received from Arias. *No, I guess we're past the point where he and I can work through our disagreements privately. Athanasius is right; Arias is beyond reasoning with. He'll never change, he'll never see reason, and he'll never abandon his beliefs. He'll have to be removed from his post and banished from preaching but in a way that won't disrupt his congregation or force his followers to come after me.*

A servant knocked on the door and brought a fresh flagon of wine to replace the one that Alexander had nearly emptied. *This is why I need to wait for Hosius' reply. He'll know how to get Arias out of the way without creating a situation that'll split the church apart.*

Arias watched his acolytes leave his chamber. He had spent three hours with them, teaching them The Way. *They're good students. They'll make fine priests one day.*

Glancing at the window, he noticed that it was dark. *Hosius should have received my letter and sent back his reply already. It should be here in a matter of days. I'm curious to read what he says about how I should work with Alexander to resolve our differences.*

Arias stood up and crossed over to the window overlooking the courtyard. *Alexander and I don't agree on many things, but I know that we both have what's best for the churches in our hearts. We can build on that. No matter what we disagree upon, we're still brothers in Christ, and that's a bond that can survive any* disagreement. *I'm sure that we can resolve our differences – or at least find a way to live with them for the good of everyone. I don't want our disagreements to cause a rift between the churches; I could never allow that. Alexander is my brother, and I am his. Our Master would never want our problems to disrupt our mission to teach The Way to the faithful. He commanded us to love one another, and I intend to do just that.*

Arias closed the shutters, sat down on the side of his bed, and prayed. *Heavenly Father, I know that Your will is supreme. Help me to know Your will so that I may obey and embrace it. You see Your creation as very good, and I must do the same. Alexander is part of that creation. You see him as good, and so must I. I don't want my problems with Alexander to jeopardize Your churches. Help me to remember that it's not the man Alexander that I oppose, it's his beliefs and the doctrine that he's attempting to force on all true believers and followers of our Master, Jesus. Give me the strength to put aside my own wants and do what You need me to do. This I will do willingly. Thank You for the opportunity to serve You and to guide others to serve You. Being in Your service is my greatest joy. I exist only to serve You. Guide my thoughts and actions so that my service is according to Your divine purpose. And help me to show Alexander and his followers the errors of their ways so that all of the churches may return to the true faith and proper worship of You and Your son Jesus. Strengthen me in this endeavor so that I do not fail You. Amen.*

CHAPTER 5

Late in the afternoon on the eighth day of their journey from Gades, the two warships steered into Portus, the great port just south of Rome at the mouth of the Tiber River. From where he stood on the upper deck of the galley, Athanasius saw a series of walls being built to provide greater protection to the sprawling central hub of Roman commerce.

The size of the port was impressive. For centuries, Rome had wanted a deep water port, and in the end, the Emperor Claudius had it dug in one of the greatest engineering triumphs that the empire had ever seen. Two man-made basins and a man-made island for the harbor's lighthouse made up the bulk of the harbor, and the warehouse district that surrounded the harbor was so vast that it could easily be mistaken for Rome herself.

Athanasius and Titurius remained on board the galley while Hosius and Sebastian went ashore to meet with Sylvester, the Bishop and Patriarch of Rome. The eight-day journey to Thessalonika required extra supplies, and it would take time for the crew to procure and load the supplies. The warships would be docked all night, all of the next day, and the next night, leaving Portus the following morning.

Athanasius was grateful for the time alone. He and Hosius had spent so much time together, working on the detailed plans for the new church, that he had gotten little rest. Once Hosius and Sebastian had disappeared into the crowds, Athanasius returned to his compartment and slept until well after sunrise the next morning.

Arias and Andrew visited the family of the boy struck by the chariot near the church at Baucalis. The boy was fully healed and full of energy, but he had no memory of the accident. The boy's parents couldn't contain their gratitude for their son's healing.

As Arias and Andrew returned to the church, Andrew asked, "Why doesn't the lad remember the accident?"

"Because the accident has no power over him," Arias replied. "Why should he remember something that's powerless to do him harm? To remember it is to think about it, and to think about it is to make it real. The lad is healed. That's all anyone needs to remember."

"But the lad doesn't remember being healed," Andrew protested.

"Why should he? If he doesn't remember being in an accident, what purpose would it serve to remember being healed from the injuries?"

Andrew nodded, and the two men continued walking. Arias was silent for most of the time.

"Is there something troubling you, Arias?" Andrew asked finally.

Arias looked at Andrew and smiled. "Is it that obvious?"

"Yes, it is," Andrew replied.

"I'm thinking about Alexander. It's long overdue that we stop fighting and start working together as brothers to find common ground between us. I overheard a messenger the other day refer to it as 'Arias' feud with Alexander.' I don't want a feud to exist between us. We're all part of Jesus' ministry, so we should be able to work together even if we disagree on certain issues."

"How are you going to get Alexander to agree to work together with you?"

"I'm thinking of inviting him to dine with me here. There are few discussions that can't be improved upon over a fine meal. Instead of throwing words at each other in letters, perhaps it's time to sit down and reason *together*. It's not a long distance for him to travel, and perhaps it'll do him good to get away from his church for a while. If I decide to invite him, will you carry my invitation to him in the morning and wait for his reply?"

"Of course, Arias," Andrew replied.

The two men walked the rest of the way to the church in silence.

Alexander re-read the invitation from Arias to dine with him. *Didn't I have the same thought only a week ago? He acted on it, and I didn't. He seems to genuinely want to work with me to resolve our differences. Don't I want the same thing?*

Alexander re-read the invitation for the third time, hoping for the inspiration to answer Arias' question: "Will you do me the honor of visiting with me at my church and dining with me as brothers in common fellowship?"

Why am I resisting his invitation? Do I resent that he approached me first, or have I been lording it over Arias that I was selected as bishop and Patriarch instead of him? Is that why I've treated him so harshly? Is that why I'd rather that he just learn his place and accept my authority? I wish Athanasius were here. I've missed his council these weeks since he's been gone. At least he should be back here with Hosius' reply before I'd have to dine with Arias.

Finally, Alexander called for Andrew, who was waiting outside of Alexander's chamber. Andrew entered and waited.

Alexander looked up at Andrew and said, "Please convey my gratitude to Brother Arias for his kind invitation, and tell him that I will be pleased to meet and dine with him next week."

"Yes, sir," Andrew said.

Arias was shocked. "He agreed to come?"

Andrew nodded, "He did, and he seemed grateful for the invitation."

"Did you see Athanasius anywhere?" Arias asked.

"No, I didn't. If he were there, he stayed out of sight until I left."

That's interesting. Athanasius is always there unless Alexander has sent him on an errand. I wonder where he's gone this time.

"No matter," Arias said aloud. "Please call for Botherik. We have much to do before Alexander arrives next week."

Hosius and Sebastian returned to the warship shortly before the two galleys were to leave Portus. Once the two ships were outside the safety of the harbor, Hosius sent for Athanasius.

"How was your visit with Sylvester?" Athanasius asked when he entered Hosius' cabin.

"It was a success." Hosius smiled and held up a scroll. "He wrote a formal request to the Emperor asking him to summon a council of bishops and help us resolve the theological differences within the churches. Now that one of the Patriarchs has requested the Emperor to intervene – especially the Patriarch of the Imperial City – it should be easy to convince Constantine to agree."

"Will Sylvester attend the council personally?" Athanasius asked.

Hosius shook his head. "He's too old and feeble to make a trip like that – even by sea. He'll send representatives, but I'm afraid that the council may also need to appoint Sylvester's replacement if he hasn't improved by then."

Gesturing for Athanasius to sit down, Hosius asked, "So what have you been working on since I've been gone?"

"Well, you've been keeping me so busy that I wanted to use the time to catch up on my sleep, but I didn't get any rest at all." Athanasius reached for the stoppered jug of wine sitting on the cabin's deck. He poured the wine and offered Hosius a cup. "I spent the whole time wrestling with three things: the Emperor's authority over the churches, the churches' power to compel obedience, and the ways to convert people of other religions to Christianity. The Emperor can order everyone to convert, but doesn't mean that the people will abandon their individual faiths and comply with the imperial orders. I think we need to identify ways to help the people make the transition."

"Have you identified any of those ways?" Hosius asked.

Athanasius nodded. "A few."

"Tell me."

"Well, the first idea is an easy one. Throughout the northern provinces of the empire, many of the pagans worship in groves of trees because they're considered to be sacred to their gods. If we build our churches in those groves or on the edge of those groves, then the people will still be coming to the groves to worship, but they'll be worshiping Christ, rather than their pagan deities."

Hosius nodded. "I like that. It's simple."

"Another idea is to denigrate some of the pagan deities. For instance, those blond giants who live far to the north worship a god named Odin. He wears a horned helmet and is referred to as 'the great horned god.' Now in the Revelation of the Apostle John, there are several passages referring to 'the beast' as a creature having horns. If we preach that worshipping a horned god is actually worshipping the beast, then we can show them how worshipping Christ is the better way."

"It's not a bad idea," Hosius said. "But you know that the Revelation of John wasn't written to be taken literally. It was a letter written to the persecuted Christians in Jerusalem in a coded language that only they'd understand. It was John's way of giving them courage and hope about their plight. The references to 'the beast' refer to a specific thing happening in Jerusalem at the time that John wrote the letter."

"True," Athanasius acknowledged, "but most people don't know that. The writings in the Revelation of John speak of heaven, the beast, calling the faithful to paradise, the signs and portents signaling the end of the world… these are myths shared by many of the pagan religions. If we incorporate them into our doctrine, then the converted will see that we believe many of the same things, and they'll have an easier time accepting Christianity."

"Good point," Hosius acknowledged.

"I've also been thinking about some of the other pagan deities. Many pagan religions have a hierarchy of gods, like Jupiter being the king of the Roman gods. We want the people being converted to see Christ as the King of Kings, the highest god in the hierarchy. But to do that, we may need to incorporate some of pagan gods into our theology. For instance, Hermes, in addition to being the messenger god, is also the god of crossroads and travelers throughout the empire. If we had a being in the hierarchy that served the same purpose, then it would be easier to help the people convert to Christianity."

"I understand what you're suggesting," Hosius said, "but there's no reference in the gospels or the epistles to a hierarchy. How would we get the bishops to agree to this?"

"Actually, there is a hierarchy of sorts," Athanasius stated. "You have Jesus at the top, his apostles directly below that, then his disciples, and then the saints."

"But the term 'saints' only refers to the faithful followers of Jesus during his lifetime and the lifetime of the apostles," Hosius pointed out.

Athanasius thought about this as he took a sip from his cup of wine. "What about assigning certain saints with the designation of *Patron Saints*? As patrons, they would have specific duties, like in my example of Hermes. The Patron Saint of travelers and crossroads would be responsible for providing God's blessings to those who travel. The church would provide an alternative to the worship of specific pagan deities, and the converted would see that their beliefs are still being respected by their new religion."

Hosius refilled his cup. "It's ambitious," he commented finally. "I think you're on the right track, but we may need to give it more thought before we present it to the Patriarchs. What else?"

"Well, we might need to adopt certain pagan rites for the same reason that we absorb pagan deities. One example happens late in December each year. Throughout most of the empire, the Winter Solstice is a night of high worship. The converted will continue their pagan worship on that night unless we have a Christian rite to replace it."

"What rite would we use?" Hosius asked. "There's nothing specific to Christianity that happened at that time of year."

"I don't know," Athanasius admitted. "It doesn't coincide with the crucifixion or the resurrection, and Jesus was born in the late spring or early summer. When the new rites and ceremonies for the church are defined, I'd suggest finding one that can coincide with the Winter Solstice, but I don't have one to suggest to you."

"Okay, I'll keep that in mind. Do you have any other ideas related to converting people to Christianity?"

Athanasius nodded. "Just one. According to the doctrine of the Divine Trinity, Jesus is God. His father is God, but his mother is Mary. Everything we know about Mary shows that she was a descendent of King David, just as Joseph was. But she became the mother of God when Jesus was born."

"So what?"

"So, most religions on earth that I've studied have one thing in common: they all have a Mother Goddess – the Queen of the Universe. Northern pagans have the Earth Mother Goddess, and the Roman pantheon has Vesta as the Virgin Goddess of Chastity and Cybele as the Great Mother Goddess who's the mother of the other gods. In Christianity, Mary is the mother of God. We may need to make her divine so the pagans will see that their most powerful deity is part of our religion as well."

"Mary had a human mother and a human father," Hosius protested. "How can she be divine with human parents?"

"Jesus had a human mother and a human father," Athanasius countered. "But Mary didn't conceive by Joseph; she was a virgin like Vesta when she conceived Jesus. Maybe she wasn't conceived by her human father, either."

Hosius waved his hand dismissively and shook his head. "She simply sprang from her mother's womb through an act of divine creation? How could that be possible? Or are you suggesting that God impregnated Mary's mother to give birth to Mary, who is his daughter, so he could come into the world as Jesus from Mary's womb, making Mary also his mother? And if Mary is the Queen of the Universe, then wouldn't she also be the wife of God, who is the King of Kings? That's stretching things a bit, don't you think? It sounds more like Egyptian mythology than Christian theology. I'm not sure that I'd ever get the Patriarchs to agree to this."

Athanasius nodded slowly. "I didn't say it made sense, but if we want to make it easier for pagans to convert, then we have to at least acknowledge the concept of the Mother Goddess somehow."

"Okay, let's put it aside for now. You mentioned that you were also thinking about the Emperor's authority over the churches?"

"Yes, but I haven't worked it out yet," Athanasius replied. "I just can't find anything in the gospels or the epistles that would give the Emperor – especially a pagan emperor – authority over the Christian churches."

"Then you're overthinking it," Hosius said, kindly. "It's in the gospel of Matthew."

"Where?" Athanasius asked.

"When Jesus responds to those who asked if it were lawful for Jews to pay tribute to Caesar. Jesus asked them whose face was on their coin, and they replied that it was Caesar's. Jesus told them to render therefore unto Caesar the things which are Caesar's; and unto God the things that are God's."

"What does that have to do with Constantine's authority over the churches?" Athanasius asked, recalling his own thoughts about those passages.

"Who commissioned this new church that we're creating?"

"The Emperor," Athanasius replied.

"Then we need to render to the Emperor the things which are the Emperor's. He rules the empire, we're part of the empire, and we're building a religion to serve his purposes. Who else could be the head of the churches?"

"But will the Patriarchs go along with that? Especially since Constantine has never been baptized?"

Hosius thought about this. Then he shook his head. "No. We'd have to remind them about Constantine's vision of the Christ granting him victory on the eve of the Battle of Milvian Bridge twelve years ago. That led to Constantine issuing the Edict of Milan the following year, which allowed the free worship of Christianity throughout the empire. The Emperor became the defender of the faith at that point, so it could be argued that Christ appointed the Emperor to be the head of his new church. And if Christ made that appointment, then no baptism would be necessary."

Athanasius smiled. "I think the Patriarchs would accept that."

"So do I," Hosius agreed. "Now what are your thoughts about the church's power to compel obedience?"

Athanasius took a sip of wine. "If the church is supposed to control the hearts and minds of the people on behalf of the Emperor, then it has to have the ability to enforce its will on the people. We use words like 'heresy' and 'blasphemy' to describe ideas that we don't approve of, but what do we do about the heretics and blasphemers? Remove them from the church? That's no threat. It won't keep the people in line. We need something stronger; we need fear to make the people obey the church."

"Fear of what?" Hosius asked. "In the first Epistle of John, it says that 'There is no fear in love; but perfect love casteth out fear: because fear hath torment. He that feareth is not made perfect in love.' How does fear become part of the doctrine of the church?"

"The faithful have nothing to fear," Athanasius admitted. "But the unfaithful do have something to fear – eternal damnation. In the Gospel of Matthew, it says that 'And when he saw a fig tree in the way, he came to it, and found nothing thereon, but leaves only, and said unto it, Let no fruit grow on thee henceforward for ever. And presently the fig tree withered away.' Jesus saw something that was unworthy to live, and he destroyed it. The church would need the same power over men – the threat of being destroyed for being unfaithful will make the people obey."

"And what about Jesus' declaration that 'I will have mercy, and not sacrifice: for I am not come to call the righteous, but sinners to repentance,' in the Gospels of Matthew and Luke?" Hosius asked.

"The church *will* call the sinners to repentance, but what of those who don't repent? What of those who spread evil within the church? Who openly defy the doctrine of the church? Who encourage others to do the same? Their sin must be purged in a way that serves as a warning to others who'd follow. It's not enough to cast the unrepentant from our midst; we must be able to condemn to death those who pose a threat to the church, and therefore a threat to the Empire."

"So you're suggesting that committing a sin would be the same as breaking the law, but instead of being judged and punished by the Emperor or the courts, the sinner would be judged and condemned by the church?" Hosius asked. "I don't know if the Emperor will relinquish that kind of secular power to the church."

"Even to secure the Imperial Church's place in the empire?" Athanasius asked.

Hosius shrugged his shoulders. "All we can do is present it to the Emperor and see how he reacts."

Alexander paced anxiously in his chamber. *Athanasius should have been back by now with Hosius' reply to my letter. He's had more than enough time to reach Hosius and return. How am I supposed to dine with Arias if I don't know what Hosius wants me to do? What if I do something that disrupts Hosius' plans? He's not one of the Patriarchs, but we all defer to him. He's the*

Emperor's oldest friend and the reason that we can openly worship throughout the empire. I can't risk meeting with Arias until I know what Hosius wants me to do.

Alexander continued pacing. *I'm supposed to leave in an hour. Do I reschedule with Arias? I don't know when Athanasius will return – especially if Hosius isn't at his church and Athanasius has to search for him. What if Hosius is on a pilgrimage? It could be weeks before Athanasius returns.*

Alexander's foot caught on the edge of a chair, and he stumbled. *I'll wait until the last possible moment for Athanasius to return before I leave to see Arias.*

Alexander angrily got back to his feet. *But if Athanasius doesn't arrive, then what do I do? I can't commit to anything with Arias until I know what Hosius advises. Without Hosius' reply, any conversations with Arias would be pointless. I can't go to Arias if Athanasius doesn't arrive in time.*

Alexander struggled with his thoughts. When the sun began shining in his eyes though the western windows, he realized how late he was. *I've lost track of the time. I should have left more than an hour ago. I'll never reach Arias' church on time, and it's too late to send a messenger saying that I can't make it tonight. I'll have to send a messenger either tomorrow or the next day with my apologies for missing dinner. Arias will understand. These things happen. And besides, it's not like our discussions would have accomplished anything because I don't yet have Hosius' reply.*

Alexander watched the sun set in the west. *Where is Athanasius?*

CHAPTER 6

Arias, Andrew, Barnabas, and Euric sat on cushions around the low table in the center of the room. The aroma of the food on the table made Arias' three acolytes' mouths water. The candlelight reflected off the brass plates and flagons, giving off a golden glow around the room. Everything was ready for their guest's arrival.

Except that their guest had not yet arrived.

"He's not coming," Euric whispered.

"He'll come," Arias said confidently.

"He's more than an hour late," Barnabas pointed out. "I agree with Euric. He's not coming."

"He'll come," Arias insisted.

Andrew remained silent.

Arias thought he heard the sound of a chariot, and he rose from the table to look through the window. He watched for quite a while, but there was no sign of Alexander. *He promised that he'd come. I extended him an invitation as a brother. How could he not come?*

Andrew, Barnabas, and Euric watched Arias stare out the window.

After a while, Arias' shoulders slumped. *He's not coming.*

Arias was devastated. *I guess Alexander doesn't want to resolve our differences. His mind is closed.* Suddenly Arias needed to be alone so he could commune with God for guidance. He turned and slowly left the room.

"Arias...?" Andrew called after him.

Arias held up his hand to signal Andrew not to speak. "Please enjoy the meal, and make sure you share it with the servants. I'll send for you tomorrow."

The three acolytes watched Arias disappear down the corridor to his chamber. Andrew looked around the table and said, "Suddenly, I'm not feeling hungry, and I don't want any food that was supposed to be shared with Alexander this night."

Barnabas and Euric looked at the food on the table and nodded. The three acolytes left the room with the feast untouched.

Arias reached his chamber, closed the door behind him, and fell to his knees. *Dear Lord, what do I do now?*

Arias woke the next morning later than usual. He had spent most of the night praying for guidance, but the only answer to his prayers was three words: *Love one another.*

Arias got out of bed and dressed quickly. *What else can I do? I can't let Alexander's actions change who I am or how I behave. If he has a problem with me, then it's his problem. I don't have to make it my problem. But if I stop loving him or treating him like a brother, then that IS my problem, and I'd be the one disobeying our Master's commandment. I must have faith that things will work out according to God's plan.*

Arias felt more at ease. He offered a prayer of thanks for God's guidance, and then he sat at his desk to meditate and prepare for the day.

Athanasius stood on the upper deck of the galley as Byzantium came into view. The previous evening, Athanasius and Hosius had finished writing down all of the initial plans for the Imperial Church. Hosius was still in his cabin, reviewing the drafts one last time. He wanted to be certain that they had addressed each of the Emperor's expectations for his new church.

As the warships rowed toward the principal city of the eastern empire, Athanasius saw workers rebuilding the walls and buildings burned during Constantine's siege. There were several damaged warships pulled up on the shore outside of the harbor, but most of the damage to the harbor itself had already been repaired.

Hosius joined Athanasius on deck as their galley rowed toward the docks. "Impressive, isn't it?" he asked the young priest.

Athanasius nodded. "Yes, it is. Have you been here before?"

"Many times," Hosius replied. "And each time it's like seeing it anew. The city is in a constant state of change, and if the Emperor decides to make it his Imperial City, then it'll probably triple in size over the next few years."

"Speaking of the Emperor, when do you think he'll summon you to meet with him?" Athanasius asked.

Hosius pointed at the main road leading from the city to the harbor. Athanasius looked where Hosius was pointing and saw a squad of imperial guards marching in tight formation down the hill from the city toward the docks.

"I think the Emperor has dispatched his guards here to summon me immediately," Hosius said. "I want you to come with me. I may need you to explain a few of your ideas to the Emperor if he asks any questions."

"Of course, Hosius," Athanasius said.

"Good. The scrolls are in a small chest just inside my cabin. Go get the chest, and bring it up on deck. I want to leave with the guards as soon as we've docked. Tell Sebastian and Titurius to follow us to the palace once the galley has been unloaded."

Athanasius ran to Hosius' cabin, grabbed the chest, relayed Hosius' instructions to Sebastian and Titurius, and returned to the main deck just as the sailors tied the galley to the dock. He walked over to Hosius, who was standing next to the gangway.

The squad of imperial guards approached the galley. "Hosius of Córdoba?" The leader shouted.

"I am Hosius," Hosius replied.

"The Emperor commands you to come with us immediately."

"I am the Emperor's obedient servant," Hosius said as the sailors extended the gangplank to the dock so Hosius and Athanasius could disembark.

Hosius left the warship first, followed by Athanasius who carried the chest filled with the plans for the Imperial Church. They joined the imperial guards on the dock. The guards formed up around the two men and quickly escorted them up the hill to the city.

Emperor Constantine stood just inside the window of his temporary palace that looked down the main street leading to the harbor. He spotted the guards returning up the hill, and he saw Hosius with them.

Good. He's finally here. It took six weeks for the ships that I sent to return. They made good time! Hosius had better have the answers that I'm looking for.

Hosius and Athanasius were escorted to an antechamber and told to wait. Athanasius was fascinated by the number of imperial guards and legionnaires that he witnessed as he and Hosius made their way from the port to the Emperor's palace. *I don't remember seeing this many soldiers the last time I visited Rome, but then again Rome hadn't just been besieged.*

The antechamber was the same size as Alexander's chamber in Alexandria, and it was lit and warmed by six bronze braziers. The antechamber had two doors – the one through which they had entered and a larger one on the opposite wall. There were windows along the walls to the left and the right, and imperial guards stood at their posts in each corner and in front of the larger door. *That must lead to the Emperor's rooms.*

Hosius looked calm as he waited, but Athanasius was nervous as he glanced around the room, admiring its opulence. *If this is what the antechamber looks like, I wonder how splendid the Emperor's private chamber must look.*

Finally, they were ushered through the larger door into the Emperor's audience chamber. When the chamberlain closed the door behind them, Athanasius heard a stern voice coming from the shadows to his right.

"It's about time you arrived."

"I can assure you, Great Emperor, that we didn't tarry along the way," Hosius replied respectfully.

There was silence in the room, and then Athanasius heard laughter. "It's good to see you, Hosius!" the Emperor said as he stepped into the light. Constantine was a tall, muscular man – built like someone who had spent his life as a soldier. His black hair was short and wavy, and his dark eyes were piercing even when he laughed.

Hosius and Athanasius bowed. "It's always a pleasure to see you, Great Emperor," Hosius replied.

"We're alone, Hosius," Emperor Constantine said. "Drop the formalities and sit down. I see you brought someone with you."

"Yes, this is Athanasius from Alexandria," Hosius said as he took a seat. "You've met him before, but it was years ago."

Constantine gestured for Athanasius to take a seat. "What's in the chest?"

"The plans for your Imperial Church," Hosius stated. "They're only a first draft, but I think you'll see that we've been hard at work crafting an institution that will control the hearts and minds of your citizens, just as you wanted."

"So, you've finished creating my church for me?" Constantine asked.

Hosius hesitated for a moment. "Not exactly. I've defined it, but I still have to get the churches around the empire to agree to it."

Constantine slammed his fists onto the arms of his chair. "What's the delay?!" he demanded, getting red in the face. "I've been waiting for nearly twelve years for you to keep your end of the bargain. I don't plan to wait any longer."

"A schism has developed between the churches," Hosius began, "and we don't have it worked out yet. Most of the churches have accepted the new doctrine of the Divine Trinity. Alexander, the bishop of Alexandria and one of the Patriarchs, has been instrumental in getting the other bishops and priests to accept the divinity of Jesus. But there's a large faction led by Arias, a priest in Baucalis near Alexandria, who refuses to accept the doctrine of the Divine Trinity. Arias and the others believe that Jesus was the Son of God only, and they won't budge from their beliefs."

"So what are you going to do about it?" Constantine asked angrily.

"Actually, I think that *you're* going to have to do something about it," Hosius replied.

"What are you talking about?" Constantine asked. "I'm not a Christian."

"No, but you're the head of the church," Hosius said.

Constantine looked dumfounded. Hosius continued. "When you agreed to allow Christians to worship openly throughout the empire, you became the champion of the churches and the defender of its faith. And when you revealed your intentions to make Christianity the imperial religion, you became the secular head of the church. That gives you the right to summon a council of bishops from across the empire to settle religious and other matters for the good of the church. I don't believe that these two factions will reach an agreement on their own, so I think that you'll need to step in, call for a council of the bishops, and preside over the meetings that'll decide on the unified doctrine to be preached in all of the churches. And to make certain that the council's decisions are binding on all churches, you'll carry the full authority of the empire to punish all who refuse to conform to the new doctrine."

"Are you suggesting that I crucify any who refuse?" Constantine asked.

"No, I'd recommend banishing them," Hosius replied. "If you condemn them, you could create martyrs, and that could make the schism grow larger, rather than ending it altogether."

"Stating that I'm the head of the church goes back to that myth you created about my vision of Christ before the Battle of Milvian Bridge, doesn't it?" Constantine asked.

"Well, who better to be the head of the church than someone who had a military victory after being visited by Christ in a vision?" Hosius asked innocently.

"Did you create that myth with this in mind, or is it a happy coincidence?"

"A little of both," Hosius replied. "I knew that you'd need spiritual authority when it came time to unite the churches under a new theology, and the time has finally arrived."

Constantine smiled. "And you're certain that the Divine Trinity will be the approved doctrine once the council is over? There are reasons why it's necessary for the god of Rome's state religion to have actually walked on the earth. People can't grasp a deity who is somewhere in the heavens – the 'unknown god' as they used to call it when Jesus' followers first reached Rome. They need to worship a god who has actually been here and knows what life is like down here. They need a god with a face, not some supreme being out among the stars."

"With you presiding over the council meeting, I can assure you that the approved doctrine will be the one you want."

"And do you think that the bishops – especially the patriarchs – will agree with me presiding over the meeting?" Constantine asked.

Hosius handed Constantine the letter from Sylvester in Rome. "The patriarch from your Imperial City has already requested that you summon the bishops and preside over the meeting to end the disagreement between the churches."

Constantine read the letter and then looked at Hosius. "And what about Arias and Alexander?"

"Alexander will agree to the plans for the church as long as he gets the doctrine of the Divine Trinity adopted. Arias will never agree to anything that we have planned for the churches, so he'll have to be banished from the churches and from the empire once the council meetings are over. Once he's gone, along with any of his followers who won't join with us, there will be no opposition to the new doctrine. Then we can get to work transforming this loose collection of Christian churches into the unified Imperial Church that you need in order to control the people of your empire."

Constantine re-read the letter from Sylvester. He was silent for quite a while. Then he said, "Before I summon the bishops to a meeting, I want you to personally talk to Arias and Alexander one more time. Try to get them to agree. If they do, then we'll use Arias to convince the rest of the opposition to put aside their disagreement for the good of the churches. If Arias won't agree with Alexander, then I'll summon the bishops, and the council will decide what the one doctrine of the churches will be."

Hosius bowed his head to hide his smile. "It will be done as you command, My Emperor."

"Good. Now show me your plans for my church. How will it help me control my people?"

Hosius and Athanasius spent two full days with Constantine, reviewing the plans, making the changes that Constantine wanted, and creating new plans based on additional requirements that occurred to Constantine during their discussions.

The night before they were to sail to Alexandria, Hosius and Athanasius ate in their chamber alone. "Do you think our meetings with the Emperor went well?" Athanasius asked.

Hosius nodded enthusiastically. "Yes, I do. I don't think that they could have gone any better."

"What do we need to do before we leave in the morning?"

"Nothing," Hosius replied. "We'll write the letters to the bishops and the patriarchs on the voyage to Alexandria. When I return to Byzantium with news that Alexander and Arias couldn't reach an agreement, the Emperor will send them by Imperial Courier."

"When will the meeting take place?" Athanasius asked.

"Next May," Hosius replied. "It'll take six months to prepare the site, send out the invitations, and have the attendees make their travel arrangements. The Emperor selected his summer palace in Nicaea as the location, which is a shrewd choice. Most of the bishops in the Eastern Empire support the Divine Trilogy theology, while bishops in the Western Empire tend to believe that Jesus is not divine. Holding the meetings in Nicaea will make it easier for the eastern bishops to attend and harder for the western bishops to attend. That should help us attain the outcomes we desire."

"How long will the council last?" Athanasius asked.

"Between the meetings with the bishops to establish the theology, and the meetings with the Patriarchs to agree to the plans that Emperor Constantine just approved, we should be there for about a month."

"Will only bishops be allowed to attend?"

"With two exceptions, yes," Hosius replied. "But the bishops may travel with as many retainers as they need, so long as the churches can still function in their absence."

"Who are the two exceptions?"

"The first one is Arias," Hosius replied. "Even though he's not a bishop, he's the leader of the opposition, so he must be there. Besides, he was almost appointed as Bishop of Alexandria and a Patriarch of the churches, so his presence is vital to our plans."

"And the second exception?" Athanasius asked.

"You, of course," Hosius said, smiling. "You'll be there as one of Alexander's retainers, but I also have a special task for you to perform during the council meetings."

"What is it?"

"Alexander is the champion of the faction supporting the Divine Trinity," Hosius replied. "I need him to appear to be the voice of reason – the calming influence in the midst of the storm. I don't want him to debate Arias directly. I want you to debate Arias and his beliefs. You draw out Arias and make him look foolish, and Alexander will provide the calm reason to guide the council to the conclusion that we want them to reach."

"Won't that make me look just as foolish as Arias?" Athanasius asked.

Hosius put a hand on Athanasius' shoulder. "Don't worry about that. You'll be named Alexander's successor by the end of the meetings with the Patriarchs. Your place in the new church will be secured."

The next morning, a squad of imperial guards escorted Hosius and Athanasius back to the harbor where the same two warships that brought them to Byzantium were waiting to take them to Alexandria. Sebastian and Titurius were already on board when they arrived.

The warships rowed out of the harbor before mid-day. The captain estimated that it would take nine days to reach Alexandria, and Athanasius was eager to return home.

During the voyage, Sebastian, Titurius, and Athanasius helped Hosius transcribe letters to all of the nearly eighteen hundred bishops of the Christian churches. The letters included an invitation from the Emperor to attend the council meeting, attended by however many retainers were necessary for the journey, and directions to the palace at Nicaea. Hosius knew that some of the bishops wouldn't be able to attend the council, but most would gladly obey the imperial summons.

On the morning of the ninth day after leaving Byzantium, the great harbor of Alexandria appeared on the horizon. Fifty-one days after boarding a ship for Carthago, Athanasius was finally home. The warships rowed into the harbor shortly before mid-day, and soon they were docked in the part of the harbor reserved for the Imperial Navy.

As Hosius disembarked, the captain said, "Remember, sir, we leave for Byzantium in five days at first light. You must be back on board by then."

"I'll be here," Hosius promised. Then he followed Athanasius onto the dock, followed by Sebastian and Titurius. Athanasius went to hire a wagon to carry them and their belongings to the church at Alexandria. Athanasius also hired two messengers – one to inform Alexander of their arrival, and one to let Arias know that Hosius would be visiting him in two days. When Athanasius returned to the dock, the sailors loaded the wagon, and the four men rode away from the harbor toward the city to meet with Alexander.

A short distance away from where the warships had docked, Peter, a priest from Ptolemais, disembarked from a merchant ship with a letter from Bishop Secundus to Arias. As he searched for transportation to Baucalis, he noticed a wagon being loaded next to two Imperial Navy galleys. He recognized the faces of two of the men in the wagon. *That's Hosius of Córdoba and Athanasius of Alexandria. What are they doing together on an Imperial warship?*

CHAPTER 7

Arias saw the messenger approaching the church at a gallop. By the time the messenger brought the horse to a stop, Arias was waiting for him on the edge of the courtyard. The messenger slid off his horse and approached Arias with the horse in tow.

"Are you Arias the priest?" the messenger asked.

Arias nodded. "I am Arias. Do you have a message for me?"

The messenger reached into his leather bag and handed Arias a scroll. Then he mounted his horse and rode off, kicking up a cloud of dust as he went.

Arias looked at the scroll and recognized Hosius' seal. *My reply from Hosius has finally arrived. It took nearly two months, but it's here.* He broke the seal and unrolled the message.

> *Brother Arias,*
>
> *Greetings, old friend. I have just arrived in Alexandria. Emperor Constantine has ordered me to meet with Alexander and you to find a resolution to your differences. I will meet with Alexander first out of respect for his post, and I will meet with you at your church in Baucalis in two days' time.*
>
> > *Hosius, Bishop*
> > *Church of Córdoba, Hispania*

"Is that from Hosius?" Andrew asked.

Arias looked up and noticed for the first time that his three acolytes were standing next to him. He smiled and showed them the letter.

"The Emperor?" Barnabas asked when he finished reading it. "Why is the Emperor getting involved in disputes between the churches?"

Arias shrugged. "I have no idea. I know he's taken a great interest in the churches since issuing the Edict of Milan, but I've never heard of him getting personally involved like this."

"Perhaps the Emperor is finally going to be baptized," Euric suggested, "and doesn't want to pledge himself to a religion that can't agree on its own doctrine."

"That's possible," Arias said. "I guess we'll know in two days when Hosius gets here."

Arias and his acolytes crossed the courtyard to the small garden next to Arias' chamber. When they heard a chariot approaching, Arias turned and watched the chariot stop and a man jump off the back.

"Brother Peter!" Arias shouted, running toward the man.

"Brother Arias!" Peter responded, smiling. "It's good to see you again."

The two priests embraced. As Peter acknowledged the three acolytes, who were standing a short distance away, Arias asked, "What brings you to Baucalis? What news is there from Secundus? Can you stay and dine with us?"

Peter shook his head and handed the letter from Secundus to Arias. "I'm sorry, but I can't. The chariot's waiting to take me back to the port. My ship home sails with the evening tide. I have to get back."

Arias nodded. Peter leaned forward and added, "But I should tell you what I saw at the port this morning. Hosius of Córdoba arrived on a galley of the Imperial Navy. I saw him heading into Alexandria."

"I know that already," Arias said, holding up the letter from Hosius. "He's coming to see me in two days after he meets with Alexander."

"Well, did you know that Athanasius was with Hosius on that galley?" Peter asked.

Arias stared at his friend. "No, I didn't. What's Athanasius doing with Hosius?"

"I don't know, my friend," Peter replied. "But if Athanasius is involved, it can't be good."

Peter grasped Arias by the arm. "Watch yourself, Arias. Secundus is concerned; it's all in his letter. The churches are at a crossroads, and I'm afraid of what's going to happen if the churches take the wrong path."

Peter climbed up onto the back of the chariot. The charioteer cracked his whip, and the horse team started moving. Peter waved to Arias as the chariot turned around and headed for the port. Soon, the chariot disappeared in the dust from its wheels and the horses' hooves.

Arias looked at his confused acolytes and walked toward the garden. *I need to read Secundus' letter. Perhaps he can shed some light on what's going on.*

Alexander was waiting at the entrance to his church when the wagon carrying Athanasius, Hosius, Sebastian, and Titurius arrived.

"Brother Hosius, I can't believe that you're here!" Alexander embraced Hosius. "Your messenger only just arrived. I've had no time to prepare a proper welcome."

Hosius smiled. "No need, Brother Alexander. I'm here on orders from the Emperor. In two days, I meet with Arias, and then I sail back to Byzantium five days from now."

Looking at Athanasius, who was paying the wagon driver, Hosius added, "Sorry I kept your aide for so long, but he found me just as I was obeying an imperial summons to meet with Emperor Constantine at Byzantium, so I had him come with me. It wasn't until we left Byzantium for here that I knew what my answer to you would be, and now I can deliver that answer personally."

Alexander nodded and smiled as he led everyone inside. Servants appeared and took everyone's personal belongings to the rooms that Alexander had set aside for his guests.

After a quick lunch, Hosius met privately with Alexander. "The Emperor wants an end to the disagreement between you and Arias," Hosius stated.

"I think Arias does, too," Alexander said. "He invited me to dine with him two weeks ago to find a way to put our differences aside, but I didn't want to have any discussions with him until I'd heard from you."

"So you didn't go?" Hosius asked.

Alexander shook his head. "No, and I forgot to send my apologies for not attending."

Hosius hid a smile. *Perfect!* Then he said aloud, "I'll convey your apologies to him when I see him."

"Thank you, Hosius."

"Think nothing of it," Hosius said. "However, even though the Emperor has ordered me to try to get the two of you to reach an agreement, it's important that you don't."

"Why not?"

"Because if you don't, then the Emperor will be forced to summon all of the Christian bishops to meet and decide what will be the one theology of the churches. It's important that this council of bishops takes place."

"Why?" Alexander asked.

"Because Arias' faction will never agree on their own to accept the Divine Trinity. But if the rest of the bishops reject Arias' beliefs, then the Emperor will banish Arias and his supporters, and the Divine Trinity will become the cornerstone of our new doctrine."

Alexander leaned back and smiled. "After all these years of trying to get the Divine Trinity accepted, you're telling me that it's finally going to happen, and that the way to make it happen is to refuse to resolve my differences with Arias?"

Hosius nodded. "Exactly. Constantine will preside over the council meetings, and by the time the meetings are over, you'll have your doctrine, and the Emperor will have his church."

"*His* church?"

"Constantine has already committed to make Christianity the official state religion of the empire. In his role as Emperor and defender of the faith, he'll be the secular head of the church, and the Patriarchs will be the spiritual heads of the church. Don't forget that he's the one who allowed Christians to freely worship inside the borders of the empire, thanks to a vision of Christ he had on the eve of battle. He sees it as his mission to help the church grow in numbers and in influence across his empire, and that's why he looks at Christianity as *his* church. With his help, there's no end to what we can accomplish."

Alexander nodded. "I understand."

"Good," Hosius said. "Because there will be two sets of meetings going on at the council. The bishops and Patriarchs will have one set of meetings to establish the unified doctrine for all churches. The Patriarchs will also meet separately to discuss the way that Christianity will work as the state religion of the empire. Our new role will require us to do things differently than we do now, and it will be for the Patriarchs to work out those details."

"As long as the Divine Trinity is part of the new doctrine, you'll have my support. It's vital to me that Jesus be acknowledged as God on earth. How else could miracles be performed if not by God?"

Hosius and Alexander met for several hours. Hosius explained what Athanasius' role in the council meeting would be, and he revealed a few of the details that the Patriarchs would be discussing in private.

Alexander didn't completely understand everything that Hosius told him, but he trusted Hosius completely. *He has the best interests of the churches in his heart, and he has the ear of the Emperor. I'm certain that everything he's suggesting will be for the best. He'll have my full support.*

Arias re-read Secundus' letter. It raised more questions than it answered, but one thing was now known. There was a growing movement to have Arias, and anyone else who opposed the Divine Trinity doctrine, banished from the churches and from the empire. *There doesn't seem to be room for disagreement any longer. I've spent my entire life practicing my faith the way it was taught to me. Now a group of fools wants to change our faith, and they want me banished because I believe things should remain as they are? What is happening to the churches?*

Arias prayed for guidance. *Heavenly Father, show me the way that I should go. Is it Your will that I should bend to the opinions of the bishops? Is it Your will that I abandon the churches so that I may preserve Your commandments and the teachings of Your son, Jesus? I serve You, and Thy will be done.*

As he communed with God, two passages from the Gospel of Matthew came to him.

Enter ye in at the strait gate: for wide is the gate, and broad is the way, that leadeth to destruction, and many there be which go in thereat: Because strait is the gate, and narrow is the way, which leadeth unto life, and few there be that find it.

Then said Jesus unto his disciples, If any man will come after me, let him deny himself, and take up his cross, and follow me. For whosoever will save his life shall lose it: and whosoever will lose his life for my sake shall find it. For what is a man profited, if he shall gain the whole world, and lose his own soul? or what shall a man give in exchange for his soul? For the Son of man shall come in the glory of his Father with his angels; and then he shall reward every man according to his works.

Arias nodded silently. *The bishops are taking the easy way that will lead them to their destruction. But God doesn't want us to take the easy way; He wants us to strive and work so that we may learn and be rewarded in heaven. I will stand firm in my faith, even if it means turning my back on the churches. After all, the churches are institutions of men. They were once created to honor God and the words and works of our Master, but even so, they're man's creation. I will leave them in the hands of other men if I must. Those who desire to learn The Way from me can easily find me wherever I am. I will continue to teach as I was taught, even if I risk the condemnation of the bishops and the empire. The chief priests of Judea condemned Jesus, and if I face the same fate because of my faith, then I'm in good company indeed.*

"Should I come with you, Hosius?" Athanasius asked as Hosius prepared to travel to Baucalis.

Hosius smiled but shook his head. "No, it's best if you remain here. Your presence will put Arias on his guard, and I need to convince him that everything's fine and that the council of bishops is his best opportunity to engage in a thoughtful debate about the Divine Trinity. He must never suspect that the true purpose of the council is to make certain that his beliefs are eradicated from the churches forever."

"I understand," Athanasius said.

Two hours later, Hosius and Arias sat together in Arias' chamber. Botherik brought in a fresh flagon of wine, setting it on the edge of Arias' desk before withdrawing from the room and closing the door.

"Your acolytes seem to be learning quickly, Arias," Hosius said. "They're a credit to their teacher."

"It's not their teacher," Arias corrected Hosius modestly. "It's their closeness to God. Andrew should be ready for his own church in another two to three years. Barnabas and Euric will be ready in less than four. I couldn't be more pleased with their progress."

"How long were you an acolyte?" Hosius asked.

"Five years," Arias replied.

Hosius nodded, collecting his thoughts. Before he could ask his next question, Arias said, "Forgive me for being blunt, Hosius, but I understand that there are several bishops calling for my banishment from the churches and the empire, along with anyone else who continues to preach and teach The Way as our Master did. I also understand that Athanasius was on the same warship that brought you from Byzantium to Alexandria. Forgive me if I find your presence here somewhat ominous, under the circumstances."

Damn! He knows about the banishment. Hosius held up a hand as if reassuring Arias that everything was fine. "I'm here on the orders of Emperor Constantine. My sole purpose in being here is to help you and Alexander find a resolution to your disagreements. But since you bring up the rumor of banishment and my traveling with Athanasius, let me address those first."

Arias nodded, and Hosius continued. "I was leaving Hispania for Byzantium when Athanasius arrived with a letter from Alexander. Like you, he was seeking my counsel on how to handle your differences. Athanasius was instructed to wait for my reply, but I couldn't give him a reply until I had met with the Emperor because his summons was to discuss you and Alexander. Athanasius traveled with me, and I returned to Alexandria with him, so I could reply to Alexander's letter and your letter in person. There's nothing more to that story. As for the rumors of banishment, it's just that – a rumor. Many bishops are angry that you speak out so forcefully against the Divine Trinity, but then again, many bishops support you and your position. Emperor Constantine asked for my thoughts on the idea of banishing priests and bishops who don't conform to the doctrine of the churches, and I reminded him that the churches can't agree on a single doctrine. Until there's a single doctrine, there's no basis for banishments, and he agreed."

"Why is the Emperor getting involved in the churches?" Arias asked.

"Because he wants our religion to be the principal religion in the empire. When he had his vision of the Christ telling him that he'd be victorious in battle, he knew that he was communing with the one true God, and he saw it as his life's mission to unite the empire and defend the churches dedicated to that God. But how can he promote the churches to all of the peoples of the empire if the churches can't agree on a single doctrine? That's why he sent me here – to find a way to end the disagreements so there is only one doctrine preached by all churches."

"You know my position on the Divine Trinity, Hosius. It hasn't changed, and it won't change. I cannot accept any doctrine which declares that Jesus is God when Jesus himself denied that he is God. The truth is that Jesus was a prophet, a teacher, and the son of God."

Hosius smiled warmly. "I know, Arias. Alexander is as unmovable as you are. My mission here has been a failure... unless I can give the Emperor a way to do what I cannot. I have an idea about that, and I'd like to have your thoughts on the matter."

"Certainly," Arias said.

"Thank you. It has always been my experience that differences are best resolved in person. Don't you agree?"

"Yes," Arias replied, "but Alexander has resisted all of my attempts to meet and discuss our issues."

"Yes, I'm aware that he didn't show up for a meeting with you two weeks ago. Did he ever give you an explanation as to why he didn't come?"

Arias shook his head. "He still hasn't said anything about it."

"Shameful," Hosius said sympathetically. "It seems pointless to me to have the two of you meet to discuss your differences. And even if you did resolve your issues, there are others who believe as both of you do. How do they resolve their differences? No, the answer is not to have you and Alexander talk to each other. I think the answer is to have all of the bishops and Patriarchs meet together, and, as a group, discuss and debate the points of our theology upon which we disagree. Then, as a group, we can decide on what the theology for the churches will be going forward."

"It's been many years since we've had a meeting like that," Arias commented.

"I know," Hosius said enthusiastically. "It's long overdue, don't you think? If we're going to be united churches and the official religion of the empire, then shouldn't the leaders of the churches all take part in defining what the united churches will preach? Think about it. You'll be able to present your view of theology to the bishops and Patriarchs all at the same time. They'll hear it from you personally, not from someone who may or may not present your beliefs correctly. Alexander will also get to present his beliefs, but then the entire leadership of the churches will be able to calmly and conscientiously reason among themselves. And you'll be there to help guide them as they decide on the official theology of the churches for the next thousand years!"

Arias appeared surprised at what Hosius had suggested. He was silent for a moment, and then he asked, "Will the Emperor be willing to host a council meeting to end the disagreements?"

Hosius furrowed his eyebrows. "I don't know," he lied. "But I think I can convince him. It gives him what he wants, and it does it in a way that's fair both to you and to Alexander. He may not agree at first, but I'll wear him down. Eventually, he'll see things my way."

Arias smiled. "If you can convince the Emperor, then you'll have my complete support."

"Thank you, Arias. There's one more thing to consider. I have no doubt that, should the Emperor agree to a council meeting, he'll demand that the decisions reached by the council be binding on every Patriarch, bishop, priest, and acolyte. Can you live with that?"

Arias nodded. "All I've ever wanted is for my brothers to hear what I have to say. I'm certain that if I can explain my position to the leaders of the churches, I'll be able to convince them to preserve The Way as our official theology."

Hosius nodded supportively. *Ah, if only you knew what's going to happen to you at the council meeting, my dear Brother Arias. No one is going to listen to you. No one is going to be convinced of anything by you. Your theology will be expelled by the time the council meetings are over. Then you and your supporters will be banished.*

Athanasius was waiting for Hosius when he returned from Baucalis. "How did it go with Arias?" he asked.

Hosius smiled a tired smile. "As expected. He supports the idea of a council meeting. He thinks that he'll finally get to present his beliefs to a friendly forum. He has no idea what he's in for. Oh, by the way, he heard about the call for his banishment, and he knows that you arrived in Alexandria on the same ship as me. I smoothed things over. He suspects nothing."

"What happens now?" Athanasius asked.

"I return to Byzantium, tell the Emperor that I failed to get Alexander and Arias to agree on anything, and have him call for a council of bishops to settle the matter."

"And what do you want me to do until then?"

"Keep whispering in Alexander's ear," Hosius replied. "Make sure that he does not meet with Arias personally, and make sure that any communications from Alexander to Arias only serve to make matters worse between them."

"I can do that," Athanasius said cheerfully.

"I know you can, my boy. I know you can."

CHAPTER 8

Two days later, Hosius boarded his Imperial Navy galley shortly before dawn. The captain of the warship immediately ordered the ship to get underway. The other Imperial Navy galley, which had escorted Hosius' ship to Alexandria, waited near the mouth of the harbor. Soon both galleys were rowing away from the port to return Hosius to Byzantium.

Hosius went to his cabin and stayed there for most of the morning. His mind wrestled with what Athanasius had proposed to him the night before. *"Wouldn't the council meetings go more smoothly if Arias weren't there?"* The comment appeared innocent enough, but Hosius knew the real meaning behind those words.

It's more than just uninviting him from the meetings or having something happen to keep him from making the journey to Nicaea. Athanasius is suggesting that Arias be condemned by the church and the empire for heresy and blasphemy. I know that Athanasius wants the churches to have the power to condemn and purge heretics and blasphemers, but are we ready to purge one of our own? Athanasius used the story of Jesus condemning the fig tree that bore no fruit to justify the need for this power, but is this how we'll wield the power for the first time?

Hosius silently shook his head. *If the Emperor or the Patriarchs condemn Arias to death, then it'll make him a martyr, and his supporters will never accept any changes to the theology. Others will follow Arias' supporters if it's said that we killed a priest because we're afraid of his beliefs. It'll make the entire council meeting a complete waste of time, and Constantine will blame me. No, we cannot risk making a martyr out of Arias.*

Hosius filled his cup with wine, drained it, and refilled it. *But what if Arias is killed in a way that doesn't look like it was by the hands of the Patriarchs or the Emperor? What if he should meet with an unfortunate accident on the way to Nicaea? If Arias can be ambushed on his way to Nicaea in a way that looks unrelated to the council meeting and cannot be linked back to Constantine or the Patriarchs, then it might be worth the risk. Constantine's hands would be clean, as would the Patriarchs' hands. Arias' supporters would lose their most eloquent champion, but they'd have no reason to blame anyone at the council meeting for his death. The Patriarchs could immediately proclaim that Arias' death was God's will for heresy and blasphemy, which might make Arias' followers afraid to continue resisting the Divine Trinity as our official doctrine.*

Hosius took another drink and set his cup next to the wine jug on the floor of his cabin. *Am I ready to abandon the plan I've spent years working on? It has been my goal all along to have Arias humiliated at the council meeting and then banished along with his followers. But what's more important? Having Arias look like a fool, or getting the new theology and the plans for the church approved by the council? It would certainly be easier to conduct the council session without Arias there. He's a powerful, persuasive speaker, and it's possible that he could convince others to join him in opposing the Divine Trinity, especially if more bishops from the Western Empire than I've anticipated are able to attend the meetings. I've always planned for Constantine to make the final judgement regarding the Divine Trinity, given that the council will not be able to reach a unanimous decision, but it could be a disaster if he chooses the Trinity over the objections of a majority of the bishops in attendance.*

Hosius closed his eyes, unable to decide what to do. *I have a week to think about Athanasius' proposal before we reach Byzantium. Maybe by then I'll have a workable plan to present to Constantine.*

The two warships rowed into Byzantium harbor late in the afternoon, eight days after leaving Alexandria. Even though they had arrived early, a squad of imperial guards waited on the docks to take Hosius to the Emperor.

The sun sat low on the horizon as the guards escorted Hosius into the Emperor's antechamber. The lit braziers bathed the room in a soft orange glow that matched the sunset. Even though Hosius had been preparing for this meeting during the voyage from Alexandria, he felt nervous. There was still a chance that Constantine might decide to punish Hosius for his failure.

The doors to Constantine's private chamber opened. Two men exited and hastened across the antechamber to the corridor beyond. Constantine's chamberlain, an imposing man named Vibius, motioned to Hosius, and Hosius followed Vibius through the doors.

"Hosius of Córdoba, my Emperor," the chamberlain announced in his deep, rumbling voice.

"Leave us, Vibius," Constantine said.

The chamberlain exited the room, closing the doors behind him.

Constantine sat across the room at the end of a long table that was covered with scrolls and maps. Hosius stood still, waiting for the Emperor to begin the conversation.

"Don't just stand there, Hosius, come here and sit down," the Emperor said finally.

"Yes, my Emperor," Hosius said respectfully.

"And stop being so formal when we're alone," the Emperor grumbled.

Hosius sat next to the Emperor. "As you wish, Flavius."

Constantine smiled and poured Hosius a cup of wine. The Emperor's birth name was Flavius Valerius Aurelius Constantinus Augustus, and while the empire knew him as the Emperor Constantine I, Hosius was one of the few people who could get away with calling him Flavius in private.

"You made good time getting back here," Constantine said.

"We had good winds and used the sail," Hosius replied, referring to the single sail mounted on the upper deck of each galley.

"How did your meetings go with Alexander and Arias?"

"Not well. They're unmovable from their positions. I'm afraid that a council of bishops is the only option now." Pulling out a scroll from the pocket in his robe and handing it to Constantine, Hosius added, "Alexander has also sent you an official request to call for and preside over a council of church leaders to resolve the dispute."

Constantine took the scroll and read Alexander's letter. "Things are going just the way you wanted, aren't they?"

"I don't understand what you mean…"

"Oh shut up, Hosius!" Constantine interrupted, slamming the scroll on the table. "Do you honestly think that I didn't know you've been positioning things to force me to call for a council of bishops?"

Hosius was shocked. He felt his face turning red.

Constantine's gaze softened. "Fortunately, I happen to agree with you, so I didn't stop you. But you should have confided in me that you didn't want Alexander and Arias to resolve their differences so I'd be forced to summon the council."

"You had a war to fight, Flavius. I didn't want to bother you with church matters when you had more important things to worry about."

"And you couldn't have mentioned it when you were here the last time?" Constantine asked. "You had my complete attention then."

"I'm sorry, old friend. I…"

"I know," Constantine said, holding up his hand. "You weren't sure that I'd agree with you, so you set things in motion to leave me no choice, right?"

Is Constantine truly angry with me? Did I go too far this time? Hosius nodded.

"Don't do that again, Hosius."

"I'm sorry, Flavius."

"You're forgiven, as long as the council meeting gives me what I want," Constantine said. "Is there anything else I should know about?"

Hosius mentioned Athanasius' suggestion that Arias be killed on the way to the council meeting.

"Don't you think it'll seem a bit too convenient that I'm forced to call a council meeting because of Arias and his views, and then Arias gets killed on his way to that meeting?" Constantine asked. "If the meeting is supposed to discredit Arias' views, then shouldn't he be there? If he's not there to defend his position, won't there be those who believe that his views were never given a fair hearing? Won't that invite them to join with the opposition to the Divine Trinity, making it even harder to reach agreement on the unified doctrine of the churches?"

"I hadn't looked at it that way," Hosius admitted. "I was focused on making it look like a random occurrence, so it could never be linked back to you or the Patriarchs."

"Random occurrence?"

"Yes. For instance, if he takes an overland route, have the caravan attacked by thieves who kill Arias and others. And if he takes a sea route, have the ship attacked by pirates."

Constantine leaned back in his chair. "The overland route would be easier to make work," he said. "It's too easy for ships to miss each other."

"I agree," Hosius said. "And since it would happen just before the council meetings begin, all anyone would know is that he didn't show up for the meetings. It would be some time before news of his death reached Nicaea and the rest of the empire."

"And by then the council would have already approved the Divine Trinity," Constantine said, nodding. "I'll have my church, and the people will have a god to worship that they can understand – a knowable god rather the 'unknown god' of Arias."

"Exactly. But in answer to your earlier question about making it harder to reach an agreement on the unified doctrine, I don't expect the bishops to reach a unanimous agreement on the issue of the Trinity, regardless of whether or not Arias is in attendance. In the end, *you'll* have to declare which doctrine will become the official doctrine. Your role as Head of the Church and President of the Council will allow you to do this."

"*I'm* going to choose the official doctrine?" Constantine asked.

Hosius nodded. "The council meeting will be like a trial, and you'll be the judge. Both sides will present their arguments. If the bishops can't reach consensus, then you, as judge, will make the final decision. It's the only way any of our issues will get resolved."

"Why am I hearing this for the first time, Hosius," Constantine demanded. "Did you *forget* to mention it until after I agreed to summon the council meeting? One more thing you set in motion that would leave me with no choice?"

Hosius lowered his eyes, terrified that this time he *had* gone too far. Both men were silent, but Hosius felt Constantine glaring at him.

After what seemed like hours, Constantine said, "All right. We'll talk more about this later. Are the invitations to the council meeting ready to be sent?"

"All eighteen hundred, yes," Hosius replied. "They just need your seal."

"Give them to my secretary in the morning. He'll have them sealed and dispatched."

"Very well." Hosius' hand trembled slightly as he took a drink. "Is there anything else that you wanted to discuss tonight, Flavius?"

"Just one thing," Constantine replied. "I think that the imperial church needs a symbol."

"Do you have one in mind?" Hosius asked.

"No, that's why I wanted to discuss it with you. I want everyone baptized as a Christian to receive a token to wear that identifies him as a Christian. The symbol would be prominently displayed on the outside and the inside of each church, and it would become central to the ceremonies and activities performed by the churches. Any ideas on what we could use for that symbol?"

Hosius thought about it for a while. He and Constantine discussed several ideas, but then a solution came to him. "A cross," Hosius said.

"A cross? Like the ones I used at Milvian Bridge?"

"Yes!" Hosius was excited. "We've already established the legend of your vision of Christ as the reason you carried crosses into battle and painted them on your legionnaire's shields. Why not extend that myth to make the cross be the symbol of the church?"

"How will an instrument of torture and death be received as the symbol of a church dedicated to a god who rose from the dead?" Constantine asked.

"Without death, there is no resurrection," Hosius pointed out. "And since this is the imperial church, shouldn't it honor the victorious Emperor whose vision of Christ led him to carry crosses before him into battle, the Emperor who ended the persecution of Christians throughout his empire?"

"And if I give the churches the power to purge non-believers," Constantine added, "the cross could also be seen as a warning to those who oppose the doctrine of the churches."

"I hadn't thought of it that way, but it would send a clear message about the consequences of disobedience," Hosius acknowledged.

Constantine stared at Hosius, deep in thought. Then he stated, "I like it."

"Good," Hosius said. "I'll add it to the list of things to discuss with the Patriarchs."

Constantine nodded happily. "Have you dined?" he asked.

Hosius shook his head. "There wasn't time."

Constantine shouted for his chamberlain. "Vibius!"

"How may I serve you, my Emperor?" the chamberlain's voice boomed when he opened the doors and stepped inside. Hosius realized that Vibius must have been standing right outside of the doors to respond so quickly.

"Bring meat," he commanded. "We're hungry."

"Yes, my Emperor." Vibius left quickly to tell the servants to fetch the food.

Platters of roasted meat, steamed vegetables, flagons of wine, and fresh bread were soon placed on the table by a small army of servants. The meal was excellent. Hosius asked about Constantine's military campaign and his plans for the city. The Emperor discussed the siege of Byzantium at length, obviously still pleased with the outcome.

"I've spent most of my time lately strengthening the defenses of the eastern provinces," he said as servants removed the platters of food and placed fresh flagons of wine on the table. "Licinius stripped the provinces bare of all of their legions, and the last thing I need right now is an invasion."

Constantine talked for another hour about his plans for redeploying the legions, restoring Byzantium, and dealing with the few rebels that were still in hiding in the region. When Constantine drained one of the flagons of wine, he looked at Hosius and smiled. "You're tired, my old friend. I forget that you only just arrived this afternoon. Have Vibius escort you to your chamber. We'll talk again in the morning."

As Hosius stood to leave, Constantine added, "Give Vibius your notes on the detailed plans for my church, and ask him to bring them to me. I'd like to review them again."

"Of course, Flavius. But don't stay up all night reading them. You need your sleep, too.

"I have an empire to rule," Constantine said. "I'll sleep after I'm dead."

The next morning, Hosius had Sebastian and Titurius take the invitations to the Emperor's secretary, Sextus Valerius Rutilus, a brilliant man who had served the Emperor for more than twenty years. In all, almost two thousand invitations were being sent by imperial messenger to the bishops of the Christian churches – including the bishops who resided outside of the empire's borders. Hosius estimated that less than five hundred bishops would answer the summons and make the journey, but more than two thousand people would descend on Nicaea for the council meeting because of the priests, acolytes, and servants that would accompany each bishop on his journey.

The Emperor summoned Hosius shortly after breakfast. When Hosius arrived, Constantine was sitting where he had been the night before, reading through the scrolls that Hosius and Athanasius had written on their voyage from Gades to Byzantium.

"I'm amazed at how detailed these plans are," Constantine said when Hosius sat down at the table. "You've thought of things that never occurred to me. I particularly like your ideas for using the churches to gather information about my citizens."

"Athanasius deserves much of the credit, Flavius," Hosius said. "I was mostly focused on the theology of the churches. Athanasius crafted most of the more *practical* suggestions for how the church could serve you and the empire."

"Then he's to be commended," Constantine stated. "I can't help but notice that much of what's written here is how to keep the people controlled through fear. Instead of fearing Rome and her legions, you're going to have everyone afraid of the church."

"Not the church as much as the eternal damnation that they'll face for disobeying God's church," Hosius explained. "We don't want the people to be afraid of the church itself. We want them to flock to the church and obey the church out of fear of displeasing God. We want them terrified of what will happen to them if they ever challenge or defy the church. The plan is for the church to dispense God's punishment for their sins, rather than the punishment of the church itself. But the church will also dispense God's forgiveness for their sins. That way, we'll make them dependent on the church for their eternal well-being."

"That's a subtle distinction," Constantine noted. "Do you think the people will see the difference?"

"Once the priests are properly trained to explain it to them, yes."

Constantine nodded and picked up another scroll. "I also see notes about creating an official version of the writings of the prophets, the gospels, and the epistles. I think that's a good idea – especially if it contains the changes that'll be approved by the council of bishops. But I don't see anything here about what language the official version will be written in."

Hosius was confused. "That's because I had planned for the new versions to be written in the same languages as the old versions."

"And how many languages is that?" Constantine asked.

"Well, there's Greek, Aramaic, Hebrew… perhaps one or two others."

"Shouldn't the official version be in the official language of the empire, since it is, after all, the imperial church?"

"Latin?" Hosius asked. "But not everyone in the empire speaks Latin. If we're going to start translating the prophets, gospels and epistles into other languages, we might as well translate them into every language spoken where there's a church."

"Why?" Constantine asked.

"So the people will understand what the priests are preaching to them," Hosius replied.

"But eventually, the entire empire *will* speak Latin. Until then, if the priests can read and speak Latin, then *they* can translate the passages to their congregations. Besides, I see from your notes that you were never planning on letting the people *read* the prophets, gospels, and epistles for themselves, right?"

Hosius nodded.

"Then using Latin for the official versions shouldn't be a problem, should it?" Constantine insisted.

"As long as the priests all read and speak Latin, no."

"Then add that to your list of things the priests need to be taught."

They talked for a while longer, and then Constantine stood. "I have to review the legions being sent to Judea."

"When may I return to my church in Córdoba, Flavius?" Hosius asked.

"I prefer that you stay here until after the council meetings," Constantine said. "I need you here to plan the meetings and prepare me to sit in judgment of theological issues. If I'm to give the appearance of impartiality, then you must give me guidance."

"Of course, Flavius. I'll send messages to my church to let them know not to expect me before summer."

Constantine nodded and strode out of the chamber. Hosius made additional notes on one of the scrolls about training for the priests. Several minutes later, as he prepared to leave Constantine's chamber, he heard shouts of "Hail Caesar!" from the street below. *That must be the legions. Only the military and the Senate still refer to the Emperor as "Caesar."* Hosius stepped over to the window to watch.

Constantine, now wearing his full armor, had exited the palace and stepped onto the back of his waiting chariot. Eight more chariots, serving as his escort, moved in unison as the Emperor's chariot sped off toward the legionnaire encampment.

The processional disappeared, and Hosius left the Emperor's chamber and went to find Sebastian and Titurius.

Three weeks after the Emperor's secretary dispatched the invitations to the council meeting, Arias heard a chariot approaching as he tended to a small tree in the garden outside his chamber's window. He put down the knife he was using to trim off a broken branch and stepped into the courtyard to see if the chariot was coming to the church.

A moment later, the chariot slowed as it approached the courtyard. When it stopped, an imperial courier stepped down and walked to Arias.

"Arias, the Priest of Baucalis?" the courier asked.

"Yes, I'm Arias."

The courier handed Arias a sealed letter. Arias saw the imperial seal on the outside.

"Thank you," Arias said. "Safe journeys to you."

The courier nodded and returned to the chariot. The charioteer flicked the ear of the lead horse with his whip, and soon the chariot had disappeared in a cloud of dust.

Arias walked back to the garden, grabbed the knife, and went to his chamber to read the letter. Once seated at his desk, he broke the seal. Inside were the official invitation to the council of bishops and information about how best to reach Nicaea. The invitation mentioned that lodging and money for travel expenses would be provided to all attendees. There was also a personal note from Hosius.

Brother Arias,

Greetings, old friend. As you can see, I managed to convince the Emperor to summon the council of bishops to resolve the differences between you and Alexander. And as I suspected, he's insisting that the decision of the council be binding. But I have faith in your power of persuasion.

At the request of the Emperor, I'll be remaining in Byzantium until it's time to leave with the Emperor for the council meeting. Please let me know how you plan to travel to Nicaea, so I can be watching for your arrival.

Safe journeys, my friend.

Hosius, Bishop
Imperial Palace, Byzantium

Arias put down the letters and smiled. *That was kind of Hosius to send me a personal note. He's a good friend.*

Arias shouted for Andrew, Barnabas, and Euric. When they arrived, he shared with them the letter and the invitation.

"The council meeting is less than three months away. I want you to start looking into caravan routes and sea routes to Nicaea that will get us there a week or two before the meetings start. I'd like to get our travel plans made quickly, so I can let Hosius know when to expect us."

"Are we going with you?" Andrew asked.

"Yes, I want all three of you to accompany me; Botherik, too. We have a lot to do before then, and your studies will continue as planned, so plan your time carefully."

The three acolytes left Arias' chamber. Arias looked at Hosius' letter again. *I wonder if I should sail to Byzantium and meet with Hosius there before going overland to Nicaea. That's the faster route. But if we take the overland route, we'll be able to stop at Jerusalem and Antioch. I might be able to meet with the two Patriarchs there. I'd like to have their support; I won't get any from Alexander, and something tells me that I'm going to need all the support I can get.*

CHAPTER 9

Athanasius was returning from the market when an imperial courier stopped him just outside the entrance to the church. "Are you Athanasius of Alexandria?" the courier asked.

Athanasius nodded. "Yes. Do you have a message for me?"

"A private message," the courier said softly. "And it's only for your ears."

Athanasius looked around. There were a number of people nearby, so he gestured for the courier to follow him down an alleyway.

"What is your message?" he asked when they were alone.

"You are to proceed with your suggested plan to keep someone from attending the meeting. Tell no one, and don't let anything get traced back to you." The courier handed Athanasius a heavy leather bag about the size of a small melon. "This should cover the costs."

Athanasius took the bag, and he could tell from the sound that it was filled with coins. "Is there more to the message?"

The courier glanced around quickly. "Only that the person who gave me the message wanted me to tell you that discretion is critical and that you're on your own if anything is discovered."

"I understand. Thank you."

The courier nodded and strode toward the main street. Athanasius secured the bag of coins in the fold of his robe, and by the time he reached the street, the courier had disappeared into the crowd.

Athanasius walked back to the church. *Hosius wants ME to have Arias killed? Why isn't the Emperor taking care of this? I'm a priest, not an assassin.*

Athanasius thought back to his conversation with Hosius. *I guess I can understand why they're putting this on me. After all, keeping Arias from reaching Nicaea was my suggestion. Because I also suggested that the church be given the authority to purge sinners, I guess they want to know if I can do this. If I can't arrange for someone to be killed, then how can I purge heretics and blasphemers from this earth? Hosius must be teaching me that even suggestions have consequences. Well, if he and the Emperor are testing me, then I'll show them that I can pass their test. Arias will never reach Nicaea.*

Athanasius entered the church and walked to his chamber to hide the bag of coins. *Now all I have to do is find out how Arias is traveling to the council meeting, so I can arrange for an accident.*

Two weeks after receiving the invitation to the council meeting, Arias sat in his chamber with Andrew, Barnabas, Euric, and Botherik. "What have you found?" he asked, referring to the travel arrangements to Nicaea.

"I looked at the sea routes," Andrew said. "There are two that will work for us, but one is more expensive than the other. There is a ship leaving Alexandria on April 22nd for Byzantium. It arrives in Byzantium nine days later, and from there, it's a nine-day overland journey to Nicaea. So assuming that it doesn't take more than four days to arrange the overland transportation once we reach Byzantium, it should take no more than twenty-two days to reach Nicaea. There is another ship leaving for Ephesus a day later on April 23rd. It arrives in Ephesus seven days after that, and it's a twelve day overland journey from Ephesus to Nicaea. We'd get to Nicaea at least a day sooner than if we took the ship to Byzantium, but it's more expensive. Both sea routes get us to Nicaea about two weeks before the first council meeting."

"I looked at the overland routes," Barnabas said. "There's a caravan leaving Alexandria before dawn on April 5th. It will pass through Jerusalem and Antioch before reaching Nicaea on its way to Byzantium. It should take about thirty-seven days to reach Nicaea, which gets us there a week before the council meetings start."

Arias nodded. "I've heard that Alexander and Athanasius are sailing for Byzantium on April 22nd. As much as I wanted to travel with Hosius from Byzantium to Nicaea, I don't want Alexander and Athanasius overhearing our conversations. It sounds like the caravan is the best plan, assuming that the supplies we need are less expensive than the cost of sailing to Ephesus."

"It's less expensive," Barnabas assured Arias. "There are several local merchants who have offered to let us travel as part of their party and share their food. All we need to do is arrange for our own camels."

"Do we know if anyone else attending the council meetings will be taking this caravan?" Arias asked.

Barnabas shook his head. "Not that I've heard."

Arias was pleased with his acolytes. "You've all done well, and I thank you. Barnabas, I'd like you to send messages to Eustathius, the Patriarch of Antioch, and Macarius, the Patriarch of Jerusalem, and let them know when we should be arriving in those cities. Let them know that I'd like to speak with them if they haven't yet left for Nicaea."

Barnabas nodded.

Arias looked at Euric. "Euric, I'd like you to arrange for camels. I think ten or twelve should be enough for us to make the journey."

"Yes, Arias," Euric said.

"Botherik," Arias said to his servant, "Go find Athanasius and let him know that we're taking the caravan departing on April 5th."

"As you wish, Arias, but I thought that Hosius wanted you to contact him directly with your travel plans."

"That's true," Arias said, "But I received a letter from Athanasius a few days ago. Hosius has asked him to gather all of the travel arrangements from the attendees in this region."

Botherik nodded. "Yes, sir."

Athanasius was at the church in Alexandria later that afternoon when Botherik arrived. "Thank you for the information," Athanasius said when Botherik gave him Arias' travel plans. "I'll pass it along to Hosius."

"You're welcome, sir," Botherik said, bowing as he left Athanasius' chamber.

Athanasius watched the servant leave, smiling. *Perfect. All I have to do now is find someone to attack the caravan and kill Arias for me.*

Arias was tending to his garden when he saw two men enter the courtyard. He didn't recognize them at first, but as they approached him, he saw their faces clearly – Jacob and Marcus. Both men lived in a village about an hour away, and they and their families attended services regularly at the church in Baucalis. Arias stepped into the courtyard to greet them.

"Welcome, my brothers," he said warmly. "What brings both of you here today?"

"Happy tidings, Brother Arias," Jacob replied. "My son, Anthony, is betrothed to Marcus' daughter, Mary."

"Congratulations!" Arias smiled. "May the blessings of almighty God be on them both and on your houses. But you didn't come all the way here just to tell me that."

Marcus grinned. "Indeed not. We've come to ask you to solemnize the marriage."

"I'm honored," Arias said. "When is the joyous event to take place?"

"The 3rd of April," Jacob answered. "We'll be holding the ceremony at Marcus' house at midday, and then we'll feast until the following morning."

Two days before I leave for Nicaea. That works well for me. Aloud, Arias said, "Wonderful. I'm leaving for a council of bishops in Nicaea on the 5th, so I won't be able to stay for the feast. But I look forward to sharing the happy day with you both."

The three men talked for a while longer. Arias offered Jacob and Marcus food and wine, but they politely declined and left to return to their village. When Arias walked back to the garden, Andrew was there waiting for him.

"Did I hear something about a wedding?" he asked.

Arias nodded. "Anthony and Mary are betrothed. The wedding is on April 3rd. I'll want you to go with me."

"Finally," Andrew said. "I was beginning to think that Jacob and Marcus would never agree to the betrothal."

Arias laughed. "I think they just wanted to make sure that Anthony and Mary are ready for marriage."

"And Jacob wanted to make sure that Marcus could afford a proper wedding," Andrew added.

"That, too," Arias agreed.

Both men laughed, and Arias went back to tending the garden.

Athanasius hadn't spent much time in that part of Alexandria, and he certainly had never spent time in the company of men like the one that sat in front of him.

At the suggestion of one of the soldiers of the city garrison, Athanasius had gone to an establishment on the far side of the harbor that attracted an unsavory clientele. The building was made of rough-hewn stone. He told the barkeep that he wanted to hire men for a job, and the barkeep pointed to a table in the back corner. As Athanasius approached the table, he saw a large, well-armed man sitting in the shadows. Athanasius took a seat across the table from the man.

The man looked up at Athanasius. "Whaddya want?" he asked gruffly.

Athanasius glanced at the cracked plaster on the walls behind the man's head. "The barkeep sent me here. I'm looking to hire some men."

The man chuckled. "Why would *you* want to hire someone like *me*?"

"Because I need some rough work done, and it cannot be linked back to me."

The man took a swig from his tankard and wiped his mouth with the back of his hand. "Rough work, ya say? What's the job?"

"May I count on your discretion?" Athanasius asked.

"Ha!" the man laughed. "People like me don't live long if they can't keep their mouth shut. I won't tell no one what's said here except for my men, and only if I take the job. Is that good enough for ya?"

Athanasius nodded. "There's a man, a priest, named Arias. On April 5th, he's leaving Alexandria in a caravan for Nicaea. I want you to be his escort."

"Ya want me to get him to Nicaea safely?" the man asked. "What's rough about that?"

"You don't understand," Athanasius said, lowering his voice. "I want to make sure that he doesn't get to Nicaea. And I don't want his body or the bodies of his traveling companions to ever be found. Is that rough enough for you?"

The man smiled an evil smile. "Relax, sonny. No need for ya to get yerself in a twist. The job's easy enough, but it's not cheap. I gotta pay my men, and I gotta make sure that we don't get caught. Are ya sure you can afford the work?"

Athanasius placed the bag of coins on the table.

The man grabbed the bag and pulled it toward him. He opened it and looked inside. His eyes opened wide as he stuck a finger in the bag and moved the coins around, as if to make sure that they were all real.

"Ya must really want this priest dead," he said in a hushed voice.

"I do," Athanasius said. "Will you take the job?"

The man stared at Athanasius as the lamplight made the shadows dance across part of his face. Finally, he tied the bag of coins to his belt and said. "Ya, I'll take the job."

He snapped his fingers. Three men got up from another table and joined Athanasius and the man. "My name is Chephren. These are Pakhom, Setna, Sneferu. The rest of my men are outside. Give us the details of the job."

Athanasius told the men when the caravan was leaving and from where, and he gave them the location of Arias' church. "I don't want word reaching Nicaea before the end of May," Athanasius cautioned, "and I don't want Arias talking to anyone who isn't traveling with the caravan. Kill him just before you reach Jerusalem."

"Anything else?" Chephren asked.

"No," Athanasius said, getting to his feet.

"How do I let you know when the job is done?"

"Just do the job and forget that you ever saw me," Athanasius said. "I can't be seen talking with you, and I certainly don't want any message about this in writing."

"I'm yours to command," Chephren said, shaking the bag of coins. He and his men laughed as Athanasius left the establishment.

Athanasius took a winding route back to the church to make sure that he wasn't followed and that no one saw him. *That wasn't so hard. Hiring someone to kill is easier than I thought. I wonder if killing is equally easy.*

"What do you think of this guy, Chephren?" Pakhom asked after Athanasius had left.

"I think he's willing to pay a lot of money to make a problem go away," Chephren replied. "He must be someone very important to be able to pay this much, and the person he wants us to lose in the desert must be someone of equal importance. If we do a good job, maybe there's more work for us in the future."

Chephren looked around and noticed that there were more patrons that usual. "Let's get outta here. Too many ears."

He tossed a copper coin to the barkeep as they left, and he and the others left the establishment to find the rest of their men.

On the morning of April 3rd, Arias and Andrew set out for the wedding. Barnabas, Euric, and Botherik remained at the church to pack and load the camels for the journey to Nicaea. Arias wanted to reach the caravan's camp the night before it was to leave. "I don't want to risk being late," he told them.

Arias and Andrew reached Marcus' house an hour before the wedding started. Arias had already met with Anthony and Mary earlier in the week to counsel them on how to live according to God's word. Now he met with them individually to see if they had any last-minute questions. Both the bride and bridegroom seemed a bit nervous, but Arias could tell that they were ready to begin their life as a married couple.

The ceremony was beautiful. Marcus had spared no expense on the comfort of their guests. After Arias had finished solemnizing the marriage, he and Andrew stayed for an hour to share wine and meat. Then they wished the couple well and left the feast to return to Baucalis.

It was late in the afternoon when they arrived back at the church. The camels were packed and tethered at the far end of the courtyard.

Andrew followed Arias inside. "Thank you for accompanying me today, Andrew," Arias said as he turned toward his chamber. "I don't know about you, but I'm exhausted. We should both get as much rest as we can. We have a long journey ahead of us."

Several hours after midnight, Arias woke and heard shouting. He sat up just as Botherik entered his chamber.

"Oh, good. You're awake, Arias. Come quickly."

Arias dressed and followed the servant to the courtyard. Marcus and another man were there looking worn-out and anxious.

"My brothers," Arias greeted the two men. "What brings you here at this hour? Is everything well?"

"No," Marcus said frantically. "Please, you must come back with us right now! Something terrible has happened. Most of the wedding party has fallen ill, and Jacob is near death. I don't know what has happened, but you need to come and heal them."

By this time, Andrew, Barnabas, and Euric had joined them in the courtyard. "We'll come immediately," Arias said to Marcus.

Arias turned to his acolytes. "I want you all to come with me. We'll take the camels. That way we can leave the village and go straight to the caravan. Run and get your belongings and any supplies that you need to take with you."

"I'll get your things, Arias," Botherik offered.

"Thank you, Botherik."

A short while later, Arias, his three acolytes, Botherik, Marcus, and the other man from the village were mounted on the camels and heading for the village.

Arias prayed as they left Baucalis. *Oh, Heavenly Father, in Your kingdom there is no illness. Man, made in your image and likeness, cannot have anything that You cannot have. You cannot be ill, so Your creation cannot be ill either. The malady that seems to have struck the wedding party is not of Your creating and therefore has no power. You are the only power, and You are love. I rejoice in Your tender care for Your children, and these people are Your children. No illness can touch them, only Your word, and Your word is peace, joy, and health. There is no illness.*

Arias arrived at the village an hour before dawn. Anthony ran out to meet Arias and the others. "It's the wine," he said, helping everyone tether the camels. "There's something wrong with the last cask that we opened. Everyone who drank from it is ill. Those of us who didn't are fine. My father drank the most. Please save him!"

Arias put his hand on the frantic bridegroom's shoulder. "Everyone is fine, Anthony. God loves his children and keeps them from harm. Think on that."

Arias and his acolytes entered Marcus' courtyard, where the feast had taken place. Botherik stayed with the camels. At Arias' request, Marcus, Anthony, and the other guests who were well, remained outside.

Arias had taught his acolytes how to heal through The Way. He directed them to tend to the other guests, and he went to find Jacob. When Arias reached the groom's father, he saw that Jacob's deep olive skin was pale, and his eyes were staring far away. His breathing was labored and shallow. Arias knelt next to him and prayed. Then he placed his hand on Jacob's chest and whispered. There didn't seem to be any change in Jacob's condition. Arias kept his hand on Jacob's chest and continued whispering.

The sun rose in the east and climbed higher in the sky. Arias didn't move.

After another hour, Jacob's breathing became regular, his eyes returned to normal, and the color of his skin became less pale. "Bring me water," Arias shouted. Anthony brought a flagon of water and a chalice. Arias poured water in the chalice and held up Jacob's head so he could sip it.

"Father!" Anthony cried.

"Jacob is fine, Anthony," Arias said, kindly. "There's nothing to fear."

"Thanks be to God!" Anthony said as he hugged his father. Looking up at Arias, he added, "You have blessed my wedding day twice. Thank you, Arias!"

Arias smiled. "All thanks belong to God, Anthony. Praise Him, and you will never lack for blessings."

Anthony stayed by his father, and Arias went to the next person who needed his help.

Arias and his acolytes ministered to the sick at the wedding feast for the rest of the day and well into the night. Everyone was healed and able to return home.

Arias sat down to a quick meal with his acolytes and Botherik once their work was finished. "How far do you think we are from the caravan site?" Arias asked.

"At least two hours," Botherik replied.

Arias nodded. "That's a long way to travel at night even if we weren't already tired. If we stay here tonight and leave early in the morning, we'll be more rested, and we should still be able to reach the caravan site before sunrise."

Botherik and the acolytes agreed. "The moon will have risen by then," Barnabas commented. "That should give us enough light to see where we're going and to find the caravan site."

Arias shared their plans with Marcus. "I have a place for you to sleep," Marcus offered.

"Thank you, my friend," Arias said. "We are in your debt."

"Not at all," Marcus said as he led them across the courtyard. "It's the least I can do for all that you've done for my family and friends."

An hour before sunset, eight riders entered the courtyard of the church at Baucalis. "I'm looking for Arias, the Priest," the leader bellowed.

One of the younger servants ran out to the courtyard to meet them. "Arias is not here, sir," the servant said.

"Where is he, and when did he leave?" Chephren demanded. "We're his escort to Nicaea."

"He left early this morning, sir. He took all of the camels. He must be with the caravan already."

Chephren turned his mount, and he and his men rode away at full speed. *Damn! Now we'll have to search the entire caravan to find him. I knew we shouldn't have waited so long to get here.*

Several hours after sunrise, Arias and the others awoke in one of Marcus' guest rooms on the far side of the courtyard. Arias rose and dressed. *We've missed the caravan! I never intended to sleep so late. The caravan will be leagues away by now. It'll be nearly impossible to catch up with it.*

"I'm sorry, Arias," Marcus said, bringing Arias a loaf of fresh bread. "I overslept and forgot to wake you."

"Think nothing of it, my friend," Arias said kindly, taking the bread from his hand. "Yesterday was a long and unusual day for all of us. You were up late looking after your family and guests. We should have left for the caravan last night."

"Can you still reach it in time?" Marcus asked.

"Doubtful, and it seems foolish to race off into the desert after them without knowing exactly which path they took. No, we'll return to Baucalis. There are other ways to get to Nicaea that are faster."

Arias ate quickly and then went around the village to check on the guests that had been healed the day before. Satisfied that they were doing well, he returned to Marcus' house.

"How is your father?" he asked when he saw Anthony.

"He is well, Arias," Anthony replied gratefully. "He slept peacefully, and he just finished eating. His appetite is as it always was."

"Good," Arias said. "And how is Mary this morning?"

Anthony blushed. Arias put his hand on the young man's arm and smiled. "That's all I need to know."

As they crossed the courtyard, Anthony pointed out a wine cask at the far end. Dogs and cats were drinking from it. "That's the last cask of wine that was opened," he said. "The animals have been drinking from it all night and all morning, and not one of them has gotten sick from it."

"If it were poisoned, you'd think that the poison would affect them," Arias commented.

"I know," Anthony agreed. "The animals have been eating the leftover food, too, and they're fine. How could the food or drink harm the guests and not the animals?"

"I don't know," Arias admitted. "Perhaps the poison was not in the food or the wine, or perhaps there never was a poison.

It's not important what caused the illness – only that the illness is gone and everyone is fine."

"You don't think it's an omen that the marriage is doomed, do you?" Anthony asked.

"If that were the case, then your guests would have died," Arias said kindly. "But your guests were healed, and that could only happen if God were in this place, giving his blessings to all who were here with you. Be assured, your marriage is blessed, and your union will flourish and bless others for many years to come."

Arias left Anthony staring at the wine cask and went to join the others where the camels were tethered. *It's interesting that an illness sprang up so suddenly and then went away just as suddenly with no trace of what caused it. It's almost like we were supposed to be here, rather than with the caravan. But why would God not want us to be with the caravan?*

CHAPTER 10

Arias, Andrew, Barnabas, Euric, and Botherik returned to the church in Baucalis shortly after noon. They tethered the camels on the far side of the courtyard and started unloading their supplies.

"I don't think that we'll need the camels any longer," Arias said. "See if you can sell them back where you bought them."

"I'm sure I can, Arias," Botherik said.

"Do you want me to make arrangements for us to sail to Byzantium with Alexander and Athanasius?" Andrew asked.

"No, I think we should take the ship to Ephesus leaving on the 23rd. That's eighteen days from now, it's a shorter journey, and it gets us to Nicaea with plenty of time to meet with the Patriarchs and the bishops who oppose the Trinity."

"I'll start arranging passage to Ephesus today," Andrew promised.

"I'll send a message to the bishop there," Arias said. "Perhaps he can provide us lodging while we arrange to get from Ephesus to Nicaea."

Arias was helping Barnabas unload the camels that carried their tents when one of the servants came running toward them.

"Arias, you're back! What are you doing here?"

"We missed the caravan," Arias explained. "We'll have to go to Nicaea by ship."

"But what about your escort?" the servant asked.

"What escort?"

"Eight riders showed up late yesterday afternoon. They said they were your escort to Nicaea. I told them that you had already left to meet the caravan, and they rode off. Didn't they find you?"

"We never made it to the caravan," Arias said. "Most of the guests at Anthony and Mary's wedding fell ill after Andrew and I returned. We were there, tending to the sick, until late last night. When we awoke this morning, the caravan had already left Alexandria hours earlier. So we came back here."

Arias look at Barnabas, "Did you hire an escort for us?"

Barnabas shook his head, looking confused.

Turning back to the servant, Arias asked, "Did the escorts say who hired them?"

"No, Arias. They just asked where you were, and then they rode off when I told them that you had left already."

Arias nodded. *That's strange. Who would have hired an escort for us? Surely not Alexander. Perhaps Hosius sent one. I'll have to ask him when I see him in Nicaea.*

"Do you think they left with the caravan this morning?" Euric asked.

"I don't know," Arias replied. "It might take them a while to search the caravan before they realize that we're not there."

"Will they come back here when they can't find us with the caravan?" Andrew asked. "Should I arrange passage for them to sail with us to Ephesus?"

Arias thought about this for a moment. Then he shook his head. "No, let's wait and see if they return here first. It could be days before they realize that we're not with the caravan and just as long to ride back here looking for us. I don't want to wait that long to secure our passage on the ship to Ephesus."

"Yes, Arias," Andrew said.

Arias and the others finished unloading the camels and putting the supplies away.

Chephren and his men quickly realized how difficult it would be to find Arias and his traveling companions. The caravan was immense, with hundreds of merchants transporting their wares and flocks to be sold in cities along the caravan route. There were also a large number of pilgrims journeying to Jerusalem. But worst of all was the fact that Chephren and his men had never seen Arias before.

"It won't do much good to search for him while the caravan is moving," Setna said after noon on the first day out of Alexandria. "It's too easy to miss someone."

"I agree," Pakhom said. "We should wait until the caravan stops before we search for him."

"But we'd only have a few hours of light each day to search by," Chephren protested. "It'd take weeks to find him."

"It'll take longer if we try to find him while we're moving," Pakhom pointed out. "We don't know what he looks like, so we have to ask everyone we see if they know him. Folks are too busy to talk to us while the caravan is moving."

Chephren glared at his men. *Damn! This job is starting badly. We missed him at his church, and now we can't find him while the caravan is moving.* "Okay, fine. Wait until the caravan stops. But as soon as we stop, I want ya to spread out and find him!"

Arias was sitting in his garden when Andrew returned from the port at Alexandria.

"Good news, Arias," Andrew said. "I've booked our passage to Ephesus. We can't arrange for the overland travel until we get there, but at least the first part of the journey is taken care of."

Arias smiled. "Thank you, Andrew. I feel like there's something else that we're supposed to do before we leave, but I can't think of what it is."

"Well, if you think of it, just let me know," Andrew said. "Did Botherik sell the camels?"

Arias nodded. "Yes, he had no trouble selling them back to the merchant who had sold them to us. The merchant is a member of the congregation here, and he gave Botherik a steep discount on the original sale price. Now he can sell them to someone else at their full price. His generosity toward us has been repaid."

A week after the caravan left Alexandria, Chephren met with his men at their campsite.

"He's not here, Chephren," Pakhom stated.

"Ya searched the entire caravan?" Chephren asked angrily.

"Yes," Chephren's men said.

"I met several merchants who knew him," Setna added. "He was supposed to travel with 'em, but he never made it. They think he must have missed the caravan."

"The servant at the church told us he'd left already for the caravan!" Chephren insisted.

"The servant was wrong," Pakhom said. "They clearly went somewhere if they had camels, but it wasn't to the caravan."

Chephren glared at the campfire. *Now what do we do? We can't find this Arias, so we can't finish the job. But I don't know who hired us, so I can't tell him that the job wasn't done. Should we go on or turn back to Alexandria? We have enough food and wine to get us to Jerusalem, but it's a long trek back to Alexandria from there. And we're not exactly welcome in Jerusalem, so going there to look for work isn't a good idea.*

"Okay, we'll leave the caravan in the morning and go back to Alexandria," Chephren said finally. "We have enough money to last until we find more work. Agreed?"

His men all nodded.

"Good. Get some sleep. I want to be gone by first light."

Athanasius felt very happy as he made preparations to sail to Byzantium with Alexander. *Arias should be dead by now – his body and the bodies of his companions lost in the desert for all time. Hosius and the Emperor will be pleased. Arias' followers will be much easier to control at the council meeting with their champion absent. Perhaps the Patriarchs will give me Arias' church at Baucalis as reward for my faithful duty.*

Chephren and his men stopped at the top of a ridge and looked down on the city of Alexandria.

"The city never looked so good," Chephren said, wiping the dust from his face with a rag. "I need to wash the desert off of me and grab something to drink that's stronger than this wine we brought."

His men laughed. With Chephren in the lead, they rode down to Alexandria.

Athanasius and Alexander boarded the ship taking them to Byzantium just before midday. Alexander went directly to his compartment to rest. He didn't like sea travel. Athanasius knew that he'd see little of Alexander during the voyage.

Athanasius enjoyed sea travel, and his favorite parts were leaving and entering the harbors. He stood at the rear of the merchant galley so he could watch Alexandria grow smaller in the distance as the ship rowed north.

As the galley pulled away from the dock, the sailor next to Athanasius tapped him on the shoulder.

"Forgive me, sir, but I think there's someone on the dock trying to get your attention."

Athanasius looked at the dock and saw a man waving his arms. It was Chephren, the man he had hired to kill Arias. *What's he doing back in Alexandria so soon? Leave it to mercenaries to do the job quickly so they can take on other jobs.* Athanasius waved to him.

Chephren cupped his hands around his mouth and shouted something.

"Can you understand what he's saying?" Athanasius asked the sailor.

"Not all of it, sir," the sailor replied. "I think he said something about a job being done and then something about a caravan."

Athanasius smiled. *Arias IS dead. I can tell Hosius that there's no doubt.* He nodded to Chephren and leaned on the railing along the rear of the galley's upper deck, watching the port and the city grow smaller in the distance.

Chephren had been wandering the docks of Alexandria, looking for any merchant who was unloading a large cargo and might want to hire some guards. As he approached a galley being loaded, he saw a face in the distance that he recognized. The man was boarding a galley that was preparing to leave the dock. Chephren got closer and remembered where he had seen it before. It was the man who had hired him to escort and kill the priest.

I should tell him that we didn't get the job done.

Chephren pushed his way through the crowd and reached the ship just as it was rowing away from the dock. He saw the man standing on the back railing of the galley. "Hey!" he shouted, waving his arms to get the man's attention.

After a few moments, he saw the man notice him and wave. "The job's not done!" Chephren shouted. "He wasn't with the caravan!"

Getting no reaction from the man, Chephren shouted it again. This time, the man on the galley nodded to him. *Good, he heard me, and he didn't seem too upset that the priest is still alive.*

Chephren didn't give the matter another thought. He turned to make his way along the rest of the docks, looking for anyone who needed to hire his men. Not finding any work, he returned to the establishment where he had been hired to escort Arias.

"Barkeep, a jug of your strongest," he said, reaching into the bag on his belt and extracting a coin. He flicked it to the barkeep and took a seat at his favorite table in the back. *Easiest money I've ever made.*

The next morning, Arias, Andrew, Barnabas, Euric, and Botherik boarded their ship for Ephesus. The docks were illuminated by torches and braziers in the pre-dawn darkness, and a gentle breeze rocked the galleys moored to the docks, making a strange rhythmic thumping sound that filled the harbor.

"I guess the ship that Alexander and Athanasius took to Byzantium left yesterday," Andrew commented as they were escorted to their compartments.

Suddenly, Arias remembered what he was supposed to do when Andrew booked their passage. "I completely forgot to tell Athanasius about the changes to our travel plans. He still thinks we're with the caravan."

"I wonder if he'll be surprised to see us waiting for him in Nicaea," Andrew commented, chuckling.

The galley to Ephesus made good time. At midday on the eighth day of their voyage, they rowed into the port at Ephesus. The galley was unloaded quickly, and soon Arias and his companions had found transportation into the city.

It was a short ride from the harbor to the church at Ephesus, where Arias planned to seek lodging until finalizing the arrangements for the overland journey to Nicaea. Arias had sent a letter to Menophantus, the Bishop of Ephesus and a faithful Follower of The Way, to be expecting them on the first of May.

When they arrived at the church, Menophantus came out to meet them, followed by several other bishops. Menophantus' greying hair was so long and wiry that it made him look like an aging lion when the air was damp and warm. Arias recognized the other bishops instantly as he greeted Menophantus – Secundus of Ptolemais, Paulinus of Tyrus, Actius of Lydda, Theonus of Marmarica, and Zphyrius and Dathes from the Pentapolis.

"What are you doing here, my friends?" Arias asked after he had introduced his traveling companions to the assembled bishops.

"We had already planned to meet here in Ephesus before going on to Nicaea," Secundus said. "When Menophantus said that you had missed your caravan and were coming this way, we decided to wait for you."

"So we'll be making our own caravan to Nicaea," Actius said. "Everything's all arranged. We'll leave here the day after tomorrow."

Menophantus gestured for everyone to enter the church. "Let's find you a place to sleep inside, and then we'll eat. There's much to discuss."

The meal was simple, but delicious. Menophantus' priests had roasted a lamb and served it with fresh bread, savory herbs, and figs. Once they had finished the meal, the priests and acolytes traveling to Nicaea withdrew, so Arias and the bishops could meet in private.

"Do we know where Eustathius of Antioch and Macarius of Jerusalem stand?" Arias asked.

Menophantus shook his head. "I haven't heard, but I can't imagine that they'll support us against Alexander."

"There's something strange about the Patriarchs and the bishops from the east," Secundus said. "Always has been. Maybe it's a remnant of the old religions here, but they have a strange perspective on miracles. They just can't conceive of how ordinary men can perform them. They were the first to embrace the idea that Jesus is God and that the apostles only worked miracles because of the gift of divine power that they received after the resurrection. In their minds, miracles ended with the apostles and have never been performed since. They get indignant when you tell them that the healing works of Jesus are still performed today in many of the churches."

"And Alexander grew up surrounded by that kind of thinking," Arias noted. "It may be why he has been pushing the Divine Trinity idea ever since he was an acolyte. He looks at God in the same way that the Israelites did – except that, instead of God sitting on a mountaintop and appearing as a burning bush, he walked along the Sea of Galilee disguised as a man. For some reason, he and the others need to have a god that has walked the earth. They can't conceive of God as a spirit who fills all space."

"It's astounding how easy it has been for them to convince others that Jesus is God," Actius commented. "Followers of Jesus seem to be taking a huge step backward. It's like they need a god that they can touch and hold. They don't feel God in their hearts; they don't hear him speak to them. Honestly, I think Rome lifting the persecution of us was the worst thing that could have happened. Our religion is becoming more Roman every day. Before long, there will be giant statues of Jesus and the apostles in our churches for us to worship like the Romans do with statues of their gods."

Paulinus looked shocked. "Do you really think it'll come to that?"

"Look around," Actius said. "Every day the churches get farther from The Way that our Master taught us. The bishops from the west aren't yet as corrupted as the eastern bishops have become, but it's only a matter of time if the Divine Trinity gets approved as the official theology of the churches."

"And isn't it interesting that the council meeting is being held in the east?" Theonus asked. "It's like Emperor Constantine wants to make it more difficult for the western bishops to attend."

"So what do we do to stop the corruption of the churches?" Arias asked.

"I don't know," Menophantus admitted. "But we'd better figure something out before we reach Nicaea."

The galley carrying Alexander and Athanasius arrived in Byzantium the next afternoon. Hosius was waiting for them on the dock with an escort to take them to the church at Byzantium. Alexander's disposition improved once he was on land again, but he was still weak from the journey. Hosius instructed the escorts to take Alexander and his acolytes and retainers to the church. Hosius wanted to talk to Athanasius in private.

"Did you get my message?" he asked once Alexander and the others were out of sight.

Athanasius nodded. "I took care of it. Arias made arrangements to travel with a caravan, and I hired an escort to make sure that he arrives at his *final* destination."

"Good," Hosius said as the two men left the harbor and climbed the hill leading to the church. "How far will he get?"

"He didn't make it to Jerusalem," Athanasius replied.

Hosius looked at Athanasius. "You have confirmation already?" he demanded.

"I do," Athanasius replied happily. "The man I hired for the job spotted me from the dock just as our ship was rowing out of the harbor at Alexandria. He shouted to me that the job was done."

"You hired someone who knows who you are?" Hosius hissed.

"No, it was a happy accident that he saw me. I never gave him my name, and I made sure that he didn't follow me back to the church."

Hosius relaxed. *We can't afford to have anything link Arias' death back to us.*

"When do we leave for Nicaea?" Athanasius asked, changing the subject.

"Four days," Hosius replied. "We're traveling with the Emperor and two cavalry cohorts that are being assigned to the far eastern borders. The cavalry won't be ready to leave before then. We should arrive in Nicaea on the fourteenth of May – the fifteenth at the latest."

"I'm looking forward to the council meeting," Athanasius said.

"Me too," Hosius said. "Especially now that we won't have Arias to worry about."

CHAPTER 11

Arias and the bishops, along with their retainers, left Ephesus as the orange glow of the sun rose above the horizon. In all, there were fifty people in the caravan and one hundred and fifty camels.

As the caravan reached the edge of the city, Arias saw ten well-armed riders ahead.

"Ah, our escort is right on time," Menophantus of Ephesus said to Arias and the bishops. "I thought it would be prudent to have guides protecting us on the journey."

Menophantus spoke to the leader of the escorts. The leader then took his place at the front of the caravan while his men positioned themselves along the sides and at the rear of the riders and the camels carrying the supplies for the journey.

Arias and the bishops didn't speak much to each other while the caravan was moving. There were too many priests, acolytes, and servants traveling with them who might overhear their conversations.

At the end of the first day of their twelve-day overland trek to Nicaea, Arias and the bishops sat around a small campfire a short distance away from the others.

"Where did you find the escorts?" Secundus of Ptolemais asked.

"They're all members of my congregation at Ephesus," Menophantus replied. "They each volunteered to get us safely to Nicaea and back."

"Someone hired escorts for me when I was supposed to be taking the caravan from Alexandria to Nicaea," Arias commented. "I had left the church to minister to members of a wedding party who fell sick, and when the escorts arrived, one of my servants, who didn't know where I had gone, told them that I'd left for the caravan already. They rode off and never returned. I don't know if they're still with the caravan, or if they finally realized that I wasn't there and turned back."

"Who hired them?" Actius of Lydda asked.

"I have no idea," Arias replied.

"You can bet that it wasn't Alexander," Theonus of Marmarica said, his thick eyebrows moving closer together as he looked suspicious. "He certainly wouldn't do anything to help you arrive at the council meeting safely."

"You don't think he'd do anything to *keep* Arias from arriving, do you?" Paulinus of Tyrus asked.

"No," Theonus replied. "Athanasius might, but not Alexander. He's a devout follower of Christ, even if his theology is flawed. He'd never condone an act of violence. Besides, he's too confident in his position to be worried about Arias attending the meeting. He believes that the council will embrace his theology and denounce ours."

"Perhaps Hosius sent the escort," Actius suggested.

"That's possible," Arias agreed. "He came to see me a couple of months ago on the Emperor's orders. The Emperor wanted the problems resolved between Alexander and me, but that was a hopeless errand. Hosius' failure to get us to agree is what led to the Emperor calling for the council meeting. Anyway, Hosius made it clear that he wanted me at the meetings to be the champion of our cause. He said that I'd be able to convince many of the bishops to side with us against the Trinity doctrine. I believe that he'd want me to arrive safely."

"Do you trust Hosius, Arias?" Menophantus asked. "He's the Emperor's lifelong friend and confidant, and in the end, he'll do whatever the Emperor wants."

"I do trust him, Menophantus," Arias stated. "He's always been a good friend to me. I know he has to remain neutral because he and the Emperor will be presiding over the council meetings, but I think he wants us to succeed."

"I've heard him openly support the Trinity doctrine," Secundus said. "And don't forget that Athanasius traveled with him from Byzantium when he came to see you. One of my priests, Peter, saw him disembark with Hosius at Alexandria."

"I asked Hosius about that when he came to see me," Arias said. "Alexander sent Athanasius to Hispania with a letter and gave him instructions to wait for a reply. Hosius had just been summoned to Byzantium by the Emperor, and he told Athanasius to come with him since he had to meet with the Emperor before he'd have a reply for Athanasius to bring back to Alexander. That's why they were traveling together."

"So Athanasius traveled with Hosius from Hispania to Byzantium and then to Alexandria?" Secundus asked. "That's nearly two months that they were together. Doesn't that concern you?"

"Should it?" Arias asked. "I think it's more likely that Hosius influenced Athanasius' views, not the other way around."

"You're a trusting soul, Arias," Secundus said.

"I live my faith," Arias stated. "How can I honor my commitment to our Master and The Way if I don't see the good in everyone? I have to believe that Hosius is on our side, and that the council meeting will provide us a forum to present our arguments and persuade the council to see things the right way. To believe anything else would be to admit that the council meeting is a sham, and I can't believe that the churches have gone so far down the wrong path that they'd summon us to a council just to ridicule us openly before the Emperor."

Arias looked at the faces of the bishops, but he could tell that they were unconvinced. "Well, I still have faith in Hosius," he insisted. "Why allow me to attend a meeting only for bishops if not to give me the chance to present our position on the theology of the churches?"

"I hope you're right, Arias." Menophantus sounded doubtful. "The future of The Way depends on our success at the council meeting."

"I'm right," Arias said confidently. "Trust in God to show us what to say and do, and trust Hosius to give us the opportunity to be heard."

The Emperor's procession from Byzantium to Nicaea was an inspiring sight. Hosius, Alexander, and Athanasius rode near Emperor Constantine and his imperial guards. One cohort of legionnaire cavalry rode in front and along the flanks of the imperial party, while the second cohort rode just behind the imperial party. The reflection of the rising sun on the armor of the guards and legionnaires was almost blinding as the procession rode east on the first morning of the journey. It was the first time that Emperor Constantine had left Byzantium since his legions had made him the absolute master of the Roman Empire when they defeated Licinius' army.

"Any last-minute instructions?" Athanasius asked after he had reined his mount closer to Hosius so they could talk privately.

"No, other than to remind you that your role during the council meetings is to challenge Arias' supporters at every turn, and make them look like fools to the other bishops. They'll be prepared to offer evidence from the prophets, the gospels, and the epistles to support their statements, so be sure that you have compelling evidence from the same sources to support yours. The council meetings will be a theological battle, and our side must win in the end. The Emperor will not tolerate failure on our part."

"Has the Emperor approved our plans for the imperial church?" Athanasius asked.

"Yes. In fact, when I pointed out to him the parts that you suggested, he was very complimentary of your work. He told me to tell you that you're to be commended for your contributions."

"What about the more controversial parts like the Mother Goddess and giving the churches the authority to condemn people for heresy and blasphemy?"

"He had no issues with those," Hosius replied. "He particularly liked having a Mother Goddess in our pantheon, and his preference is for Mary's own conception to have been an act of divine creation by the universe itself. He thinks it'll be easier for his people to accept the divinity of Jesus if Mary is also divine. As for condemning people for heresy and blasphemy, he's drawing up a set of guidelines for us to use so we don't overstep our authority and cross into what's the purview of the imperial government."

"Wonderful," Athanasius said. "How do you think Arias' followers will react when they realize that he's not coming?"

"It'll take them some time to reorganize and select one of their own to replace Arias as their champion during the council meetings," Hosius speculated. "We can take advantage of that time to push the Divine Trinity and ridicule their position. If we hit them hard enough at the beginning, they won't be able to recover, and we'll be able to expel their doctrines quickly."

"Do you see any problem getting the Patriarchs to agree with our plans?"

Hosius shook his head. "No. Alexander is already on our side, Sylvester of Rome is not attending but has given me the authority to cast his vote as I see fit, and Eustathius of Antioch, Macarius of Jerusalem, and Eusebius of Caesarea are all from eastern churches that favor a god who has walked on the earth rather than a spirit in the heavens. I think that they'll agree to anything that the Emperor wants as long as their version of a unified theology is adopted. Plus, I think that they'll come to enjoy the power they'll have as the spiritual heads of the new imperial church."

"That's an interesting point. Do you think the Patriarchs going forward will be content to govern the church as a council, or will they start striving for sole control over the churches?"

Hosius smiled. "A supreme leader of the churches? It's possible that may happen in the future, but I think that, as men of God, they'll see the wisdom of keeping the power out of a single hand. Power corrupts, after all, and we need to keep that sort of corruption away from the church."

"I wonder if Alexander has any idea that we've been using him for all of these years," Athanasius whispered.

"I doubt it. Alexander has always been a simple-minded person. He's so focused on the myth of the Divine Trinity that it's a wonder he can hold another thought in his head. As long as we give him what he wants, he'll give us what we want so he doesn't have to think about it."

"*Myth* of the Divine Trinity?" Athanasius asked. "You mean you don't believe that Jesus is God?"

"I didn't say that," Hosius replied smoothly. "But you have to admit that Arias' arguments against the Trinity make sense. For nearly three hundred years, the churches believed that Jesus is the son of God, not God himself. The Divine Trinity is a relatively recent reinterpretation of the gospels and the epistles. Is Arias wrong because he believes what the churches have always believed, or is Alexander wrong because he's interpreting things differently than the churches have in the past?"

"If you doubt the Trinity, then why support it?"

"Because my focus all along has been on making Christianity a religion that can thrive and grow in the empire," Hosius explained. "To do that, I have to give Constantine an imperial church that will help him rule his empire. Constantine believes that the Divine Trinity will be easier for his people to accept, so I support it and the bishops who want it to be the official doctrine of the churches."

Athanasius persisted. "But *do* you believe in the Trinity?"

Hosius laughed. "Oh, Athanasius, of course I do. But I don't let my beliefs get in the way of my responsibilities to the churches. I convinced the Emperor to allow us to worship openly without fear of persecution, and I convinced him to make us the state religion of the empire. And all it took to do that was to promise him a unified theology for the churches – the unified theology that *he* supports. And that's what I'm doing. In thirteen years, we've gone from being an underground movement living in constant fear of discovery to becoming the official religion of the greatest empire the world has ever known. That's *my* legacy to the churches."

Athanasius nodded, and the two men rode on in silence.

Arias, the bishops, and all of their retainers made good time on their journey, arriving in Nicaea mid-afternoon on the twelfth day after leaving Ephesus. Arias and the bishops immediately rode to the church at Nicaea to meet with Theognus, the bishop there.

When they arrived, they were happy to find that Eusebius of Nicomedia and Maris of Chalcedon were already there. These two bishops, along with Theognus, were also devout followers of The Way and supporters of Arias.

"Any news of Hosius?" Arias asked once they were all seated in Theognus' chamber.

"He's expected here tomorrow," Theognus replied, brushing a fly off his tanned, bald head. "He's traveling with the Emperor."

"Are Alexander and Athanasius with him?" Arias asked.

"Yes."

Arias nodded, and Secundus gave Arias an I-told-you-so look.

"Any word on the number of bishops from the western churches that will be attending?" Menophantus asked.

"Not many," Theognus admitted. "Fewer than four hundred bishops have sent messages to confirm that they're attending, and most of those are from the eastern empire. We're definitely in the minority."

"Arias believes that Hosius will make sure that we're given a fair hearing," Secundus said.

"I wish I could agree with you, Arias," Theognus said. "You're the only one of us who counts him among your friends. He's never been a friend to me. He's the Emperor's man first and a bishop second. Never doubt that."

"That may be true," Arias admitted, "but regardless of his position on the Trinity doctrine, he made sure that we all attended. Now that we're here, what we do is up to us. We'll present our views on the theology of the churches. No one has to listen to us, but they can't stop us from speaking out on what we believe."

"If Hosius is helping the Emperor preside over the meetings, couldn't he control whether or not we get to speak out?" Eusebius asked.

Each of the bishops began talking over each other with their own dire predictions of what Hosius or the Emperor might do to prevent them from speaking out against the Divine Trinity.

Arias held up his hands. "It's not a question of whether Hosius and the Emperor will do anything to stop us. We have no choice but to make certain that we're heard. The correct understanding of our Master's words and works are at stake. The Way that we and the churches have faithfully followed for nearly three hundred years is at stake. If we don't stand up for the true theology, then by the end of this council, all that our Master said and did will have been for nothing, and The Way will die. When it's our turn to stand before God and answer for our lives, will we say that we cowered in the face of opposition or that we stood and fought for what's right? Now, I still believe that Hosius is on our side, but even if he isn't, it doesn't change the fact that we have to fight for our beliefs, and if the numbers are stacked against us, then we have to fight that much harder."

"I'm so grateful that you're here to speak for us, Arias," Theognus said. "Between your eloquence at persuasion, and your faith, what can stand against us?"

The other bishops nodded in agreement. Arias accepted the compliment with a smile, but deep inside, he felt anxious. *Is Hosius really on our side? He's never given me a reason to doubt his sincerity, but I seem to be the only one who believes it. Did he want us here so we could speak out against the Trinity in a safe and convivial setting, or is there something else going on here that I haven't seen?*

The Emperor's procession arrived at Nicaea the day after Arias did. Trumpets sounded all across the city as the Emperor and the imperial guards entered the gates and rode to the palace where the council meetings would be held. The two cohorts of legionnaire cavalry remained outside of the city. They'd be leaving two days later to join the rest of their legions along the eastern borders of the empire.

Hosius, Athanasius, and Alexander accompanied the Emperor to the palace. Alexander and the other Patriarchs were being housed at the palace, as were Hosius and Athanasius. Once Hosius, Athanasius, and Alexander were settled in their chambers, they went to find food before going to the church at Nicaea.

'Even though Bishop Theognus is one of Arias' supporters, it's only proper that we pay our respects to the head of the church that's helping to host the council meeting," Hosius explained when Athanasius questioned the need to visit the church.

"Do you think that Arias will be there?" Alexander asked.

Athanasius and Hosius looked at each other. Then Hosius replied. "I have no idea, Alexander. Arias left with the caravan more than a month ago. I guess it depends on how fast they moved and how many stops they made along the way."

Alexander nodded and sliced another wedge of cheese for his bread.

Hosius hid a smile. *Good. Alexander still has no idea what Athanasius arranged to be done to Arias. The council meetings will start in a few days, and then Arias' supporters will realize that he's not coming. Without their champion, they have no hope of convincing anyone to join their side. Alexander will return to*

Alexandria and realize that Arias has disappeared. Athanasius will be given the church at Baucalis, and that'll be the end of the opposition within the churches.

An hour later, Hosius, Alexander, and Athanasius left the palace and walked to the church at Nicaea. Imperial guards were posted all around the palace, and legionnaires from the nearby garrison patrolled the streets. The sudden addition to the city of hundreds of bishops, priests, acolytes, and servants put a strain on city resources. Wagon trains of food and wine arrived daily to feed the city's guests, and casks of water were being brought in to prevent the local wells from being drained dry.

There was quite a crowd standing outside the church when Hosius and the other two men arrived. "I guess we're not the only ones who stopped by to pay their respects," Hosius said to Alexander and Athanasius.

They waited patiently for their turn to greet Theognus, who was standing outside the main entrance to the sanctuary and greeting the visitors to his city. When he noticed Hosius, he raised his hand and walked toward them.

"Welcome to Nicaea, Brother Alexander, Brother Hosius," he said warmly when he reached them. "Brother Athanasius, it's good to see you again," he added.

"You seem to be busy today, Brother Theognus," Hosius said pleasantly.

"Yes, everyone decided to come and pay his respects today." Theognus gestured to the crowd. "It's been like this since just after sunrise."

"The Emperor wants to know if there's anything that you need," Hosius said.

Theognus shook his head. "Please convey my thanks to the Emperor, but I think that we have everything well in hand. Supplies of food have been arriving daily, and space has been made for the tents, horses, wagons, and camels."

"Are many of the attendees staying at the church?" Alexander asked.

"About seventy altogether," Theognus replied. "Most of them arrived from Ephesus yesterday."

Hosius nodded. *Ephesus? That would mean that Menophantus is here. I'm guessing that the rest of Arias' supporters are staying at the church.*

Hosius was about to say something when he heard someone shouting his name. He turned and faced the crowd. He scanned the faces, and then he saw a familiar-looking man approaching him and calling his name again.

He recognized the face, but it took a moment for his mind to comprehend what he was seeing. The pleasant smile on his face froze. *This can't be! He's supposed to be dead! How can he be here?*

Hosius glared at Athanasius, who stared at the man approaching through the crowd. Athanasius' face was ashen, and the expression on his face was a mixture of confusion and terror. Athanasius looked at Hosius. His mouth opened, but no sound came out.

"Brother Hosius," the man said when he finally made his way through the crowd. "It's good to see you. Brother Alexander, Brother Athanasius, welcome to Nicaea!"

Hosius steadied his nerves. He smiled broadly to hide his shock before turning to face the man. "It's good to see you, too, Brother Arias."

CHAPTER 12

"Explain yourself, Athanasius!" Hosius demanded when the two men reached the privacy of Hosius' chamber in the palace. "I just had a conversation with a man who is supposed to be dead!"

"I…" Athanasius began.

"You did tell me that he's dead, didn't you?" Hosius interrupted. "I didn't imagine it, did I? You told me that you had confirmation from the men you hired, right? Because that's what I told the Emperor. Did I just make it all up in my mind?"

"Hosius, I…"

"Perhaps Arias has miraculously risen from the dead! That's it, isn't it?" It was difficult for Hosius to hide his sarcasm as he ranted. "Perhaps we should make Arias our living god and worship him instead of Jesus! Because if the men you hired *did* kill him, then he must be god, right?"

"Hosius, I don't think that's…"

"Oh shut up, Athanasius," Hosius snarled, pacing angrily. "Do you have any idea how the Emperor's going to react when I tell him that Arias is still alive? Can you even begin to imagine his response when I say, 'Oh Great Emperor, I'm sorry; I was mistaken. I thought Arias was dead, but he's actually very much alive and here in Nicaea'? It'll be a miracle if he doesn't kill us both!"

Athanasius sat silently, waiting for Hosius to stop shouting.

Hosius stopped pacing and stared at the silent Athanasius. "Well, what do you have to say for yourself?"

"I honestly thought he *was* dead," Athanasius blurted out. "The leader of the men I hired told me that he was dead."

"The one that shouted to you from the docks at Alexandria?" Hosius asked.

Athanasius nodded.

"Is it possible that what he *actually* shouted to you was 'Arias is *not* dead'?"

Athanasius swallowed hard but said nothing.

"What a mess you've made of things, Athanasius," Hosius said, pacing again. "You wasted my money, and you have nothing to show for it. Maybe I should send *you* to explain things to the Emperor. I'm certain he'll want to reward you for your faithful service to him."

Athanasius watched Hosius pacing.

"Eliminating Arias was the key to our plans," Hosius muttered to himself. "Take away their champion, and the opposition crumbles. But now their champion is here and ready to rally the opposition against us. That's a complication that we didn't want."

"So what if Arias is still alive and is here?" Athanasius demanded loudly. "What does it really change? For months, we've been preparing to take on Arias in the council meetings. Killing him was only decided upon recently. So what if that part of the plan failed? We're still ready to take him on in open council. It might make presiding over the meetings more difficult, but between you and the Emperor, we'll still get what we want. Arias and his supporters will be defeated, and the imperial church will be born."

"Can you guarantee to the Emperor that we'll still succeed with Arias here?" Hosius asked.

"Could you guarantee that we'd succeed with him absent?" Athanasius countered.

Hosius stopped pacing again. "No," he said reluctantly.

"Then we're no worse off than we were before when we thought that Arias was dead," Athanasius stated.

Hosius nodded slowly. "I guess I could tell the Emperor that the assassins lied to you. He'll want retribution, though. What was the name of the man you hired?"

"Chephren."

"An Egyptian?"

Athanasius nodded.

"Well, he should be easy enough to find. All right, I'll tell the Emperor what happened. You make sure that you're ready to take on Arias during the council meetings. One more mistake, and we'll both be crucified when this is all over."

"Did anyone notice how Hosius and Athanasius reacted when they saw Arias outside of the church this afternoon?" Theognus asked Arias and the bishops when they were alone in his chamber late that afternoon.

Secundus laughed. "Athanasius looked like he'd seen a ghost."

"And Hosius looked like he'd just swallowed horse dung," Theonus of Marmarica added. "He recovered quickly with that fake smile of his, but he was clearly surprised."

"Why would they react like that?" Menophantus asked.

"Maybe they didn't expect Arias to be here," Secundus suggested.

"Why wouldn't they expect me to be here?" Arias asked. "Hosius made sure that I was invited. And Athanasius knew that I was coming; I told him as soon as I had made arrangements to join the caravan."

"But did you tell him that you missed the caravan?" Secundus asked.

Arias shook his head. "I forgot to. I only remembered as we were boarding the ship for Ephesus."

"Then were Hosius and Athanasius surprised to see you because they thought you'd still be on your way with the caravan, or were they surprised because they didn't expect you to arrive at all?" Theognus asked.

"I don't like what you're implying, Theognus," Arias said, frowning.

"Then I won't imply," Theognus said. "I think that they arranged to have something happen to keep you from arriving here in Nicaea."

"I won't listen to this!" Arias said.

"Then who hired that escort, and what were they really supposed to do?" Secundus asked. "No one else had an escort hired for them. Why you? If they expected you to be here, they'd have reacted differently. If they were surprised that you made it here so soon, they'd have reacted differently. Athanasius looked like he'd seen a dead man standing in front of him. Explain that to me!"

"I can't," Arias said. "I can't."

"Well, I can," Menophantus stated. "You're the leader of the opposition to the Trinity doctrine. They're worried that you'll convince others to join us in our opposition to making the Trinity part of the official theology of the churches, so they made arrangements for you to never be able to speak out against them again. With you gone, they knew that we'd be easy to defeat in the council meetings. And now that you're here, they'll have to find another way to keep you from interfering with their plans."

Arias put his head in his hands.

"What do we do?" Theognus asked.

Arias looked up. "If this council meeting is a lie, if everything Hosius told me is a lie, then we're facing a difficult fight to preserve The Way. But I'm not ready to give up. There are nearly four hundred bishops in the city right now. They can't all be part of some conspiracy. If we can convince them to continue following The Way in accordance with our Master's teachings, then we can still prevail."

"And if we can't convince them?" Menophantus asked.

"That's up to God," Arias stated. "His will be done."

Hosius wasn't sure what to expect when he was finally ushered into Emperor Constantine's private audience chamber at the far end of the palace.

"What's so important that you had to see me immediately, Hosius?" Constantine demanded. "I'm in the middle of something important."

"I apologize, Great Emperor," Hosius replied, not knowing if anyone else was in the chamber. "But I thought that you needed to know as soon as possible."

"We're alone, Hosius." The Emperor smiled. "Relax, and tell me whatever it is that has you so nervous."

"Arias is still alive."

Constantine gripped the arms of his chair tightly as he stood up. His smile faded from his face. "You told me that he was dead."

"I know, Flavius, and I'm sorry. The assassins that Athanasius hired told him that they'd done the job. They didn't."

"And you're *sure* that he's still alive?"

"I spoke with him earlier today," Hosius replied.

Constantine paced for a moment. Hosius watched him carefully, trying to determine how Constantine would react to the news. Constantine stopped pacing and stared at Hosius.

"What does this mean to our plans?" Constantine asked. "Will I still get my church?"

He took the news better than I expected. Hosius relaxed and cleared his throat. "Yes, Flavius. It'll mean more work for Athanasius and me, but in the end, you'll get what you want."

Constantine nodded and sat down. Then he looked up at Hosius and said, "Why don't I dispatch one of my assassins and kill Arias here?"

"I would advise against that, Flavius."

"Why?" Constantine demanded.

"Because there's no way to do it so that it looks like an accident unrelated to the council meetings. If the bishops find out that the leader of the opposition was killed here when the city is filled with your guards and legionnaires, they'll know that you were behind it. No, it's best to let him live for now. If you still want to kill him after he's been exiled, though, I'm sure that it could be done in a way that keeps the bishops from ever finding out."

Constantine smiled. "Anything else?"

"There's the problem with the assassins that Athanasius hired. They took the money, and then they lied about finishing the job. It's bad enough that they didn't do what they were paid to do, but they also know that someone wanted them to kill Arias, and they know what that person looks like."

"So what are you suggesting?" Constantine asked.

Hosius looked at the Emperor. "They're a problem, Flavius. The problem needs to go away."

"What's their leader's name?"

"Chephren," Hosius replied.

"Very well. I'll send a dispatch to the legionnaire encampment at Alexandria and order this Chephren and his men beheaded. Who knows, maybe sticking their heads on pikes and displaying them near the harbor will serve as a warning to Athanasius when he gets home about what happens when *I* have to make *his* problems go away."

Hosius swallowed and nodded.

Constantine picked up a pencil and wrote a note on a piece of scrap paper on his desk. Then he put down the pencil and looked up. "Tell me something, Hosius. When did you become so bloodthirsty?"

"I'm not bloodthirsty, Flavius," Hosius replied. "I'm just mindful of the stakes involved. These men are dangerous, and I don't want anything to suggest that you were involved in a plot to kill a priest."

"Very well, Hosius," the Emperor said, waving his hand dismissively. "You may leave. But make sure that you use the next few days to prepare yourself for dealing with Arias in the council meetings."

"It will be done, Great Emperor," Hosius said, bowing. He turned and quickly exited Constantine's chamber.

Theognus approached Arias' chamber at the church and saw that Andrew and Barnabas were standing in front of the door.

"I need to speak with Arias, my Brothers," he said to them.

"I'm sorry, Brother Theognus," Andrew said. "Arias is praying and asked not to be disturbed until the evening meal."

"He's been praying for more than a day," Theognus said.

Barnabas nodded. "He's seeking God's guidance for the council meetings. He hasn't eaten or slept since he closed the door and asked us to keep anyone from disturbing him."

Theognus nodded. "Please have him come and see me as soon as he emerges."

"We will, Brother Theognus," Andrew promised.

Hosius entered Athanasius' chamber and found the priest busy scribbling notes.

"Good news. The Emperor is not going to kill you… yet."

Athanasius looked up, startled. "I'm sorry, Hosius. I didn't know you were there! How did he take the news about Arias? And what do you mean he's not going to kill me yet?"

"He took the news well… considering. He's not happy about having to clean up your mess, and he's going to have the men you hired taken care of. His primary concern is about getting his church."

Hosius glanced at the notes that Athanasius had been writing. "How are your preparations for the council meeting coming?"

"They're going well," Athanasius replied. "But I'm concerned about something."

"What concerns you?" Hosius asked, taking a seat across the table from Athanasius.

"Most of the authority we cite to justify the doctrine of Jesus' divinity comes from Paul's epistles. Arias and his followers use the gospel of John and John's epistles as their justification that Jesus is not divine. John was the faithful apostle who never abandoned or betrayed Jesus. Paul was never one of Jesus' apostles and only spent a brief moment with him on the road to Damascus. Arias and his supporters have always used that fact to discredit our belief that Jesus is divine."

Hosius shrugged. "I know this."

"Well, how do I defend Jesus' divinity against Arias' assertion that John is a better authority than Paul?"

Hosius stared at the young priest. "Look to the gospels."

"I've spent the last two days trying to find evidence in the gospels for our doctrine, but there isn't any. It all comes from Paul."

Hosius continued to stare at Athanasius. "Then you need to use Arias' arguments against him."

"How do I do that?" Athanasius appeared confused.

"By taking every passage from the gospel and epistles of John that Arias will reference, and use them to prove that they mean the opposite of what Arias says they mean. If Arias says they prove that Jesus and God are distinct entities, show how they say the opposite. Make John your authority for declaring the divinity of Jesus."

"But how? Arias is right; John draws clear distinctions between Jesus and God."

Hosius shook his head. "If you think Arias is right, then perhaps I should tell the Emperor and the Patriarchs that you're not the right person for this task."

"Don't tell him that, Hosius," Athanasius protested. "I can do this. I just need your guidance."

Hosius thought about this for a moment. Then he leaned forward. "Then give the bishops another way to interpret those passages. If Arias says that a particular passage proves that Jesus is not God, then show how the passage actually proves that Jesus *is* God."

"That won't be easy," Athanasius said.

"It had better be if we're going to get the council to approve our new theology," Hosius countered. "There can't be any doubt in the minds of the bishops by the time we're done. Every passage in the gospels and epistles must provide proof that our new theology is correct, or we'll be inviting dissent for the next three centuries. That's unacceptable to the Emperor. He'll probably reward your failure by displaying your severed head on a pike on the walls of his palace."

Athanasius swallowed hard and nodded. "I'll find a way to make it work."

Late in the afternoon of May 19th, Theognus and Hosius sat across the table from each other in the Emperor's audience chamber, reviewing the final agenda for the council meetings. Emperor Constantine sat at the far end of the table, watching and listening.

"I placed the questions of the divinity of Jesus and the Divine Trinity at the top of the agenda," Theognus explained. "The outcome of those discussions will determine how the rest of the discussions go, and since Arias and Athanasius will not be invited to any of the other sessions, I thought it best to get those issues resolved first."

"Are you planning for the Emperor to attend all of the meetings?" Hosius asked.

"No," Theognus replied. "I was under the impression that you only want the Emperor there when the key issues are presented and when they're being voted upon."

Hosius glanced at the Emperor, who nodded. "Agreed," Hosius said. "When will the Patriarchs hold their meetings?"

"Those meetings will be held each morning, beginning tomorrow," Theognus replied. "I thought that you wanted the Patriarchs to be able to guide the discussions and debates by having reviewed the issues in advance of the full council."

"Quite right," Hosius acknowledged. "Now what about the opening ceremony?"

"The processional of the bishops will begin one hour after the mid-day meal. As of today, there are three hundred and eighteen bishops who will be attending the meetings. There is no assigned seating in the central hall of the palace except for the Emperor's seat, your seat, Hosius, the seats for the scribes, and the seats for Arias and Athanasius during the initial sessions." Turning toward Emperor Constantine, Theognus asked, "How do you wish to enter the council chamber, Great Emperor?"

Hosius answered for Constantine. "The Emperor wishes to demonstrate his respect for the bishops attending the meetings. Once the bishops are in their places and seated, the Emperor will enter the central hall from the rear, rather than through the front entrance that the bishops will use. The bishops will stand when he enters, but the Emperor will allow them to take their seats before he sits."

"Very well," Theognus said. "Once the Emperor is seated, the council meeting will be officially opened by the president. Will that be you or the Emperor making those remarks?"

"Does the Emperor need to make any opening remarks?" Hosius asked.

"Under the circumstances, yes," Theognus replied.

"What circumstances are those," Constantine demanded, speaking for the first time since the meeting began.

"Great Emperor, there are other issues between the churches than just the questions of Jesus' divinity and the Divine Trinity. There have been petty squabbles between various bishops for years – some going back to when certain churches were first dedicated. Almost every bishop here in Nicaea has brought with him a list of grievances against the other bishops, priests, or churches. They've been arguing with each other since arriving in the city, and they're looking to you to resolve those grievances."

"During the council meetings?" Constantine asked.

"Yes, Great Emperor. You are their Emperor and the head of the churches. They look to you for guidance and for justice."

Constantine gave a pained look to Hosius.

"There's not going to be enough time to settle the theological issues facing the council if we get caught up in personal disagreements between the bishops," Hosius said. "Perhaps the Emperor *should* make the opening remarks to admonish the bishops to remain focused on the larger issues at hand. If there's time once those issues are resolved, then the bishops may present their grievances in open council."

Theognus smiled. "I think that would be the best course of action."

Constantine nodded.

"Fine," Hosius began. "The Emperor will welcome the bishops and admonish them to focus on the theological issues that must be resolved. Then you, Theognus, can give your opening remarks as the host bishop. I'll give the final opening remarks to outline the agenda and how the debates will proceed."

"Perfect," Theognus said. "Will Arias and Athanasius be attending the opening session?"

"Yes," Hosius replied. "They're part of the first agenda item, so they should hear the opening remarks."

"I'll let them know," Theognus promised.

Constantine gestured to Hosius, signaling the end of the meeting.

Hosius stood up. "I think that's all for now, Theognus. We can address any last-minute details in the morning."

Hosius escorted Theognus to the door, and both men exited the audience chamber.

The next morning, Hosius and Athanasius met privately with Alexander of Alexandria, Eustathius of Antioch, Macarius of Jerusalem, and Eusebius of Caesarea. "Welcome to Nicaea," Hosius said to the assembled Patriarchs.

"Where is Sylvester of Rome?" Alexander asked.

"Ah, because of his failing health, he's unable to attend." Hosius held up a letter written by Sylvester. "But he has appointed me to act in his place."

The Patriarchs nodded their consent.

Hosius introduced Athanasius to the Patriarchs. "Athanasius will be serving as the scribe for our meetings. We have much to discuss, and he's already familiar with most of what I'll be presenting to you."

"What is there for us to discuss in private that can't be discussed in front of the full council?" Macarius asked.

"I'm glad you brought that up," Hosius said. "The full council was called to settle the disagreements regarding church theology. We have another task to complete; one that will redefine our churches to the world!"

"What are you talking about, Hosius?" Eusebius demanded.

"As some of you know, the Emperor has taken a great interest in the churches…"

"About that," Eustathius interrupted. "This is the first time that a potentate has attempted to interfere with the doctrine or the inner-workings of the churches. Why are we allowing this?"

"Because no other potentate has ever been visited by God and been given such a clear vision of what God wants him to do," Hosius replied. "Emperor Constantine sees himself as the defender of our faith. Christ led him to military victory, and in return, the Emperor has lifted the prohibition on the worship of Christianity throughout the empire, he made war on those who wanted to keep that prohibition in place, and now he's ready to do one more thing that will secure our religion for centuries to come."

"What's that?" Alexander asked, already knowing the answer.

"Emperor Constantine is going to make Christianity the state religion of the empire."

With the exception of Alexander, the Patriarchs looked stunned at this news. Hosius leaned back, letting the significance of his statement sink in.

"Now you see why we have to discuss redefining our churches," Hosius said after a long pause. "The number of churches throughout the empire is about to increase a hundredfold, and the congregations are about to increase a thousandfold! Up until now, Christianity has been focused on living according to the commands of Christ, attracting only those who wanted to join us in our worship. Now, we're going to be converting the citizens of the empire to Christianity. We've never done that before."

Hosius took a sip if wine before continuing. "Much of what we preach and practice comes easily to us because we've studied the words and works of Jesus for most of our lives. These new converts will have no knowledge of the Christ. They'll also be coming to us with a set of beliefs based on their current religions. They won't understand Christianity immediately, nor will they easily be able to walk away from their old gods and rituals. If we're going to help them become one with Christ and his churches, we must change how we do things."

"But what will these changes do to those who are already Christians?" Macarius asked.

"Nothing," Hosius assured him. "Our existing congregations have a deeper understanding of the ways of Christ, and they'll help us convert and educate the newcomers. As the converted reach a similar level of understanding, they'll join in the effort to convert others. There will always be novices and more advanced Christians as the empire expands and new peoples are converted. The church must accommodate both."

"So how will the churches need to change to become the new imperial church?" Alexander asked.

Hosius gestured to the scrolls stacked on the edge of the table where Athanasius was sitting. "These documents detail my recommendations for creating a unified church that will serve the needs of existing and new Christians alike, while also serving the needs of the empire. Over the next several weeks, we'll go through these plans, adjusting them as necessary, until we have a design to present to the Emperor for his approval. Then we'll have the foundation upon which our new church will be built."

Shortly before the opening ceremony, Hosius was summoned to the Emperor's private chamber. When he arrived, he noted that Constantine had not finished dressing.

"I'm not wearing that, Hosius," he said, pointing to the jewel-encrusted gold robe draped over a chair. "It makes me look like some oriental potentate, rather than the Emperor of Rome. I should be wearing the purple robe."

"If you were attending this meeting as the Emperor of Rome, I would agree with you." Hosius picked up the robe. "But you're not. You're attending as the head of the churches, and you need to be dressed in a way that gives an immediate visual connection to that role. Your chair is gold, and your robe is gold. All of the light in the room will reflect off you, giving you a semi-divine appearance. I selected this robe to keep the bishops from questioning your authority over these proceedings. You need to wear it. Besides, the robe is edged in purple to remind you that you're still Emperor."

"You're an ass!" Constantine snapped, snatching the robe from Hosius and putting it on. He stared into the burnished bronze mirror in front of him, examining himself from each side and fidgeting with the collar. Then he shot a pained look at Hosius.

"Are you absolutely certain that I need to wear *this* robe?"

"Yes, Great Emperor." Hosius bowed low.

"You really are an ass, Hosius."

Hosius smiled. "And I'm yours to command."

Constantine looked at himself one more time in the mirror, and then he shrugged. "Very well. I'll wear it."

There was a knock at the door. Hosius opened the door and saw the imperial guards ready to escort him and the Emperor to the council chamber.

"It's time, Great Emperor."

Constantine joined Hosius at the door. "Fine. Let's get this started."

CHAPTER 13

"Unbelievable," Arias said as he and the bishops opposing the Trinity doctrine walked from the church at Nicaea to the Imperial Palace.

"What's unbelievable?" Theognus asked.

Arias gestured toward several clusters of bishops who were also making their way to the Imperial Palace. "For nearly three hundred years, our churches met in secret to avoid being discovered by those who'd persecute us and kill us for their amusement. The churches helped each other avoid capture, they took in refugees from churches that had been discovered, and they put their faith in God above all else. But in the thirteen years since the Emperor lifted the prohibition on our worship, look at what has happened to us. We fight among ourselves, putting our personal self-interests above our congregations, our churches, and our God. We let petty squabbles define our interactions with other churches, we take offence at the littlest of things, and we demand that everyone else bend to our will, rather than having the humility to admit that we might be the ones who are wrong. And I'm not referring to the larger questions of church doctrine; I'm talking about things as petty as who gets to enter the central hall first!"

"I understand what you mean," Theognus said. "I've had bishops coming to me all week, demanding that I put their grievances on the agenda, insisting that they enter the central hall first, and dictating where they want to sit and with whom. If I didn't know these were bishops, I'd think they were members of the Imperial Court! I mentioned it to Hosius and the Emperor yesterday, and the Emperor is supposed to address it when he opens the council meeting today."

When they arrived at the Imperial Palace a few minutes later, Theognus pulled Arias aside. "I need you to wait here, Arias. The Patriarchs will enter first, followed by the bishops. Hosius will enter next with the scribes, and then you and Athanasius may enter and take your seats on opposite sides of the hall. Your seat will be right in front of Secundus and me. Once everyone else is seated, the Emperor will enter the hall."

Arias noticed a nervous look on Theognus' face. He placed his hand on his friend's shoulder. "Have faith, Theognus," Arias said softly. "We're in God's hands, and He is in this place with us now. There's nothing to fear."

Theognus smiled, and then he hurried away to take his place in the procession of bishops entering the central hall.

Arias looked around the vestibule of the Imperial Palace while he waited for his turn to enter the hall. *If this is what one of the Emperor's lesser palaces looks like, I wonder what his palace in Rome looks like. I know the ruler of an empire is afforded certain luxuries, but this is beyond anything I've ever imagined. I'd hate to be a priest or bishop assigned to a place like this. Surrounded by such opulence and artwork, how could one remain focused on the word of God and the word and works of our Master? If we turn our churches into places such as this, how would there be room for God in our sanctuaries?* Arias chuckled at the thought of churches filled with such finery. *It'll never happen.*

Arias saw the last of the bishops entering the central hall, and he took his place behind Hosius and the scribes. Athanasius joined him, and Arias nodded politely to Alexander's chief priest. Athanasius lifted his chin curtly in a sign of disdain. *God loves you and so do I, Athanasius. I have no quarrels with you, personally. We hold to different beliefs, and by the end of these meetings, I pray that our differences will finally be put aside.*

Hosius entered the hall, followed by the scribes. Athanasius pushed past Arias and entered the hall next. Arias entered last. He looked around, saw Theognus and Secundus, and walked to his seat. One of the imperial guards closed the intricately carved door once Arias was inside. The sound of the door closing echoed throughout the hall.

Arias looked around once he was seated. The central hall was immense. The walls, which were circular, were made of smooth stone. High above the marble floor was the domed ceiling. Windows placed around the base of the dome allowed in light and fresh air. Arias estimated that the hall could easily hold more than a thousand men.

Risers of marble and timber, set up in a semi-circle, faced the door that Arias had just entered. Large pillows covered the risers for the assembled bishops to sit on. The room was set up this way to ensure that everyone could be seen and heard during the council's deliberations.

There was an opening in the middle of the risers leading to another entrance into the hall. In the center of the opening, there sat a magnificent golden chair that Arias assumed was for the Emperor. Hosius sat next to the chair on the lowest level of the risers. Across from the golden chair, about halfway between the chair and the door that Arias had entered, was the table where Sebastian and the other scribes sat. Athanasius sat in a chair on the far left of the risers. Arias' chair was on the far right.

Sunlight streamed in from one of the windows at the base of the dome, shining on the floor directly in front of the Emperor's chair.

Once everyone in the room was seated, Arias heard the doors behind the risers open. When he saw Hosius stand, Arias, along with everyone else in the hall, stood. A moment later, Arias saw Emperor Constantine enter the hall and stand in front of the golden chair. When the doors behind the risers closed, Constantine stepped forward. Sunlight from the window above reflected off of his golden robe, making him appear to glow with a heavenly radiance. Emperor Constantine smiled and gestured for the bishops to be seated.

"Welcome to Nicaea," the Emperor's voice boomed across the hall. "Most of you have traveled far to be here, and I thank you for that. Many of you have brought grievances with you that you want resolved while you're here. I have no doubt that these grievances are important to you. But this council was called to address the theological differences that threaten to split the Christian churches.

"I have achieved great military victories through Christ's guidance in order to secure the free and open worship of Christ throughout the empire. But in order to give my people the hard-won peace that they deserve, I must now heal all of the divisions within the empire – not just the political and economic divisions, but the spiritual divisions as well.

"So I ask each of you assembled here to remain focused on the theological issues to be addressed. Once these issues have been resolved, if time remains, then you may present your grievances for the council to address.

"There is one more point that I wish to make before our host bishop, Theognus, addresses the council. I expect the conduct of these meetings to proceed in a manner befitting the leaders of the Christian churches. Speakers will not be interrupted. If you believe differently than the speaker, you'll hold your comments until you have been recognized by the president of the council – either Hosius or myself – and you'll express your opinions calmly and reverently. If Hosius or I have to caution you more than once to hold your comments until the current speaker is finished making his remarks, or to keep your comments polite, you may find yourself being removed from the council meetings. Understood?"

The bishops nodded in agreement, and the Emperor sat down. Theognus walked to the center of the room. He bowed to the Emperor, who nodded politely.

"Welcome, my brothers," Theognus began warmly. He then gave the invocation. When he was finished, he returned to his seat behind Arias.

Hosius stood and addressed the council. After reviewing the agenda, he said. "This is how the discussions will proceed. We will debate and attempt to resolve one issue at a time. For contested issues, champions have already been identified to present and defend the opposing positions on that issue. Each champion will be allowed to speak and present his position to the council first. Once both sides of each issue have been presented, then the debate will begin. Those opposing a champion's comments may speak, and the champion will defend his position. Remember, we are here to debate ideas, not people. Don't make your opposing comments personal.

"Once the debate is closed on the issue, the council will vote. If there is no unanimous vote on the issue, then the presiding officer will either allow the majority to decide the outcome of the issue or bring the matter to the Emperor for his decision. The option of having the Emperor make the final decision will only be used if the vote is too close to declare a majority or if the issue is critical to the future of the churches. Because less than a fourth of the total number of Christian bishops are in attendance at this council, and because the decisions made by this council are binding on every Christian church, bishop, priest, and acolyte, there are some issues that can only be decided by the Emperor, because he alone represents all of Christendom at this council."

Hosius looked around the hall. Alexander rose and said, "I agree with the procedures for debating and resolving the issues to be presented to the council." The other Patriarchs stood to show their agreement, and then the bishops joined them. Hosius smiled and nodded to the Emperor.

"Are there any comments regarding the agenda or any items that should be brought before the entire council before proceeding with the first issue of discussion?" the Emperor asked.

Alexander immediately rose to his feet and bowed to the Emperor. Constantine gestured for the Patriarch to speak.

"Emperor Constantine, fellow Patriarchs, and bishops of the Christian churches," Alexander began, "I'm honored to be among you at this historic occasion, and I commend our great Emperor for his wisdom in summoning this council, and for his kind hospitality to those of us who answered his summons. I pray that each of us will remember why we are here and agree to put aside our own personal feelings so we may keep the greater good of the churches in the forefront of our minds."

Arias saw the hint of a smile on Alexander's face as the Patriarch glanced at him. *I agree with your sentiment, Alexander, but it's a shame that we don't agree on what the greater good is. You believe that we should change our doctrine to make Jesus and God the same being, and I believe in faithfully following The Way. I have no doubt about which of those two positions is right, but which one will prevail with the council? What will become of our religion if the wrong doctrine is adopted? What will happen to the faithful? I'm not here just to defend The Way before the council, I'm here to ensure that the faithful are not abandoned by your dangerous doctrine. I'm here to make certain that obedience to our Master is not lost forever.*

Arias kept his face expressionless as Alexander continued. "I pray that almighty God will grant us wisdom as we discuss the issues that are causing divisions between us."

Alexander sat down, and Emperor Constantine rose and bowed low to Alexander. Arias watched Alexander accept the Emperor's show of respect, wondering if it had been rehearsed.

The other Patriarchs made similar comments, and Emperor Constantine paid respect to them as each concluded their remarks. The hall appeared to be filled with nothing but good will. Then Achilleus of Larissa stood up to be recognized.

"I, too, am grateful to our host and benefactor, the great Emperor Constantine, for calling this council meeting," he began once the Emperor had acknowledged him. "But before I can participate in any discussions regarding theology, I must insist that my grievances be heard. For years, the churches in the Thessalian region have been taxed at a rate that is far higher than the churches around Antioch and Rome because the Patriarchs from both of those cities claim us as part of their territories. Until there is a clear hierarchy regarding which churches fall under each bishop and Patriarch, how can we even begin to discuss theology?"

The hall erupted with shouting. The bishops from the former Greek states voiced their support for Achilleus, while bishops from the Roman states and from the eastern provinces shouted them down, each claiming that the Thessalian churches belonged to their regions.

Hosius attempted to restore order, but the hall descended into chaos as bishops from across the empire added their list of grievances to the verbal melee.

Arias watched what was happening around him with a mixture of shame, shock, and fascination. Glancing back, he saw the bishops who opposed the Divine Trinity remaining seated. *I must remember to thank them after today's session is over. The true Followers of The Way are leading by example. They're refusing to participate in personal attacks – even those that are directed toward them. They're obeying the rules established by Hosius. Could there be a more perfect example of the differences between those who support the Trinity doctrine and those of us who oppose it? The supporters of this new theology are making a mockery of these proceedings. We, the faithful followers of our*

Master, are turning the other cheek and refusing to be distracted by the noise of discontent.

It was clear that Hosius couldn't restore order to the council meeting. He looked at the Emperor and said something that no one else in the hall could hear. Then Constantine stood.

At first, no one seemed to notice that the Emperor was standing and facing the risers. But slowly, the bishops saw what the Emperor was doing and fell silent. When everyone had stopped talking, the Emperor spoke.

"It grieves me to see such divisions within the churches. But it grieves me more that you couldn't hold the discussions of your grievances until the other items on the agenda have been resolved. It's clear to me that your passions are clouding your good judgment, so we'll end our meeting for today and resume tomorrow. When we reconvene, we'll begin with the first item on the agenda, and we'll work through all of the agenda items before there's any further discussion of grievances. Is that understood?"

The bishops nodded, and Constantine continued.

"I'm not without compassion for the issues you want discussed during the council meetings, but we have larger issues that must be addressed first. If you'll write out your specific grievances and provide them to Hosius, I'll review them all. Those that cannot be resolved by the council once the agenda items have been addressed, I'll resolve. You may not like my resolution, but at least you'll have your answer before you return to your churches. Agreed?"

Again, the bishops nodded.

Constantine bowed to the assembly and left the hall by the same door he entered. Hosius followed him out of the hall. The Patriarchs silently left the hall, followed by the bishops.

Arias and the bishops opposed to the Trinity doctrine remained behind. "I've never seen anything like that," Arias commented.

"I was embarrassed for the Emperor," Theognus said. "I'm certain that he expected better from us."

"Well, I'm very pleased that none of you joined in," Arias said. "I don't know if anyone else noticed, but at least no one can accuse us of disrupting the council meeting or disobeying the Emperor's wishes."

Theognus gestured for them to leave the hall and return to the church. As they left the Imperial Palace, several bishops from the western provinces were waiting for them. "We'd like to talk to you about your views on the Divine Trinity," they said.

Theognus invited them back to the church so their conversations wouldn't be overheard. As they left the palace, Arias was pleased. *I guess some DID notice us during the council meeting. If we can convince these bishops to join us in opposing the Trinity doctrine, and if they can help us convince others, then we should have enough support to defeat the doctrine and restore The Way as the only doctrine of the churches.*

"What's wrong with your fellow bishops, Hosius?" Constantine demanded when they were alone in his chamber. "I no sooner tell them to hold their grievances until the end of the meetings when they start verbally attacking each other! Is this what I'm going to be dealing with from now on? Churches that can't possibly get along and work together for the good of the empire?"

Hosius tried to sooth the Emperor. "Don't worry, Flavius. The meetings I'm having with the Patriarchs will take care of situations like this. Once we have the mechanisms in place to create the united church that you and I have talked about, then you'll never be bothered with grievances like this again. I promise you."

"You'd better be right, Hosius. This is not how I wanted the first day of our meetings to go."

"I think it was inevitable, Flavius. I should have realized that the bishops would want to take advantage of everyone being together to finally get their problems resolved. Perhaps I should have invited them to arrive a week early and used that extra time to just focus on their personal differences."

"And if those differences couldn't be resolved in just a week?" Constantine asked. "Giving them seven days to argue about petty problems might have driven them apart even more. Then we'd never get through the agenda, and we'd be no closer to the church that I need before they return home."

Hosius nodded. "True. Having them write down their grievances was a brilliant idea, by the way. Perhaps they'll be able to focus now that they know you're going to address their problems."

"It's the same way that I handle the Senate," Constantine said, smiling. "Honestly, I thought I was attending a Senate meeting today, except the bishops are much more polite than the senators!"

"I'll meet with the Patriarchs tonight and get them to help me control their bishops," Hosius promised.

"Good. How did the first meeting with the Patriarchs go this morning? I forgot to ask."

"That's okay, Flavius. You were distracted by your wardrobe."

Constantine glared at Hosius, and then both men laughed.

"The meeting went very well. I think the Patriarchs are with us, and there shouldn't be any problem getting them to agree to our proposals."

"Good. Then in spite of today's nonsense, you still believe that we'll have what we need by the end of the council?"

"Yes, I do," Hosius replied.

"Are you ready for today's council meeting?" Theognus asked Arias the next afternoon as they headed for the Imperial Palace.

"I am," Arias replied, confidently. "Knowing that there are other bishops ready to support our opposition to the Trinity doctrine gives me hope. Now if we can just convince the rest of them to return to The Way and forget this nonsense about Jesus being God, then we'll have fulfilled our duty to our Master."

"And what about the Emperor?" Secundus asked.

"What about the Emperor?" Arias countered. "He doesn't care about what doctrine we preach as long as all of the churches preach the same one. It's unity he wants, not a specific doctrine."

"I hope you're right," Secundus said, sounding doubtful.

"Trust in God," Arias said. "Don't give in to concern and doubt. Believe in Him, and He'll show you the way."

Arias and the bishops who followed The Way entered the Imperial Palace and took their places in the procession into the central hall.

Arias had just taken his seat when Emperor Constantine entered the hall, wearing the same gold and purple robe he had worn the day before. The Emperor bowed to the bishops and then took his seat.

The bishops had done as the Emperor asked, and the written grievances filled three wooden chests next to the table where the scribes sat. All of the bishops were sitting quietly, ready to take on the first item of business – the divinity of Jesus.

"You may begin with the first item on the agenda," the Emperor said to Hosius.

CHAPTER 14

Arias saw Hosius nod to the Emperor and then turn to face the council. "Brother Alexander of Alexandria, you have been designated as the champion for those who believe that Jesus is God."

Alexander stood and bowed to Hosius. "Brother Hosius, with your permission, and with the permission of my brothers on the council, I ask that my chief priest, Brother Athanasius, present our position on this issue."

Alexander sat. Hosius looked around the council. "Are there any objections to allowing Brother Athanasius of Alexandria to speak on Alexander's behalf?"

Hearing no objections, Hosius gestured to Athanasius to join him in the center of the hall. "You may proceed, Brother Athanasius."

Arias watched Athanasius pick up several scrolls and approach Hosius. *I wonder which passages from the gospels and epistles he'll use to "prove" his thesis.* Arias leaned forward so he could hear Athanasius clearly.

Athanasius bowed to the Emperor and to the council, ignoring Arias completely. "Great Emperor, Patriarchs, and bishops of the Christian churches, there can be no doubt that Jesus is God. The belief that Jesus and God are two separate entities is based on a misinterpretation of the Apostles' writings. God the Father, Jesus the Son, and the Holy Spirit, which is the Christ and the Word of God, are one! One being, one entity, one supreme power governing all. The Father created the heavens and the earth. The Son walked among us to take away our sins. The Holy Spirit filled the Apostles and faithful disciples so they could continue performing God's miracles on earth – the power of God granted to man, just as it was granted to the Hebrew prophets who prepared the way for Jesus' birth. Jesus even says plainly that *'I and my father are one.'* What could be clearer than Jesus' own admission of his divinity?"

Emperor Constantine applauded, as did many members of the council. This surprised Arias, but he soon discovered that the Emperor applauded every time he thought a speaker made a good point. Athanasius bowed to the Emperor, who nodded back.

"The Divine Trinity," Athanasius continued, "is not something that was recently conceived, as some here have suggested. It has existed all along, and it is well-documented in the writings of the Apostles. I offer the following evidence as proof."

Athanasius picked up a scroll. "Let us consider the idea of worship. In Deuteronomy, we read the following: *'If there be found among you, within any of thy gates which the Lord thy God giveth thee, man or woman, that hath wrought wickedness in the sight of the Lord thy God, in transgressing his covenant, And hath gone and served other gods, and worshipped them, either the sun, or moon, or any of the host of heaven, which I have not commanded; And it be told thee, and thou hast heard of it, and inquired diligently, and, behold, it be true, and the thing certain, that such abomination is wrought in Israel: Then shalt thou bring forth that man or that woman, which have committed that wicked thing, unto thy gates, even that man or that woman, and shalt stone them with stones, till they die.'* It is because of this commandment that Shadrach, Meshach, and Abed-nego refused to worship King Nebuchadnezzar and the gods of Babylon."

Athanasius picked up two scrolls. "In Paul's epistle to the Colossians, we read: *'Let no man beguile you of your reward in a voluntary humility and worshipping of angels, intruding into those things which he hath not seen, vainly puffed up by his fleshly mind, And not holding the Head, from which all the body by joints and bands having nourishment ministered, and knit together, increaseth with the increase of God.'* This passage clearly tells us that the worship of angels and other gods is forbidden. And in two separate places in the Revelation of the Apostle John, the angels sent to reveal the future to John told him not to worship them. In the second place we read: *'And I John saw these things, and heard them. And when I had heard and seen, I fell down to worship before the feet of the angel which shewed me these things. Then saith he unto me, See thou do it not: for I am thy fellowservant, and of thy brethren the prophets, and of them which keep the sayings of this book: worship God'.*"

Athanasius put down the scrolls. "So the worship of other gods is forbidden, which is understandable since there is only one true god. But the worshipping of god's angels is also forbidden, showing us that God doesn't want us worshipping anyone other than Him."

Athanasius picked up several scrolls. "But let's consider the following passages. In the gospel of Matthew, just after Jesus' resurrection, we read: *'And as they went to tell his disciples, behold, Jesus met them, saying, All hail. And they came and held him by the feet, and worshipped him. Then said Jesus unto them, Be not afraid: go tell my brethren that they go into Galilee, and there shall they see me.'* And in the gospel of Mark, when Jesus cast out the legion of devils from a man, we read: *'But when he saw Jesus afar off, he ran and worshipped him, And cried with a loud voice, and said, What have I to do with thee, Jesus, thou Son of the most high God? I adjure thee by God, that thou torment me not. For he said unto him, Come out of the man, thou unclean spirit.'* In these passages, the Apostles and the devils worshipped Jesus, and Jesus didn't stop or rebuke them. He knew the law of God that only God could be worshipped, and yet he allowed himself to be worshipped. Doesn't this show us clearly that Jesus is God?"

Emperor Constantine applauded again, and Athanasius bowed to him before continuing.

"Throughout the Apostle Paul's epistles," Athanasius said, picking up other scrolls, "and especially in his epistle to the Colossians, he writes of the fullness of God dwelling in Jesus. The gospels and epistles also refer to Jesus as our Savior, but who can save us from sin, disease, and death, other than God? Jesus fed the multitudes, turned water into wine, raised Lazarus from the dead, healed the soldier's ear, restored sight to the blind, healed lepers, and raised himself from the dead. Who could do these things other than God?"

Arias listened to Athanasius, who continued holding up scrolls, claiming that passages plainly stated that Jesus is God, and making his arguments for the Divine Trinity. *Do the council members even know that he's misquoting the passages? There is nowhere in the gospels or the epistles where it is written that 'Jesus is God overall,' that 'Jesus is our God and Savior,' or that Jesus is the 'person to whom one must pray to receive salvation.' The passages that refer to Jesus being the 'most high priest' are NOT saying that Jesus is God. If anything, it proves that Jesus is NOT God. It should be all too easy to refute all of Athanasius' arguments. The true meaning of the gospels and epistles show clearly that Jesus is the Son of God.*

After nearly an hour, Athanasius concluded his remarks to the council. "As you can plainly see, the concept of the Divine Trinity has existed since Jesus' time. It is not something that a group of Christians made up in the past few decades, as some have accused. It is fundamental to the teachings in the gospels and the epistles of the Apostles. It must be the cornerstone of our faith, if we're to continue calling ourselves Christians. The Father, the Son, and the Holy Spirit are one – one being, one entity. They're the three facets of God – the Supreme Being who created the heavens and the earth. To suggest that these three are separate and distinct entities is blasphemy and an affront to God. I urge the council to reject any such notion and declare that the Divine Trinity is the one true doctrine of our churches."

Athanasius picked up his scrolls and returned to his seat. The Emperor and many of the bishops applauded as Athanasius left the center of the hall.

Hosius walked to the center of the hall. "Thank you for your most eloquent stating of the position *for* the Divine Trinity, Brother Athanasius. We shall now take a short break, and when we return, Brother Arias will state the position *against* the Divine Trinity doctrine."

As the council members stood to stretch their legs and get cups of wine from the tables at each end of the hall, Arias' supporters pulled him aside.

"Are you ready, Arias?" Theognus asked.

Arias smiled. "Yes, I am. Athanasius' arguments were weak, and he misquoted a number of passages from those scrolls that he was holding up. It should be no problem to set the record straight with our position."

"It looked like several of the bishops agreed with him," Secundus noted.

"We knew that Alexander had many supporters on the council," Arias said. "Many of the bishops here have not held their posts very long, and many more received little or no theological training before being given their posts. They'll side with whoever has the best argument."

"Or the argument that requires the least effort on their part," Menophantus of Ephesus said. "I hate to admit this, but many of our fellow bishops have never actually read the gospels and the epistles. They want someone to tell them what's written, rather than having to read and research the scrolls for themselves. A persuasive and charismatic person could easily come along and with little effort convince them of anything. They may go along with those who support the Divine Trinity simply to keep from having to learn our Masters words and works on their own."

"Many of the churches have turned their back on the discipline required to be true Followers of The Way," Theognus said. "How can we expect the bishops to believe that healing is still being performed if they've never seen a healing before? How can we expect them to embrace the requirement of living every moment according to The Way if they've never studied and learned what The Way is?"

Arias put his hand on Theognus' shoulder. "God will lead the faithful as He always has. Those who lack the faith will fall by the wayside, and those who have the faith will attain salvation. We can't make people be faithful. All we can do is show them The Way and let them follow us as far as they're able and willing."

When the council reconvened, Hosius gestured for Arias to join him in the center of the hall. "Brother Arias of Baucalis, you have been designated as the champion for those who believe that Jesus and God are separate entities."

There were loud murmurs heard as Arias stood. Hosius held up his hand to signal for silence, but as Arias walked toward Hosius, several bishops began shouting derogatory remarks. The shouting increased. Arias waited next to Hosius for the bishops to quiet down. Once it became clear that these bishops had no intention of being quiet, Emperor Constantine jumped to his feet and faced the bishops.

"Silence!" he thundered.

The bishops immediately stopped shouting.

"You are representatives of Christ," Constantine stated sternly. "Please act like it. Would any of you want to be treated the way you just treated Brother Arias?"

The Emperor paused and looked around the hall. When he saw a few of the bishops nodding, he continued. "Then don't treat him with such disrespect. Brother Arias represents many bishops who hold to a different viewpoint of Christian theology. They allowed your position to be presented uninterrupted, now you must do the same. Whether or not you agree with Brother Arias, you must allow his position to be heard here."

Constantine took his seat and nodded to Hosius.

"You may proceed, Brother Arias," Hosius said to Arias.

Arias bowed to the Emperor and to the bishops. "Thank you, Great Emperor. Patriarchs and bishops of the churches, you have heard Brother Athanasius present the position that Jesus is God. I will now present the opposing position."

There was a low murmur from the upper level of the risers, but Arias ignored it. "Brother Athanasius stated several times that the Divine Trinity and the divinity of Jesus have been central to the Christian theology since the time of Jesus. And yet, if this is true, then why for the past three hundred years have so many of the churches preached that Jesus and God are two separate entities? Why is it only now that this *new* doctrine is being openly preached? My learned brother cites many passages from the epistles of the Apostles to prove his point that Jesus and God are the same entity. I will cite passages from the gospels that prove the opposite to be true.

"At the beginning of Jesus' ministry, he is tempted of the devil for 30 days and nights. How could the devil tempt God? If God is all-powerful, with what could the devil tempt him? More power? Why would God be tempted to worship Satan, who he had vanquished and cast out of heaven? This makes no sense if Jesus and God are the same entity."

Arias picked up the scroll containing the gospel of Matthew. "Throughout the gospels, Jesus draws a clear distinction between his Father and himself. If Jesus and God are the same entity, why would he do that? Why would it be necessary? Some suggest that he did it to disguise his true nature, but that's an *interpretation* that is not supported by the gospels themselves.

"In the gospels of Matthew, Mark, and Luke, we read: *'And, behold, one came and said unto him, Good Master, what good thing shall I do, that I may have eternal life? And he said unto him, Why callest thou me good? there is none good but one, that is, God: but if thou wilt enter into life, keep the commandments.'* In this passage, if Jesus were God, he would have simply answered the question instead of pointing out that it is God who is good and not himself.

"Further in Matthew, when Jesus is baptized, we read: *'And Jesus, when he was baptized, went up straightway out of the water: and, lo, the heavens were opened unto him, and he saw the Spirit of God descending like a dove, and lighting upon him: And lo a voice from heaven, saying, This is my beloved Son, in whom I am well pleased.'* And later, when Jesus is transfigured and the disciples saw Moses and Elias talking with him, we read: *'While he thus spake, there came a cloud, and overshadowed them: and they feared as they entered into the cloud. And there came a voice out of the cloud, saying, This is my beloved Son: hear him.'* In these two passages, the voice of God was heard by John the Baptist and by the disciples. Were they hearing Jesus say these things? If so, wouldn't the passages read that Jesus declared himself to be God? But instead, the passages refer to Jesus as the beloved Son – distinct from the Father, God.

"There are numerous other passages from Matthew that show Jesus referencing his Father as a separate entity, including when Jesus is praying to his Father. The night before Jesus is taken by the soldiers at Gethsemane, he prays to his Father. *'O my Father, if it be possible, let this cup pass from me: nevertheless not as I will, but as thou wilt.'* And his second and third prayers are similar. *'O my Father, if this cup may not pass away from me, except I drink it, thy will be done.'* Why is Jesus praying to God if he *is* God? Why is he surrendering to the will of God to be crucified if he *is* God? It makes no sense to state that Jesus is God when the gospels show him praying to his Father. Why would he pray to himself? Why would he have to surrender to his own will?

Later, when the soldiers capture him, Jesus orders his followers to put away their swords, saying: *'Thinkest thou that I cannot now pray to my Father, and he shall presently give me more than twelve legions of angels?'* If he is God, why would he have to pray to his Father for deliverance? He could have delivered himself."

Emperor Constantine applauded. A few of the bishops joined him, but most remained silent. Arias bowed to the Emperor and then continued.

"Brother Athanasius referenced Peter's writings as part of his proof of the divinity of Jesus, and yet, in the passages in Matthew before the crucifixion, we read, *'When Jesus came into the coasts of Caesarea Philippi, he asked his disciples, saying, Whom do men say that I the Son of man am? And they said, Some say that thou art John the Baptist: some, Elias; and others, Jeremias, or one of the prophets. He saith unto them, But whom say ye that I am? And Simon Peter answered and said, Thou art the Christ, the Son of the living God. And Jesus answered and said unto him, Blessed art thou, Simon Bar-jona: for flesh and blood hath not revealed it unto thee, but my Father which is in heaven.'* It seems clear to me, from this passage that Peter thought of Jesus as the Son of God and not God himself."

Arias picked up another scroll. "The Apostle John, in his gospel, provides numerous examples where Jesus refers to his Father. *'But Jesus answered them, My Father worketh hitherto, and I work'* *'Verily, verily, I say unto you, The Son can do nothing of himself, but what he seeth the Father do: for what things soever he doeth, these also doeth the Son likewise.'* *'I can of mine own self do nothing: as I hear, I judge: and my judgment is just; because I seek not mine own will, but the will of the Father which hath sent me.'* *'If I do not the works of my Father, believe me not. But if I do, though ye believe not me, believe the works: that ye may know, and believe, that the Father is in me, and I in him.'* *'Verily, verily, I say unto you, He that believeth on me, the works that I do shall he do also; and greater works than these shall he do; because I go unto my Father.'* If Jesus is God, why would he make such clear distinctions about his Father? Again, none of the passages make sense if Jesus is God, so if Jesus is God then why did he say these things?

"In the gospel of Luke, Jesus asks, *'wist ye not that I must be about my Father's business?'* And when he is on the cross, we read: *'And when Jesus had cried with a loud voice, he said, Father, into thy hands I commend my spirit: and having said thus, he gave up the ghost.'* If he is God, why would he talk about his Father's business, and why would he commend his spirit to his Father?"

"Here is the principal error with the belief that Jesus is God," Arias said after pausing for a moment to let his words sink in. "For Jesus to be God, he must also be a liar."

Several of the bishops jeered while others shouted "blasphemy" and "heresy" at Arias. Hosius signaled for the bishops to sit down and be quiet.

Once order had been restored, Arias continued. "I don't think that there is anyone here who believes that God is fallible. Indeed, one of the cornerstones of our theology is that God is infallible. If that is true, then God cannot be a liar, because lying demonstrates fallibility. If Jesus claimed that he and his Father are distinct, which he does throughout the gospels, and if Jesus is actually God in disguise as a man on earth, then Jesus is a liar every time he talks about his Father, every time he prays to his Father, and every time he tells his disciples to worship and pray to his Father. That would make God fallible, and the very foundation of our religion would crumble. When Jesus says: *'I am the way, the truth, and the life,'* he'd be lying because he cannot be 'the truth' if he is lying about being God.

"My Brothers, you can't have it both ways. Either God is infallible, making Jesus his Son and a distinct entity, or Jesus and God are the same entity, making both liars and making God fallible."

The central hall was silent. Arias looked at the faces of the bishops. He saw a few heads nodding, but many other were glaring angrily at him with their arms crossed on their chests. *They don't like hearing what I have to say, but at least they're listening. It's time to bring this to a close.*

"There's another point that I'd like to discuss. If Jesus is God, why would Jesus allow himself to be crucified? What purpose would the crucifixion serve?"

Arias took another sip of wine. "I have heard some say that Jesus was sacrificed for our sins, as if by his death our sins are removed. And yet throughout Jesus' ministry, he required repentance and reformation for the healing of sin. He said, *'I will have mercy, and not sacrifice: for I am not come to call the righteous, but sinners to repentance.'* So why would he have to die to absolve us of our sins, thereby keeping us from having to repent and be reformed? That seems utterly contrary to his words and works, and there is nothing in the gospels to support such an idea. Jesus did not have to die to forgive us of our sins.

"I have heard others say that the crucifixion was God's way of leaving the earth and returning to heaven. But he didn't leave the earth after the crucifixion; he resurrected and came back to eat with and preach to his disciples. He could have ascended at any time during his ministry. And if this were God's way of returning to heaven, why choose such a painful way to ascend? Why would it be necessary? And why would Jesus pray to his Father and call out to Him while on the cross if he's God? What purpose did the resurrection serve if Jesus is God? It serves no useful purpose.

"Others have pointed out that it is by Jesus' stripes, meaning the wounds from his lashings by the Roman soldiers, that we are healed. But how did Jesus' suffering do anything for us, especially if Jesus is God? It didn't. Jesus' suffering and eventual triumph were to show us that death is powerless. He endured this ordeal to show us that life is spiritual and that this earth-bound existence has no power over us. Jesus used himself as the example for us all to follow. This makes no sense if Jesus is God, but if Jesus is the Son of Man, as he declared himself to be, it makes perfect sense. It wasn't God's will that Jesus die on the cross. It was His will that Jesus prove the powerlessness of death through his resurrection."

Arias then held up the gospel of the Apostle John. "Lastly, I'd like to address Brother Athanasius' first point. He is correct when he quotes Jesus as saying that *'I and my father are one.'* But that doesn't mean one entity, it means a unity of purpose. And that quote is taken out of context. If you read further in the same chapter, it says: *'Say ye of him, whom the Father hath sanctified, and sent into the world, Thou blasphemest; because I said, I am the Son of God? If I do not the works of my Father, believe me not. But if I do, though ye believe not me, believe the works: that ye may know, and believe, that the Father is in me, and I in him.'* As you can see, when you look at this quotation in the right context, Jesus is not claiming to be God. In fact, there is no place in the gospels or the epistles which explicitly states that Jesus is God. Quotations given to that effect are false."

Arias put down the scroll in his hand. "My Brothers, even the most superficial reading of the gospels and the epistles shows us that Jesus is not God. There is no Divine Trinity supported by the writings of the Apostles. To say that Jesus is divine is a misinterpretation of the words of the Apostles. For three hundred years, the churches have worshipped God and honored the words and works of our Master. This new doctrine is not true. It is not based on anything but opinion and conjecture. If we adopt it as our official doctrine, we're turning our back on Jesus' very words as given to us in the gospels. Is that what you've come here to do? Is that the future you want for the churches? A theology devoid of spiritual truth, contrary to the words of the man you are trying to make a god in *your* own image and likeness? Do not do this, my Brothers. Do not call yourselves Christians while denying the words of the Christ."

CHAPTER 15

"Your man Athanasius looked like a fool today, Hosius!" the Emperor roared.

Hosius kept eye contact with Constantine but said nothing. He and the Emperor were alone in Constantine's private chamber on the far side of the palace from the central hall. The Emperor had ended the day's session after Arias concluded his remarks. Constantine maintained a calm appearance as he exited the hall, but it was clear to Hosius that the Emperor didn't feel calm at all.

"Arias made a very compelling case against the Divine Trinity," Constantine continued. "What if more bishops decide to support him and his views?"

"We knew all along that he'd make a strong case today, Flavius," Hosius answered. "That's one of the reasons why we tried to keep him from attending. But this is just the beginning. As you know, battles aren't won in the opening move. The debates start tomorrow, and that's where we'll make Arias look like the fool."

"Do you still promise me that the Divine Trinity will win the vote?"

Hosius reassured the Emperor. "Yes, I do, Flavius. We have the votes, and I still have the option to defer any split decision to you. You'll get your unified doctrine *and* your imperial church by the time these meetings are over."

"I'd better," Constantine growled.

Athanasius waited impatiently in the Patriarch's meeting chamber for Hosius to arrive. When Hosius entered the chamber and walked around the table, saying nothing, Athanasius asked, "How does the Emperor feel about today's session?"

"Not well at all," Hosius replied. "I calmed him down, but he's not happy about how poorly you did today and how well Arias did." Hosius sat down at the table across from Athanasius. "I told you to prepare your arguments so that you used Arias' points against him. You didn't do that, and Arias came away looking like the reasonable one today."

"You know as well as I do that Arias' quotes from the gospels regarding the 'Father' are nearly impossible to refute," Athanasius said. "My preparations weren't to make Arias' opening statements look foolish but to make *him* look foolish during the debates. I'm still ready to do that once the debates begin tomorrow."

"You'd better be," Hosius warned. "I promised the Emperor that he'd get his church and his doctrine by the end of the council meetings, and if he doesn't, he's going to take it out on us."

"You did well today, Arias," Theognus said when he, Arias, and the rest of Arias' supporters had returned to the church at Nicaea after the council meetings. "You spoke eloquently, and your arguments were perfect!"

Arias smiled. "Thank you. Even the Emperor seemed pleased with what I presented."

"I noticed that, too," Secundus commented.

"I was impressed with how he silenced the bishops who didn't want you to speak," Menophantus of Ephesus said. "I'm starting to feel more optimistic about our chances when this issue comes up for a vote."

Arias nodded. "You see? I told you that we have nothing to worry about. God is watching over us and the churches. We will prevail."

Hosius and the Patriarchs met the next morning to continue discussing the plans for the church that the Emperor needed to control his empire. The first topic on the agenda concerned the purging of heretics and blasphemers.

"I'm not sure that I understand what you're proposing, Hosius," Eusebius of Caesarea said. "The churches will have the authority to condemn anyone who is a heretic or a blasphemer?"

"Yes," Hosius replied. "In the past, the people who attended our services *wanted* to join us in worship. If they no longer wanted to worship with us, they simple left us and continued to search for the truth on their own. But once Christianity becomes the only religion in the empire, the people will be required to worship with us, and they cannot leave without disobeying an imperial decree. We must have a way to keep the people from leaving, but we also must have a way to enforce obedience to the will of the church. We can't have Christians causing dissent within the churches. Constantine won't tolerate any further divisions."

"So your solution is to execute the disobedient?" Macarius of Jerusalem asked. "What of Jesus' practice of healing the sinners? He didn't let the crowd stone the woman taken in adultery. If we condemn sinners, we deny them the opportunity to repent and reform, thereby condemning them for all time."

"The accused will have the opportunity to repent and reform prior to being condemned," Hosius assured them. "If they accept the will of the churches, they'll be spared, providing their repentance and reformation is genuine. It's only if they refuse to accept the will of the churches that they'll be condemned."

"And in what manner will they be condemned?" Eustathius of Antioch asked.

I discussed that with the Emperor, and he suggested burning them at the stake. He said, 'The condemned will burn in hell for all time, so it makes sense to use fire to send them on their way'."

"That's gruesome!" Alexander exclaimed. "It's a terrible way to die and horrible to watch."

"That's the point," Hosius said. "We make it terrible in order to discourage the people from committing acts of blasphemy and heresy. Otherwise, it wouldn't deter the behaviors that we're trying to prevent, would it?"

"I never thought that a religion dedicated to a man of peace would end up executing its own members," Eusebius commented.

"Neither did I," Macarius said. "Will we have to condemn our people for all infractions, or only the most serious?"

"Only the most serious," Hosius replied.

"Then we need clear guidelines for the correct punishment for each type of infraction," Alexander said. "Just as we cannot condemn someone for a minor infraction, we cannot overlook serious infractions. We need documented church law that lists the potential offences and their prescribed punishments."

Hosius glanced at Athanasius, who was busy making notes of the discussion. "I'll make sure that we create those guidelines," Hosius assured the Patriarchs.

That afternoon, once the council had reconvened, Hosius faced the attendees. "Now that we've heard from Brother Athanasius and Brother Arias, I will open the floor to debate the two positions presented yesterday. The debates are to remain congenial and respectful. Whoever wishes to speak may do so without interruption or derision. Is that understood?"

The Patriarchs and bishops nodded silently.

Arias felt optimistic. His optimism didn't last.

As soon as Hosius called on the first bishop who wanted to speak, it was clear that the bishops who supported the Divine Trinity doctrine had no intention of remaining respectful and congenial. The bishops who supported Arias were shouted down every time they challenged any of Athanasius' positions. The bishops who opposed Arias shouted him down every time he tried to answer a question.

The Emperor had to intervene several times to restore order. "If you cannot restrain yourselves," he said finally, "then I will have my guards enter the hall and restrain you."

The threat of using the imperial guards to maintain order was enough to keep the bishops well-behaved for the remainder of the day.

By the end of the day's session, Arias felt discouraged. *They couldn't find anything wrong with the message, so they attacked the messenger. Bearing false witness is one of the sacred commandments of the church, and yet that's what they did to us today. Why didn't Hosius caution them against doing that? We never attacked Athanasius and his supporters. Why did they waste their time attacking us?*

As soon as the session ended, Arias left the hall quickly, avoiding contact with anyone until he reached the church at

Nicaea. He climbed up to the roof and sat on the tiles, watching the setting sun and praying for the strength and wisdom that he'd need for the next day. *Heavenly Father, I am an instrument for Your will. Use me as You desire. Please guide me as I respond to those who oppose You, and help me remember that what I say and do is for Your glory and not my own. I am Your servant, and I obey You and You alone.*

The next afternoon, as the bishops entered the central hall, there were imperial guards standing at their posts in the corners of the hall and directly behind the Emperor's chair.

Arias noticed the guards as soon as he entered the room. *I guess the Emperor's not going to tolerate any outbursts from the bishops today.*

Once Hosius opened the day's session, Nicholas of Myra stood.

"Brother Nicholas of Myra, come forward," Hosius said, taking his seat.

Nicholas' broad shoulders and chiseled features made him one of the more handsome bishops attending the Council meetings. Nicholas walked to the center of the hall and turned toward Arias. "Brother Arias, I have a question about your position."

Arias approached Nicholas.

"One of the issues that you and your supporters have not addressed is the miracles performed by Jesus and the Apostles," Nicholas said. "Now, we *all* know that only God can work miracles, so if Jesus is not God, as you claim, then how were the miracles performed?"

"Where is it written that only God can perform miracles, Brother Nicholas? That assertion is not supported by the gospels or the epistles of the Apostles. Jesus raised the dead, healed the sick, cast out mental disorders, fed the multitudes, transformed water into wine, and overcame death and freed himself from the tomb. The Apostles performed many of the same works as our Master did. In the gospel of Luke, we read that Jesus sent seventy of his disciples to the cities that he'd be visiting, and they reported back that *'even the devils are subject unto us through thy name.'* Even the Hebrew prophets performed many of the same miracles that Jesus did. If only God can work miracles, then how did the prophets, the Apostles, and the disciples perform the same miracles?"

"The Holy Spirit, God's power, came upon all of those who performed miracles," Nicholas said.

"So Jesus gave of his divine power to his Apostles and disciples?" Arias asked.

"Of course," Nicholas replied.

"And who gave that power to the prophets?"

"God did, but in the form of Jehovah and not in the form of Jesus."

"And who gave that power to the disciples of the Apostles after Jesus ascended to heaven?" Arias asked.

"The disciples of the Apostles didn't receive the Holy Spirit, Brother Arias. *Everyone* knows that."

"Then how could the disciples of the Apostles perform miracles if they never received the Holy Spirit? How could the churches perform the works of our Master for the past three hundred years if no one has received the Holy Spirit since Jesus walked the earth?"

Nicholas laughed. "What miracles are you talking about, Brother Arias? There have been no miracles performed since the last of the original twelve Apostles died."

"You're wrong, Brother Nicholas," Arias said calmly. "Works of healing based on the teachings of Jesus are still being performed in the churches today. There is ample documentation of miracles being performed by the churches over the past three centuries."

Nicholas looked slightly annoyed at being told that he was wrong in front of the entire council. "Can you produce this documentation?" he demanded.

"I don't have it with me, but I *can* produce people who have performed healings through the power of God. Several of us are in this room right now."

"Us? Are you including yourself as one of those people?"

Arias nodded.

"Then you're saying that you're God, Brother Arias!" Nicholas said loudly. "Or are you saying that you've been touched by God?"

"Neither," Arias said. "I'm saying that you don't have to be God or touched by the Holy Spirit to perform miracles. I'm living proof, and I'm not the only one here who makes that claim."

"Blasphemer!" Nicholas shouted. Several of the other bishops shouted the same.

Emperor Constantine raised his hand, and the guard at the corners of the hall marched forward ten steps and slammed the butts of their spears onto the marble floors. The sound caught the attention of the bishops, who noticed the guards and quickly sat down.

Nicholas looked at the Emperor, and the Emperor nodded. "Proceed," Constantine said.

Nicholas bowed and then faced Arias. "So, you claim that you have performed healings in the same way that Jesus and the Apostles did?"

"Of course," Arias said with a faint smile. "Didn't our Master say, *'Verily, verily, I say unto you, He that believeth on me, the works that I do shall he do also; and greater works than these shall he do; because I go unto my Father'*? Jesus came to teach his followers how to perform the same works that he performed. I am a faithful follower of Jesus, and so I'm able to perform the works that our Master taught us to perform."

"And when was the last time you performed a so-called work of healing?" Nicholas sneered.

"Twice in the last several months. I healed a young boy who was struck by a chariot…"

"And did anyone see you perform this healing?" Nicholas interrupted.

"Yes, my acolyte Andrew was with me. The parents of the boy can also attest to the healing."

Nicholas bit his lower lip. "And the second time?"

"It was the day before I was to join up with a caravan to come here," Arias replied. "I had to go to a nearby village to heal several members of a wedding party who were poisoned by a bad cask of wine. It took most of the day to heal them all, and it caused me to miss the caravan."

"And were there witnesses to this healing?" Nicholas asked.

"Many," Arias replied. "My three acolytes, who helped me, my chief servant, the bride and bridegroom, and several other members of the wedding party, as well as many concerned neighbors."

"Your acolytes helped you?" Nicholas asked. "You now claim to be able to teach others to heal?"

Arias nodded.

Nicholas was silent for a moment. Then he asked, "Then tell me something, Brother Arias. Why is it that you seem able to do these healing works when most of us here cannot? What makes you so special? You're just a priest, after all. Most of us here are bishops. Why can't everyone here perform healings?"

"Because I study and practice every day," Arias replied. "The Way that our Master taught us is not easy. It requires discipline, study, and sacrifice. In the Revelation of the Apostle John, he describes The Way: *'And I went unto the angel, and said unto him, Give me the little book. And he said unto me, Take it, and eat it up; and it shall make thy belly bitter, but it shall be in thy mouth sweet as honey.'* That's the nature of The Way. It's sweet in your mouth when you discover that you can do the same works as our Master, but it's bitter in your belly when you realize the commitment that it takes. There are few left in the churches willing to make that commitment, but there are several of us here today who have dedicated our lives to that commitment. We see it as our duty to keep the healing works of our Master alive and integral to the mission of our churches.

"Everyone who follows The Way of our Master can perform the same miracles that he performed. That's what he came to earth to teach us. But it's a lifelong commitment to serve others. Sadly, most Christians in the churches have grown lazy over the years, which is why they've lost the ability to heal. They cover their laziness with the superstitious notion that only God can work miracles, thereby giving them a convenient justification for why they can't do what we're able to do."

Arias gestured toward his supporters. "Menophantus, Secundus, Paulinus, Actius, Theonus, Eusebius, Maris, Theognus, Zphyrius, and Dathes… all of us have performed healings through The Way that our Master taught us. We're not Gods, and we haven't been touched by the Holy Spirit. We're faithful followers of our Master's words and works, and we're proof that anyone can perform the same works if he has the discipline, the commitment, and if he's willing to put forth the effort that it takes."

Arias looked at Nicholas for a moment, and then he added, "If you can't heal others, Brother Nicholas, it's not because God didn't bestow the Holy Spirit upon you; it's because you lack the discipline to practice what our Master taught us. It's a choice, not fate, Brother Nicholas."

Arias noticed that Nicholas' face had turned bright red. Before he realized what was happening, Nicholas had stepped closer, pulled back his arm, and struck Arias' face with the back of his hand. Arias stumbled backward, caught his heel on the corner of a chair, and fell, landing hard on the marble floor.

Arias' supporters jumped to their feet, shouting for Nicholas to be punished. Other bishops, who were pleased with what Nicholas had done, shouted encouragement for Nicholas to strike Arias again.

Hosius tried to restore order. Nothing he did worked.

Constantine stood. The imperial guards rushed in and seized Nicholas. The bishops immediately fell silent. The Emperor gestured to one of his guards. "See if Brother Arias is all right."

The guard helped Arias get to his feet. "I'm fine," Arias said, nodding to Hosius and the Emperor.

Constantine faced the bishops. "This is unacceptable behavior. Guards, deliver Brother Nicholas to your captain. He's to remain locked up and guarded until tomorrow's session."

As Nicholas was taken from the hall, the Emperor continued. "This had better be the last time something like this happens. If anyone here strikes another person during a council meeting, that person will be punished. Now, clear the hall. Today's session is over. We'll resume tomorrow afternoon."

The Emperor strode out of the hall, followed by Hosius and Athanasius.

Arias' supporters immediately surrounded him and escorted him from the hall and back to the church at Nicaea.

"How do you feel?" Theognus asked once they were outside of the palace.

"I didn't know Nicholas could hit like that," Arias replied, feeling his jaw.

"It probably comes from throwing all those bags of coins through the open windows of the needy," Secundus joked.

"Well I wish he'd stick to throwing bags of coins instead of punches," Arias said.

"What is going on with these bishops?" Constantine demanded when he, Hosius, and Athanasius were alone. "It's one thing to shout while another person is talking, but to actually strike someone during the council meeting is unbelievable!"

"I'll admit that Nicholas' actions took me off guard," Hosius said. "But today's session served its purpose. Arias insulted nearly every bishop and Patriarch in the hall today, and he and his supporters look like braggarts and liars. Everyone *knows* that they can't perform miracles and healings, and to hear them claim that they can will only serve to alienate them from the rest of the bishops."

Constantine nodded. "Get your bishops in line, Hosius. Our side is supposed to appear to be the reasonable ones. So far, they've been anything but reasonable."

"Yes, Great Emperor." Hosius and Athanasius bowed as they left Constantine's chamber.

As Hosius and Athanasius walked down the hall to their rooms, Hosius whispered, "Go and check on Nicholas. Let him know that I'm pleased with his performance today."

Athanasius nodded. "Are you sure about this latest plan, Hosius? Wouldn't it be better for the Divine Trinity to be voted as our official doctrine by the majority of the bishops? You're plan is going to have more bishops voting against the Divine Trinity, which will force the Emperor to make the final choice. Won't that keep the churches divided, instead of uniting them?"

"No, we need the power of the Emperor to decide this issue. The bishops who didn't respond to the Emperor's summons could keep the churches divided for years if they don't like the outcome of the votes. We need all contention ended as soon as the decision is made, and that requires the Emperor to step in and resolve the issue."

"Won't it look strange in the minutes for the Emperor to make such an important decision for the churches?"

"Oh, the minutes won't make any mention of the Emperor casting the deciding vote," Hosius said. "This council was called to create unity, after all. Future generations will think that the bishops were all of one accord on the subject, except for a handful of Arias' followers."

"Clever," Athanasius commented.

Hosius smiled. "Thank you."

CHAPTER 16

Arias' jaw still hurt the next morning, but he looked forward to that afternoon's session. *Surely the bishops will realize that the supporters of the Divine Trinity are wrong if they're resorting to violence to silence us.*

When Arias arrived at the palace that afternoon, he bumped into Athanasius, who was hurrying from the Patriarch's meeting chamber to the central hall.

"Good day, Brother Athanasius."

"Brother Arias," Athanasius acknowledged. "How's the jaw?"

"It's a bit sore, but nothing that'll keep me silent in today's session."

Athanasius sneered but said nothing. The two men entered the hall and took their seats across the floor from each other.

Arias looked around the hall and noticed that the number of guards present had doubled. Nicholas was escorted in by four guards who then took their posts at the ends of the risers.

The Emperor entered a few moments later. Rather than immediately taking his seat, he walked to the center of the hall and addressed the bishops.

"There will be no outbursts, no mocking of anyone who is speaking, and no striking anyone in this hall today. Anyone who disobeys me will either be dragged from the hall and thrown into the street, or he'll be bound and locked up for a period of time that suits my pleasure."

The Emperor sat down and gestured for Hosius to continue the debates.

The debates lasted for two more days, and there were no incidents that required the Emperor to make good on his threats.

At the end of the last day of debate on the deification of Jesus and the Divine Trinity, Alexander rose to speak.

"Great Emperor, fellow Patriarchs, and bishops of the Christian churches," Alexander began when Hosius gestured for him to step forward and address the council, "I believe that everyone has now had the chance to speak on this issue. Brothers Athanasius and Arias have done a fine job explaining their positions and responding to questions. I believe it is now time to end the debate and bring this agenda item to a vote."

"Thank you, Brother Alexander," Hosius said. "Does anyone have any objection to ending the debate?"

The Patriarchs and bishops shook their heads.

"Very well," Hosius said. "Brother Athanasius, do you have any final comments that you'd like to make?"

Athanasius shook his head and remained seated.

"Brother Arias, do you have any final comments that you'd like to make?" Hosius asked.

Arias nodded. "I wish to thank the Emperor for inviting me to attend and to address the council, and I'd like to thank each of you for your attention and prayerful consideration of the points that I made in opposition to the Divine Trinity doctrine."

Hosius looked at Constantine. "Does the Emperor wish to make any final comments on this issue?"

Constantine rose and faced the bishops. "The empire has been divided and needs to be reunited. The Christian churches have been divided and also need to be reunited. As you cast your vote, put aside personal opinions and choose what is in the best interest of unity."

Hosius then said, "Before I call for the vote, I must ask Brothers Athanasius and Arias to leave the hall."

Arias bowed to Hosius and the Emperor, and he left the hall with Athanasius. *I knew I wouldn't be allowed to vote or be here when the vote is taken. I'll have to wait until Theognus and the others come out to know how the vote went.*

Arias waited in the vestibule of the palace while the Patriarchs and the bishops voted. Athanasius disappeared down one of the adjacent hallways. *I wonder where he's going. Isn't he curious about the outcome of the vote?*

Once Athanasius and Arias had left the hall and the doors were closed, Hosius said, "We'll now vote on the two opposing positions presented by Athanasius and Arias. I'll ask you to stand for the position you support, and remain standing until the votes are counted. Remember, if there's not a clear majority, then the Emperor will decide which position will be adopted."

The Patriarchs and bishops nodded. Hosius continued. "Those who agree with Brother Arias that Jesus is *not* God and that the Divine Trinity should *not* be adopted as the official doctrine of the churches, please stand."

Arias' supporters immediately stood. Hosius was about to ask them to be seated when a few more bishops rose to their feet. Hosius added their votes, but more bishops stood. After several moments, more than a third of the bishops were standing, including most of the bishops from the western empire. *One hundred and forty! Arias got more votes than I expected, but at least he doesn't have a majority.*

"Be seated," Hosius said. "Those who agree with Brother Athanasius that Jesus *is* God and that the Divine Trinity *should* be adopted as the official doctrine of the churches, please stand."

All of the Patriarchs and the remaining bishops stood. Hosius counted the votes. *One hundred and seventy eight. That's the majority, but with so many of the bishops from the western empire voting with Arias' supporters, the Emperor will have to make the decision.*

"The vote is one hundred and seventy eight in favor of adopting the Divine Trinity doctrine to one hundred and forty against," Hosius said. "Given that the vote is so close, I see no other option than to have the Emperor make the final decision."

Constantine slowly walked to the center of the hall. He kept his back to the bishops for several moments, and then he turned to face them. "This is a heavy burden that you've placed upon me. Ever since my vision of the Christ on the eve of battle, I've loved the churches, and my goal all along has been to restore unity between you. Brothers Athanasius and Arias each made excellent theological points in support of their positions, as did the bishops who spoke out during the debates. But I believe that the arguments *in favor* of the Divine Trinity make the most sense and are substantiated by the vision of Christ that I had thirteen years ago. There is sound theological evidence that Jesus *is* God. Therefore, I rule in favor of adopting the Divine Trinity doctrine and declare it to be the official theology of the Christian churches throughout Christendom."

The bishops who voted in favor of the Divine Trinity immediately cheered and applauded the Emperor's decision. Several of the bishops who had voted against the Divine Trinity applauded politely. Arias' supporters sat in stunned silence.

Hosius ended the session, and he and the Emperor left the hall. The Patriarchs and the bishops who supported the Divine Trinity remained in the hall, congratulating themselves, as Arias' supporters exited.

"That went exactly as planned," Hosius said to Constantine once they were alone in the Emperor's chamber.

Constantine smiled. "Yes, it did. I was worried when I saw how many of the bishops voted against the Divine Trinity, but we had the majority. You were right when you assured me that I had nothing to worry about. Now that the Divine Trinity is the official theology, we should get through the rest of the agenda quickly. How are the meetings with the Patriarchs going?"

"They're making suggestions and raising some good points, but so far they've approved everything I've presented to them. We should have all of the plans approved within the next ten days."

Constantine nodded. "I feel like celebrating tonight. Will you join me?"

"My pleasure, Flavius," Hosius replied.

"Good! Have Athanasius join us as well. It's time for him to receive a little reward for his efforts."

"I'll go get him right now." Hosius left the Emperor and headed for the Patriarch's meeting chamber where he knew that Athanasius was waiting for him.

Arias was waiting in the vestibule when Theognus and the other Followers of The Way exited the central hall. He was excited when he noticed them, but as he walked toward them, he saw on their faces that the vote didn't go well.

"What happened?" he asked

"It was close, Arias," Theognus said.

"We almost had the majority," Secundus added.

"But Hosius said the vote was too close to call, so he had the Emperor make the final decision," Theognus continued. "The Emperor sided with those supporting the Divine Trinity. It's now the official theology of the churches."

Arias was dumfounded. *How can this be? Why would God allow the churches to turn their backs on The Way? How can we allow Jesus to be worshipped as a god throughout the empire?*

Theognus put his hand on Arias' arm. "You did the best you could, Arias. No one could have defended our position better than you did. Most of the bishops from the western empire sided with us, but Alexander had more supporters here than we did."

"So what happens now?" Arias asked.

"I don't know," Theognus replied. "I imagine that all of the decisions made by the council will be documented, and we'll have to sign our names in a show of unity, but Hosius hasn't really said anything about that."

"And if we refuse to obey the council's decree to stop following The Way and start worshipping Jesus as our god?" Arias asked.

"Then we risk banishment from the churches and from the empire," Theognus said.

Arias shook his head. *I have to talk to Hosius about this. I need his advice on what to do.* He saw someone out of the corner of his eye and turned to look. It was Hosius. Arias watched him go down the same hallway where Athanasius had disappeared earlier.

"I need to talk to Hosius," he said aloud. "I'll meet you back at the church later."

Before his supporters could say anything, Arias raced across the vestibule after Hosius.

The hallway was deserted. Arias followed it, looking for any sign of where Hosius had gone. The corridor turned to the left, and Arias thought he heard voices coming from one of the rooms halfway down. As he approached the room, he heard Hosius speaking.

"The Emperor wants to celebrate our victory, and he's invited you to join us."

"The Emperor wants me there?" Arias recognized Athanasius' voice.

"You've earned it," Hosius replied. "You presented our position to the council, you helped us make Arias look like a fool in front of the Patriarchs and the bishops, and you helped our side defeat Arias' supporters. This more than makes up for the debacle with the assassins that you hired to keep Arias from attending the council."

Assassins? Athanasius hired men to kill me? Is that who the escorts were who came to the church looking for me?

Arias heard Hosius' voice get louder. He looked around quickly for a place to hide and saw a deep niche on the wall opposite the room where Hosius and Athanasius were talking. He stepped inside and hid in the shadows.

"Leave the scrolls where they are, Athanasius," Hosius said. "Your notes can keep until we meet with the Patriarchs in the morning. It's not good to keep the Emperor waiting when he's feeling generous."

From the shadows of the niche, Arias saw Hosius leave the room, followed by Athanasius. He waited until he couldn't hear their voices or their footsteps anymore.

Hosius, Athanasius, Alexander, the Emperor… they've been planning this all along. Hosius mentioned something about meetings with the Patriarchs. Are all of the Patriarchs part of this conspiracy? This council was never about giving us the chance to convince the churches to follow The Way. The outcome was already decided before the council was ever summoned. I was invited here to be humiliated by the Patriarchs and the bishops so my views would be discredited.

Arias was curious about the room that Hosius and Athanasius had just exited. He stuck his head out of the niche. Seeing no one, he crossed the corridor and entered the room.

A large table stood in the center of the room with a smaller table a short distance away at one end. Both tables were covered in scrolls. Arias picked up one.

Proposal for the purging of heretics and blasphemers? What is this?

Arias read the scroll. Then he let it drop. *They're going to give the churches the authority to condemn anyone they think is a blasphemer or a heretic? The churches will wield secular power over the people? Isn't that for the courts? And since when is breaking a precept of the churches punishable like a crime?*

Arias picked up another scroll. *Proposal for the deification of Mary as the Mother of God? Now they're saying that Mary is also divine? Based on what? This is the most absurd thing that I've ever read.*

Arias spent the next several hours reading through the scrolls on the tables. When he read the last one, he noticed a small trunk on the floor. Opening it, he found several more scrolls. He sat down and read them one by one.

Arias couldn't believe what he was seeing. *This isn't a religion they're creating. It's a tool for the Emperor to use to control the people of the empire. There's nothing Christian about it. There's nothing here that Jesus or the Apostles would ever approve of. This is the kind of church that Judas would have proposed. It betrays everything that our Master said and did.*

I've been a fool. I've been so focused on faithfully following The Way that I didn't see what was happening all around me. Menophantus and Secundus tried to warn me, but I didn't listen. Hosius played me like a child. How do I face my friends and tell them how wrong I was? How do I face my congregation?

"More wine!" the Emperor shouted as he drained the last flagon.

A servant appeared with more wine and placed it on the table before quickly leaving the chamber.

Constantine filled his cup again. Raising it, he slurred, "I want to thank you again, Athanasius, for all that you've done to help me get my church."

Athanasius nodded and smiled sleepily. "M-my pleasure, Great Em-Em-Emperor. I am your humble ser-servant."

Hosius pretended to take a long sip of wine, but he allowed little of the wine to pass his lips. *I have too much to do to get drunk tonight. I should have warned Athanasius not to drink so much.*

He's not used to the strong wine that the Emperor drinks. If he's not careful, he'll be in no shape for the meeting tomorrow morning with the Patriarchs.

Constantine refilled Athanasius' cup, and the young priest drained it quickly. A strange smile appeared on Athanasius' face, and he slowly slid off his chair and disappeared below the table.

"Ha!" Constantine laughed. "He may be a good priest, but he can't hold his wine like you and I can."

"He's still learning," Hosius said. "Give him time, and access to the good wine, and he'll soon be keeping up with you."

Constantine snorted and called for his servants to help Athanasius back to his chamber. "Put him in his bed, and let him sleep it off," the Emperor ordered. The servants bowed, picked Athanasius off the floor, and half dragged, half carried the young priest out of the Emperor's chamber.

Hosius stood up.

"No, stay, Hosius," the Emperor said. "There's more celebrating to be done."

"I wish I could, Flavius," Hosius said. "But I have things to do before I meet with the Patriarchs in the morning, and I have to prepare for the next item on the agenda for the council meeting tomorrow afternoon. But I promise that I'll celebrate with you for a whole week once the council meetings are concluded."

"I'm going to hold you to that, Hosius," the Emperor said with a wolfish grin.

Hosius bowed to the Emperor and left the room.

Hosius headed for the Patriarch's meeting chamber. The corridors were deserted, and most of the torches had been extinguished. Only a few braziers were still lit. They gave off a faint glow, but it was enough to help Hosius navigate the labyrinth of corridors that led from one end of the palace to the other.

He was so deep in thought as he walked that he didn't notice the open door to the meeting chamber or the person sitting at the large table, reading one of the scrolls detailing his proposals for the Imperial Church.

Hosius crossed the room and stopped short when he noticed that the small trunk on the floor was open and empty. *I know I left that closed.* Spinning around, he saw that the table was covered with scrolls. Then he saw the person sitting there and staring at him with a look of betrayal etched on his face.

"What are you doing here, Arias?" Hosius demanded.

The expression on Arias' face was unmistakable. Arias had discovered the truth about the council meeting's purpose.

"I'm waiting for you, Hosius."

CHAPTER 17

Hosius shrugged and started putting the scrolls back where they had been before Arias read them.

Arias was annoyed with Hosius for ignoring him. "You don't have anything to say to me?"

Hosius put down the scrolls in his hand and looked across the table at Arias. "What do you want me to say, Arias?"

Arias gestured toward the scrolls. "I want you to explain this."

"What's there to explain? The Patriarchs and I are working out the details of how the churches will work once Constantine names Christianity as the state religion of the empire."

Arias held up scroll after scroll. "Condemning heretics and blasphemers to death by burning? Rewriting the gospels and epistles to fit your false interpretations? Using priests to gather intelligence on the empire's citizens and use that intelligence against them? Giving Christianity a goddess? Converting pagan gods into saints and devils? Adopting pagan rites as part of Christian ceremonies? Moving the date of the birth of our Master from late spring to the winter solstice just so there will be a Christian celebration at that time of year?"

Arias slammed the scroll in his hand onto the table. "All of this is necessary for Christianity to be the state religion of the empire?"

Hosius took the scrolls and put them back where they had been. "You don't understand, Arias. You never did."

"Then explain it to me."

Hosius stopped and glared at Arias. "You want an explanation? Fine. Here's the explanation. For three hundred years, Christians were persecuted. They were murdered, butchered, burned, captured and used as sport for lions and gladiators in the arena… and why? Because of their faith. They believed in Jesus Christ, and for that, they became targets for anyone with a lust for blood. But thirteen years ago, that stopped. Why? Because *I* convinced Emperor Constantine to end the persecution! And in return for him granting my request, I had to promise to give him a religion that could serve the empire as well as the faithful. So if you want to know what I'm doing and why I'm doing it, think of it this way: I'm rendering unto Caesar that which is Caesar's. Why can't you understand that, Arias? Why can't you support and help me, rather than work against me?"

"Rendering unto Caesar…?" Arias began. "Hosius, the churches do not belong to Constantine!"

Hosius sneered. "No, Arias, but the Empire does. And, like it or not, we're part of the Empire. If we want to continue to live under its protections, we must be and do what the Empire demands of us."

"But what you're creating here is not a church based on The Way, based on salvation or the emulation of our Master's words and works," Arias protested. "You're creating a tool of statecraft… an instrument to control Roman citizens for the sole benefit of Emperor Constantine!"

"And that's what the Empire demands, Arias!"

Arias shook his head in disbelief. "You're betraying our Master and his Apostles, Hosius, and you're spitting in the face of every martyr who has given his life in defense of The Way. I'd rather be martyred, too, than support this church that you're creating."

"That can be arranged, Arias."

"What's that supposed to mean?" Arias shot back. "Or are you threatening to let Athanasius hire more assassins to kill me?"

Hosius looked shocked. "What are you…"

"I heard you talking to Athanasius earlier," Arias shouted. "I heard you congratulating him on how well you two manipulated the council so Constantine could have his new religion and how it made up for the debacle with the assassins who failed to kill me."

Hosius clenched and unclenched his fists. He stared at Arias for several moments. Then he said, "I don't need to hire assassins again, Arias. Didn't you read the scrolls? The Patriarchs approved condemning heretics and blasphemers. By the end of the council meetings, your position will be considered blasphemy. The churches will condemn you, Arias, not me. You'll be purged as a warning to others who defy the official theology of the churches."

"So, rather than the empire persecuting Christians, the churches will now persecute anyone who holds to a belief that doesn't agree with your new theology?"

"It's necessary for the state religion to succeed," Hosius replied.

"And what happens if the theology changes again? Suddenly, things that were acceptable in the past will become unacceptable – just like what's happening now. What happens when *your* beliefs don't agree with the new theology?"

"That'll never happen," Hosius said smugly.

"Why, because you and the Emperor are friends?" Arias asked.

"No, because I control the Patriarchs."

Arias looked confused. "So, you're the supreme head of the church? I didn't read that scroll."

"It's not written in the scrolls," Hosius said. "And I don't see the church being under the absolute control of any one man at this time. But there will come a time when, for the sake of unity, there will be one supreme head of the churches and of mankind – Christ's representative on earth."

"And that person will be you?"

Hosius smiled. "Perhaps."

"And how will you be chosen?" Arias asked.

"I will be elected by the Patriarchs. Or someone else will be. Anyway, that's for the future. There's a lot to do before then. For now, the Patriarchs are the religious heads of the churches and the Emperor is the secular head."

"And as the Emperor's theological advisor and friend, you control both."

"Exactly!"

Arias shook his head. "Hosius, for the love of God, don't do this. Our faith is supposed to be a light set upon a hill, a beacon of hope to humanity. We're supposed to live our lives according to our Master's teaching. We're supposed to spread the gospel of Christ to those who want to understand more about what we believe. By making our church the state religion of the empire, you'll force its citizens to convert to Christianity at the point of the sword. You'll water down the teachings of our Master to be more palatable to the converted. You'll absorb aspects of the empire's pagan religions into Christianity so everyone will see something familiar once they've converted. But worst of all, you'll create parts of the church that have nothing to do with the salvation of mankind. They'll be nothing more than agents of the empire and exist to help the Emperor control the hearts and minds of his citizens. You'll destroy The Way, and in the end, you'll destroy all that our Master said and did. You'll destroy any possibility of salvation for the faithful followers of Jesus today and the future."

Arias stared at Hosius for a moment. Then he added, "You're creating the anti-Christ and unleashing it on the world!"

Hosius laughed. "You are a fool, Arias. You live in the past where each church was all alone and left to fend for itself. I'm creating the future for our religion, where we are united and where our numbers are greater than anything our Master could have imagined. The Christ will be worshipped across the known world in a few short years. That's how *I* worship Christ. That's how I've proven *my* faith. That's how *I'll* receive eternal salvation."

"Calling yourself a Christian isn't enough, Hosius," Arias said with contempt. "You have to act like a Christian, too. There's nothing Christian about this new church that you're creating. There's no salvation waiting for you or your followers."

Hosius smiled. "Be that as it may, I'm the one who will still be here when the council ends. You'll either be condemned to death or exiled from the empire, and I'll be at the Emperor's side, leading the churches to a glorious future."

"Leading the churches straight to hell," Arias retorted. "Yes, you may still be here, but you won't be able to eradicate The Way from your new church. It'll continue to exist."

"Perhaps," Hosius said, "But not here. Not in the empire."

Arias stood to leave. As he walked past Hosius, he whispered, "We'll see about that."

Arias strode out of the room. As Hosius heard Arias' footsteps fade in the distance, he said softly, "Yes, Arias, we *will* see about that."

Arias left the palace and walked through the streets of Nicaea back to the church. He arrived at the square in front of the church several hours after midnight. He saw candlelight inside. *Someone is still awake. I can't face anyone right now. I need to be alone and seek divine guidance. The anti-Christ has come to the world, and I wasn't strong enough or aware enough to stop it. I need to plan my next steps carefully, or all that I've worked for my entire life will be lost.*

Arias walked past the church toward the city gates. *I need to find a quiet place to pray.*

Hosius met with the Patriarchs shortly after breakfast to continue reviewing the plans for the imperial church. He glanced at Athanasius, who looked ill. *Yes, I definitely should have warned him not to drink so much last night.*

"Before we get started," Hosius began, "I need to let you know something. Arias found his way in here last night and read the plans that we've been working on. He knows everything that we've discussed and several things we haven't discussed yet."

"How could this happen?" Alexander demanded. "Not even the bishops are supposed to know until after the Emperor announces Christianity as the state religion! He'll tell his supporters, and they'll tell others on the council."

"I know," Hosius said. "It was an accident. I should have kept this room locked, but it never occurred to me that Arias would find his way back here. He's staying at the church, so there was no reason for him to be in this part of the palace."

"What do we do about him?" Eustathius of Antioch asked.

"Nothing," Hosius said. "He's not part of any of the remaining council sessions, and no one will believe his supporters if they say anything. I just wanted you to be aware of what happened in case he should approach one of you."

"And what if he talks to the bishops outside of the council meetings?" Alexander asked. "He's very persuasive, as you've all seen."

"Good point," Hosius acknowledged. "I'd suggest that you all talk to your bishops and let them know that Arias had become unstable and that they should avoid talking to him."

The Patriarchs nodded and smiled. "That's a good plan," Eustathius said. "If the bishops think he has gone mad, they won't believe a word he says."

Hosius looked at Athanasius, who was trying to listen carefully to the conversation in spite of an obvious headache. *Maybe I should send for another scribe to take notes.*

"Have you seen Arias this morning?" Secundus asked Theognus as they were preparing to leave the church that afternoon.

"No, and neither have his servants," Theognus replied. "It doesn't appear that he returned to the church last night."

"You don't suppose that Hosius had something done to him, do you?" Paulinus of Tyrus asked.

"I wouldn't put it past him," Menophantus of Ephesus commented.

Theognus gestured for Arias' supporters to follow him outside. "Don't assume the worst. Arias may just need time alone after the vote yesterday. If he's not back by this evening, we'll send people to search for him."

Secundus nodded. "Agreed."

The bishops followed Theognus to the palace to attend that afternoon's session of the council.

Arias sat on a hillside outside of the city walls, praying. He had been there for three days, but the peace that he longed for eluded him. The people that his supporters sent to look for him had found him, and he sent them back with a message that he'd return when he was ready.

My church has been handed over to the anti-Christ. I spent my life trying so hard to live The Way that I forgot to defend The Way from those who wanted to see it gone from the earth. I've failed my God, my Master, my congregation, and myself. How do I make this right?

As Arias pondered his failures, a passage from the second prophet Isaiah came to him like a trumpet blast.

Thou whom I have taken from the ends of the earth, and called thee from the chief men thereof, and said unto thee, Thou art my servant; I have chosen thee, and not cast thee

away. Fear thou not; for I am with thee: be not dismayed;
for I am thy God: I will strengthen thee; yea, I will help
thee; yea, I will uphold thee with the right hand of my
righteousness. Behold, all they that were incensed against
thee shall be ashamed and confounded: they shall be as
nothing; and they that strive with thee shall perish. Thou
shalt seek them, and shalt not find them, even them that
contended with thee: they that war against thee shall be as
nothing, and as a thing of nought. For I the Lord thy God
will hold thy right hand, saying unto thee, Fear not; I will
help thee.

Arias felt a deep sense of peace come over him, and in that instant he saw clearly what he needed to do. *I'll make one more attempt to get the bishops to understand what they're doing, even though it'll fail. But I'll never resign my faith just to avoid exile or condemnation. I'll stand with the faithful and will preach and teach The Way for as long as I have breath in me.*

Arias felt divine serenity flowing through him. He remained on the hillside for another day, communing and rejoicing with God.

"So we're in agreement?" Hosius asked the Patriarchs when they met the next morning.

Each of the Patriarchs nodded.

"Very well," Hosius said, feeling satisfied. "All of the plans for the imperial church are now adopted, as are the revisions to the gospels and the epistles to make them easier to understand in light of our official theology. I'll inform the Emperor. Once the revised gospels and epistles are ready, I know he'll want all previous versions destroyed. There can be only one official version of the sacred texts."

"Thank you for all of the work that you've done, Hosius," Alexander said. "I think we're now ready to begin converting the people of the empire to the worship of the Christ. I have no doubt that God is smiling on our efforts to bring His word to the entire world."

The other Patriarchs agreed.

Hosius smiled. "I thank each of you. I offered suggestions, but you had to discuss and refine them, and then vote on the ones that you believe are in the best interest of the churches. You had the hardest task, and you performed it very well."

After the Patriarchs left the meeting chamber, Hosius looked at Athanasius. "Get the final revisions made to the scrolls as quickly as you can. I want the Patriarchs to sign them before I present them to the Emperor.

"Yes, Hosius," the young priest promised.

Hosius left the chamber to find the Emperor and tell him that the meetings with the Patriarchs were over and that they had agreed to everything he wanted for the imperial church.

Arias passed through the city gates just before they closed for the night. He walked through the city to the church, feeling hungry after spending four days on the hillside. But for the first time since arriving at Nicaea, he felt calm. *I may have lost the battle, but the war is far from lost. As long as one person faithfully follows The Way, then our Master's words and works are not lost. There will always be those who seek the truth, and we must be steadfast in our faith so that they'll find what they seek.*

It was dark when he entered the church. Andrew and Barnabas were sitting on a bench outside of the sanctuary, talking. When they looked up and saw Arias, they didn't recognize him at first.

"Good evening, Andrew, Barnabas," he said, walking toward them.

"Arias?" Andrew exclaimed. "Is that you?"

Andrew jumped up and ran forward. Barnabas went to find Theognus.

"It's me, Andrew."

"I barely recognized you," Andrew said. "You look different. I know that you sent word that you didn't want to be disturbed, but I was going to come myself if you didn't return by morning."

"Then I've saved you the trouble," Arias said pleasantly as Barnabas returned with Theognus and the rest of the bishops who supported Arias.

"It's about time that you returned," Theognus said. "You look like a new man. Did you find what you were looking for?"

Arias nodded and smiled. "Yes, I did. And I have so much to tell you."

"We have much to tell you, too, Arias," Secundus said.

"Is there any food around?" Arias asked. "I think this is a discussion that's better had over a meal."

"We were just getting ready to eat," Theognus said. "Get yourself cleaned up, and then join us. We'll wait for you."

"Arias hasn't been seen for several days," Hosius informed the Emperor. "It's possible that he's returned to Alexandria to seek refuge in his church at Baucalis."

"Are you sure that he's gone and not just hiding?" Constantine asked.

"No, Flavius, but why would he stay in Nicaea and hide? He knows that he's lost, he knows what the plans are for the imperial church, and he knows that there's nothing he can do to stop us. The Patriarchs have talked to their bishops and told them that Arias is going mad, so no one will listen to him even if he is still in the city."

"Still, keep searching for him. I want to make an example of him at the end of the council meetings."

"Yes, Flavius."

Arias and the bishops who were Followers of The Way talked for hours. Arias told them what he had read in the Patriarch's meeting chamber and about his conversation with Hosius, including the part about Athanasius hiring assassins. The bishops didn't believe him at first, but he finally convinced them that he was telling the truth.

When he finished sharing what he had discovered, the bishops were shocked by Hosius' betrayal. After a while, Theognus told Arias what had been happening in the council meetings.

"We've covered a lot of topics since the vote on the Divine Trinity. We've decided how to determine when Easter will be celebrated each year, and then we started working on the structure of the churches, ceremonial practices, and other practices in the churches that need to be standardized. And then the Emperor told us about the 'Creed' and the 'Canons'."

"The 'Creed' and the 'Canons'?" Arias asked.

"The Creed is the summary of the theological decisions that have been made during the council sessions," Secundus explained. "The Canons are the twenty church laws that relate to church structure and practices."

"At the end of the council," Theognus continued, "everyone will be expected to sign the Creed and the Canons. And not just the Patriarchs and bishops who attended the council. Every Patriarch, bishop, priest, and acolyte will be required to sign them."

"What if they don't sign?" Arias asked.

"They'll either be banished or purged," Secundus replied. "And by purged, I mean condemned. The Emperor is treating this like an imperial decree."

Arias nodded. Then he said, "I need to speak to the other bishops and tell them what's going on."

"They won't listen, Arias," Secundus said. "The Patriarchs have been telling their bishops that you've gone mad. They've been warned to avoid you and to report your whereabouts to Hosius."

"Then I'll address the council as a whole," Arias stated.

"Hosius will never grant you an audience," Theognus said. "You're the enemy. He's already started discrediting you during the sessions, referring to your position on the Divine Trinity as heresy and blasphemy that needs to be eradicated. Even the Emperor has said that he won't tolerate your ideas now that the issue of the Trinity has been settled. He calls your position "Arianism," and he's preparing decrees to have it banned throughout the empire.

Arias thought about this for a while. "I think I have a way around Hosius. It'll probably fail, but I can't leave Nicaea knowing that I didn't try everything I could to prevent what Hosius and the Emperor are doing."

The next morning, the Patriarchs and bishops convened in the central hall of the palace. Now that the separate meetings with the

Patriarchs were concluded, the full council would meet all day until the remaining issues were resolved.

The Emperor was absent from the morning session, but the imperial guards were still posted around the hall. Hosius called the meeting to order.

Theognus stood and asked to be recognized.

"Brother Theognus," Hosius said, "do you wish to address the council?"

"Yes, Brother Hosius."

"Very well, proceed."

"Actually, Brother Hosius, I'd like to request that someone else speak on my behalf, if you have no objections."

"I have no objections, Brother Theognus. Who do you want to speak for you?"

"Brother Arias of Baucalis."

CHAPTER 18

The hall erupted into pandemonium.

Many of the bishops shouted, "Blasphemer! He has no place in this council meeting!"

Other bishops shouted, "Let him be heard! What is there to fear from one priest?"

Hosius glared at Theognus, who silently stared back. *What is Theognus up to? Arias has been missing for days. He can't possibly be here.* After several moments, Hosius raised his hand, and the imperial guards moved forward to help restore order.

Once the bishops stopped shouting, Hosius said, "It's not appropriate for Brother Arias to address the council, Brother Theognus. He has already been given ample time to present his ideas during the debate over the Divine Trinity."

"He's not going to be presenting *his* ideas, Brother Hosius," Theognus stated loudly. "He's presenting information on my behalf. And besides, you already said that you have no objections to allowing someone to speak for me. You can't add an objection now after already agreeing to my request."

"I have no objections to someone speaking on your behalf," Hosius countered. "But I do object to *who* will be speaking. Arias has clearly gone mad. We've all seen it, and I can think of no reason to subject this council to the ravings of a lunatic."

Theognus snorted. "What are you afraid of, Hosius? That one madman will undo all that *you've* accomplished since this council first convened? Are the ravings of one priest so terrifying to you? If he's crazy, then letting him speak won't hurt anyone. If anything, it'll only convince everyone that he *is* mad. And if he's not crazy, what harm can one person do? My request stands. I wish Brother Arias to speak on my behalf."

Hosius looked around the hall nervously. Then he said, "But no one has seen Brother Arias for days. I don't want to dismiss the council while we send people to search for him. If he's not already here in the palace, then you'll have to choose someone else to speak for you."

Hosius' smile made him look like a viper. *That settles that, Theognus. Whatever you're planning, it won't work.*

But Theognus just smiled back. "He's outside the door to this hall, Hosius. Have one of the guards summon him now. No one has to go searching for him, and there will be no need to dismiss the council."

Damn you, Theognus! How did you get Arias inside the palace? The Emperor has had legionnaires and imperial guards searching for him for days. How did he manage to just walk past them? What do I do now?

Hosius and Theognus glared at each other. Finally, Hosius turned to one of the guards closest to the hall's main entrance. "See if Brother Arias is in the vestibule."

The guard immediately opened the door and peered outside. Then he closed the door and nodded to Hosius.

He IS here! Hosius looked around the hall. Several bishops were murmuring that Arias should be allowed into the hall to speak. As they got louder, more bishops joined in the call to allow Arias to speak. Hosius shrugged. *What harm can one priest do?*

"Very well," Hosius said. "I'll allow Brother Arias to speak. But from this point forward, no one other than Patriarchs, bishops, and the Emperor may address the council."

Hosius turned to the guards at the door. "Summon Brother Arias."

Arias heard the door to the hall open and saw the face of one of the imperial guards. The guard looked surprised to see him. A moment later, the face disappeared, and the door closed.

I guess Hosius wants to know if I'm out here.

A few moments later, the door reopened. "You may enter, Arias," the guard said.

Arias heard the door close behind him as he walked to the center of the hall where Hosius was standing. Even from a distance, Arias could tell that Hosius wasn't happy to see him.

"Good morning, Brother Hosius," Arias said pleasantly.

Hosius glared at him and hissed, "I don't know what you're up to, Arias, but it won't work."

"*I'm* not the one who's up to something, Brother Hosius. You are. You're corrupting everything that our Master stood for. I'm just here to make sure that everyone knows it."

Before Hosius could retort, Theognus said, "Brother Arias, you're here to speak on my behalf. Please proceed."

Hosius scowled at Theognus and Arias for several moments before finally taking his seat.

"My brothers, thank you for allowing me to speak to you one more time. I know that you're trying to finish the remaining items on your agenda, so I'll be brief. Brother Theognus has asked me to share an important matter with you."

Arias paused for a moment. "We've been betrayed!" he thundered.

The Patriarchs and bishops reacted strongly to this statement. Arias heard several of them whisper, "What's he talking about?" "How have we been betrayed" "He's mad, don't listen to him." "Let him speak!"

Hosius glowered at Arias, as if daring the priest to continue.

Arias raised his hand. "Hear me, my Brothers. While you've been meeting every day to resolve issues that are dividing the churches, Hosius and the Patriarchs have been meeting in secret to define the new Christian Church; not a church dedicated to Christ or to the salvation of our congregations, but a church designed for one purpose: to be a tool for the empire to use to control its citizens!"

Arias saw Hosius stand. But before he could interrupt, Arias continued. "I have seen their plans. They are rewriting the gospels and the epistles to conform to what they want the people to believe, rather than what the original authors intended. They plan to use the church to spy on Roman citizens and gather information that can be used against them for the benefit of the Emperor. They plan to adopt pagan deities and rites into our religion to make it easier to convert people once the Emperor announces that Christianity is the state religion of the empire. They plan to deify Mary as the mother of God so that Christianity will have a goddess. But worst of all, they plan to condemn to death by burning anyone they believe has committed an act of heresy or blasphemy. Church law will now be superior to civil law, with disobedience to the Patriarchs and the church earning eternal damnation to anyone they accuse of wrongdoing."

Arias pointed at Hosius. "My brothers, Hosius and the Patriarchs are creating a church that is no longer dedicated to the words and works of our Master, Jesus Christ. They are creating the anti-Christ and are unleashing their new beast on mankind!"

Nicholas of Myra jumped to his feet. "Liar!" he shouted. "You've gone mad, Arias. The Patriarchs are the most respected Christians on earth. How can you stand there and slander their good names with such nonsense? I have better things to do than to sit here and listen to the ravings of madman!"

Several bishops shouted in agreement with Nicholas. Arias waited calmly until they were finished. Then he continued. "Many of you have been told that I'm crazy. But if I'm lying, Brother Nicholas, then let's hear from the Patriarchs. Let them tell you what they've been doing in their secret meetings."

Hosius looked nervous. *You didn't think that I'd call on the Patriarchs to answer for themselves, did you, Hosius?*

"Yes, let's hear from the Patriarchs," Theognus shouted. "If Brother Arias is lying, then let *them* tell us what the truth is. If they're the most respected Christians in the world, then let them swear before God and this council that they'll tell us the truth."

The other bishops opposed to the Divine Trinity joined the chorus of those demanding that the Patriarchs answer Arias' accusations. Hosius raised his hand, and the imperial guards stepped closer. The hall fell silent.

No one spoke or moved for several moments. Finally, Alexander stood. Arias watched in anticipation. *Will you redeem yourself and tell us the truth, Alexander?*

All eyes were on Alexander, who looked at Arias with a mixture of contempt and scorn. Alexander gestured to his fellow Patriarchs before stepping off the riser and leading them past Arias and out of the hall. Nicholas left next, followed by most of the other bishops, including many of those who had voted with Arias' supporters against the Divine Trinity doctrine.

Soon, Arias and his supporters were alone in the hall with Hosius.

"It was a good effort, Brother Arias," Hosius said as he paused in front of Arias. "But you're too late. No one on the council will listen to you. Those who didn't think you mad before certainly will now. You've failed. Accept your ignominious defeat. Your fate was sealed long before you were even invited to Nicaea, and your name and your words will be reviled for centuries to come. In the end, *you'll* be called the herald of the anti-Christ, and I'll be remembered as Peter's faithful successor – the man who brought Christianity back into the light."

Hosius followed the Patriarchs and the other bishops out of the hall.

Arias' supporters gathered around him. Theognus put his hand on Arias' shoulder. "You did your best, Arias. No one could have done any better."

"None of them has the discipline to obey our Master's instructions," Arias said, referring to the Patriarchs and bishops who had left the hall. "Rather than change themselves to conform to Jesus' commands, the Patriarchs and bishops have changed his commands to conform to their own will! The problem isn't with our Master's instructions; the problem is the Patriarchs and the bishops!"

"But what can we do to stop them?" Secundus asked.

"We can't stop them," Arias said sadly. "All we can do is try to prevent *them* from stopping *us*."

"Stopping us from doing what?" Secundus asked.

"From preserving The Way," Arias replied.

"But the Emperor is preparing edicts to have all old versions of the gospels and the epistles destroyed," Menophantus said. "Arianism, as the Emperor now calls The Way, will be outlawed throughout the empire, and anyone caught practicing or preaching The Way will be condemned as a heretic and blasphemer."

"It's no different from how Christianity was treated for its first three hundred years," Arias said. "Christians had to hide their faith to avoid persecution at the hands of the Romans. Now the true followers of The Way will have to do the same to avoid persecution at the hands of Rome's imperial church."

"Wouldn't it be better for us to just give in to the council?" Eusebius asked.

"No, but it must appear that you're doing just that," Arias said.

"What do you mean?" Theognus asked.

Arias smiled. "When I was meditating outside the city, I finally saw things clearly. Constantine will get his church, and he'll use it to rule the empire, as will his successors for centuries to come. The people will be led farther and farther away from our Master's true words and works until they're forgotten or relegated to myth and legend."

"Then why bother fighting it?" Eusebius asked.

"Because we're the faithful followers of our Master. As long as we continue preaching, teaching, and living our lives according to The Way, then The Way will never completely disappear and be lost to the world. That's what God demands of us. The Patriarchs and the bishops may turn down the wrong path, but we don't have to follow them. All we have to do is follow our Master where he leads us."

"But if we're all exiled for following The Way, what will happen to The Way once we're dead?" Paulinus asked.

"You're not going to accept exile," Arias replied. "You're going to sign the creed and appear to stand with the Patriarchs and the other bishops. You'll appear to destroy your old copies of the gospels and epistles, and you'll openly preach what the Patriarchs demand that you preach. But you'll hide your old copies of the gospels and the epistles. You'll continue preaching, teaching, and practicing The Way in secret, and you'll pass along to new students all that you have learned, so they can pass it along to their students once you're gone."

"Why?" Eusebius asked.

"So The Way will live on," Arias explained. "There will come a day when the imperial church will lose its stranglehold on the truth. It may not be for a hundred years or five hundred years or even fifteen hundred years, but it will happen. And when it does, The Way will step out of the shadows and lead the faithful back to the true worship as shown to us by our Master. But if we don't keep it alive, then there will be nothing left to step out and lead the way when the time comes."

"An underground church hidden inside the imperial church?" Theognus tugged at his beard. "It's risky."

"But look at the cost to mankind if we don't do it," Arias said. "The risk to us is a small sacrifice in order to keep the door of salvation open for future generations."

"And what about you, Arias?" Secundus asked. "Will you sign the creed and preach what the Patriarchs command?"

Arias shook his head. "No. I'll never be allowed to return to Baucalis. Hosius has made that clear. The Emperor calls my beliefs 'Arianism', and I'm the face of the opposition to his church. If I stay, I'll be assassinated. If I pretend to give in, I'll be accused of heresy and blasphemy later, and then I'll be executed for the greater good. My only choice is to accept exile. I'll leave the empire, but I don't want any of you to follow me. You need to return to your churches and keep The Way alive. With me gone, you'll be safe."

"But for how long?" Theognus asked. "Hosius knows that we supported you and that we're faithful Followers of The Way. How long will it be before he accuses *us* of heresy and blasphemy?"

"I don't know," Arias admitted. "But hopefully it'll be long enough for you to preserve The Way in your churches."

"Is there no other choice?" Theognus asked.

"No, my friend. This is God's will. The Christian churches were supposed to be the light of the world, the city on the hill where all could come and worship. But now we have to hide our light under the bushel, letting it be seen only by those who are led to that light by God. The light has to be cared for so it doesn't go out. Then, when the time is right, the light will shine again for all to see. Just as the child Jesus had to be protected and cared for until he was ready to begin his ministry, so, too, must The Way be protected until it can take its place again as the true religion of the Christ."

Arias motioned for the others to follow him. They walked out of the hall and back to the church at Nicaea.

"Arias was here in the palace?" Emperor Constantine asked when Hosius came to see him after leaving the central hall. "What did he want?"

"Theognus of Nicaea asked that Arias be allowed to speak on his behalf. I tried to prevent it, but the old fox caught me off guard. I had to let Arias speak."

"At least we know that he's still in the city," Constantine said. "Although I'd like to know how he got into the palace past my guards."

"So would I," Hosius said.

"So what did Arias say?" Constantine asked.

"He told them what the Patriarchs and I have been working on," Hosius replied.

"What?!"

Hosius smiled. "Don't worry, Flavius. No harm was done. The Patriarchs have been telling their bishops that Arias is quite mad ever since the vote on the Divine Trinity. When Arias challenged the Patriarchs to confess, they simply walked out of the hall. The bishops followed them out. When I left, Arias was alone, apart from his core group of supporters. No one believed him, and now he looks crazier than ever."

Constantine nodded. "Good."

Changing the subject, the Emperor asked, "Is the Creed ready to sign?"

"Yes, the final drafts of both the Creed and the Canons are finished and ready for the council to sign."

"Perfect. Make sure Arias is there when the documents are presented. If he refuses to sign them, then he'll be forced to leave the church and accept exile from the empire. If he tries to stay, he'll face execution for heresy and blasphemy. I want the bishops to see that I'm serious about stamping out Arianism throughout the empire, beginning with its author."

"I'll see to it, Flavius," Hosius promised.

"Do you think Arias' supporters will sign the Creed and the Canons?" Constantine asked.

"I don't know," Hosius replied. "But even if they do, I'd watch them closely. Signing the documents is one thing, but conforming to their requirements is something else altogether. I'm not sure that I'd trust their sincerity if they sign the Creed and the Canons."

"Well, if they don't sign the documents, then they'll face the same fate as Arias. If they do sign, we'll observe them and see if they're sincere or if they're just pretending to obey. If they're pretending, then they'll face exile or execution."

Arias and the bishops who opposed the Divine Trinity were meeting when a messenger arrived at the church with orders from the Emperor that Arias was to attend the next council session.

"That's it, then," Theognus said when he read the message. "The final vote is tomorrow. Either we vote for and sign our names to the Creed and the Canons, or we face immediate exile from the empire. It's over."

"I'm sorry, Arias," Paulinus said. "I know that Hosius' betrayal was a blow to you."

Arias nodded. "Never have I been so wrong about anything or anyone. But we can't let him defeat us. For The Way to survive, it must be protected in secret. As far as Hosius and the Emperor are concerned, The Way is all but destroyed, and we need them to believe that. Officially, it'll end with the final vote of the council tomorrow. All that we've done, taught, and preached will be publically eradicated. And so will we, unless all of you agree to vote with the council. I won't be allowed to vote, but you must."

"Are you certain that there's no other choice?" Secundus asked.

Arias nodded. "None. Our duty is to our Master and The Way. Nothing else matters. You must sign the Creed and the Canons. Otherwise, your churches will be turned over to men devoted to Hosius and his cause. You can't let that happen."

"Who do you think will get your church?" Theognus asked.

"Athanasius, probably," Arias replied. "He's the best choice to undo all that I've done, and Alexander will want him to bring Baucalis back in line with his other churches."

"You should have been made Bishop of Alexandria and Patriarch, Arias," Theonus said. "Then you could have stopped Hosius' plans before they got this far."

"It wasn't meant to be," Arias said. "Everything that's happening, everything that has happened, is part of God's plan. I don't understand all of the plan, but I see my part in it clearly."

"I wish I had such a clear vision of things," Secundus said. "All I see is the abyss before us."

Arias put his hand on Secundus' arm. "The abyss is only a mist blocking your view. Once it lifts or you rise above it, you'll see the path right there in front of you."

Arias and the others talked until well after midnight before retiring. As Arias walked to his chamber, Andrew, Barnabas, Euric, and Botherik stopped him.

"It goes without saying," Andrew began, "but your fate is our fate. If you're exiled, then we're coming with you."

"Absolutely not!" Arias stated.

"This is not a discussion," Barnabas said. "We can't go back to Baucalis if Athanasius is given the church, and we can't go to any of the other churches without arousing Hosius' suspicions. They know that you're our teacher and that we're loyal to you. There's no place we can go except with you."

Arias knew that Barnabas was right, but he hated the idea that his faithful acolytes would be facing exile with him. Turning to Botherik, he asked, "And what of you, Botherik? You're my servant, not my student. Surely you'd be safe anywhere."

"Where you go, I go," Botherik replied.

Arias smiled at the four men. "Thank you, my friends. Meditate on it tonight, and we'll talk about it in the morning. I appreciate what you're saying, but I want to make sure that you've thought through what it'll mean to be separated from both the church and the empire."

"We'll meditate on it," Euric said. "But we won't change our minds."

When Arias reached his chamber, he lay down on the cot. *As much as I'd appreciate the company, I won't allow anyone to share my fate. I'll ask Theognus or Menophantus or Actius to give Andrew, Barnabas, Euric, and Botherik sanctuary in their churches. They can help preserve The Way in my absence. That would serve me far better than having them with me in exile.*

CHAPTER 19

Arias awoke early the next morning. He listened to hear whether anyone else was stirring. All was quiet. He rose and quietly packed his belongings, knowing that there'd be no time to do so later. Then he went to the sanctuary to pray.

Heavenly Father, I am ready to do as You've instructed. I'll remain steadfast in my faith. I'll reject the anti-Christ, and I'll refuse to obey the commands of the Emperor and the council to adopt a Creed that makes Your Son equal with You. I'll accept exile from the churches and the empire so that I may continue in The Way as You commanded and as Your Son showed us. I'll rejoice in my faith and in Your service. I'm not defeated. By being obedient to Your commands, I triumph over those who oppose You.

Please protect those that I leave behind who must keep The Way alive in secret. Give them the strength to face what they must face, and to endure what they must endure. Theirs is the hardest task. They protect a precious legacy. Guide them with wisdom so that this legacy endures through the ages until mankind is ready to receive it once again.

Arias joined the others for the morning meal. The council meeting wasn't until mid-morning, so Arias and the bishops opposed to the Divine Trinity had a few hours together before it was time to leave for the palace.

After the blessing was offered, Theonus spoke first. "Arias, Secundus and I have been talking. There's no way that we can pretend to obey the Creed and the Emperor's edict while continuing to practice The Way in secret. We have priests in our churches who believe in the Divine Trinity, and they'll be watching us for any sign that we still support you. We have no choice but to refuse to sign the Creed and the Canons. We'll accept exile with you and your acolytes."

"My acolytes are not accepting exile, and neither are you," Arias insisted. "I need my acolytes placed in one of the churches that'll be preserving The Way in secret, and I need the two of you to stay where you are."

"No, Arias," Secundus said calmly. "We cannot stay with our churches and do what you've asked of us. We'd be exposed in no time, and then we'd be exiled anyway. We're going with you, and it's not up to you. It's our decision."

Arias looked at the two men, hoping to think of something to say to change their minds. "I wish you wouldn't," is all he could say.

Theonus nodded. "I know, Arias, but the others have agreed to do as you asked. They'll protect The Way and keep it safe until the time is right."

Arias walked in silence with the others to the palace. He was escorted by four imperial guards who had been dispatched to make sure that he obeyed the Emperor's summons. *Is this what Jesus felt like when he was taken to see Pontius Pilate?*

When they arrived at the palace, the guards stayed with Arias until he was seated. Arias couldn't help but notice many of the bishops watching as the guards escort him into the hall. Some just stared; others snickered at him.

Hosius, Athanasius, and Emperor Constantine entered the hall. Hosius and Athanasius took their seats. The Emperor walked to the center of the hall. The sunlight reflected off the jewels on his gold and purple robe, reinforcing the illusion of divine authority.

"Brother Hosius, are the Creed and the Canons ready?"

"Yes, Great Emperor," Hosius responded.

"Read them," Constantine commanded.

Hosius picked up the first scroll and read the Creed aloud. When he was finished, Hosius then picked up the second scroll and proceeded to read the twenty Canons that had been approved by the council.

When Hosius was finished reading, the Emperor said, "What has been decided by this council is now binding on all churches, Patriarchs, bishops, priests, and acolytes across

Christendom. All who attended this council, and those who didn't attend, will be required to sign the Creed and the Canons. Those who refuse will either face banishment from the churches and the empire, or they will be purged in flame as a warning to others who would refuse."

Constantine sat down. Hosius placed the scrolls with the Creed and the Canons on the tables where Sebastian and the other scribes sat. "Will the Patriarchs step forward to sign their names?"

The four Patriarchs signed their names to the two scrolls. Hosius signed his name for Sylvester of Rome.

"Bishops and priests, come forward and sign your names," Hosius commanded.

One by one, the bishops signed their names on the scrolls. Theognus looked at Arias with a pleading look in his eyes. "Sign the scrolls, my friend," Arias whispered. "Remember what our Master said: *'Suffer it to be so now: for thus it becometh us to fulfil all righteousness'.*"

Theognus nodded and led the others to sign the scrolls. Athanasius, who had been chosen as Alexander's eventual successor that morning, signed his name last.

When everyone had returned to his seat, Constantine asked, "Have all Patriarchs, bishops, and priests in attendance today signed the Creed and the Canons?"

Hosius had kept a close count on who had signed. There were three names missing from the scrolls. "No, Great Emperor. Three have defied your edict and have not signed the Creed or the Canons."

"Whoever has not signed the Creed and the Canons, step forward," Constantine demanded.

Arias, Secundus, and Theonus walked to the center of the hall.

"Sign the Creed and the Canons," the Emperor ordered.

Arias stepped forward. "I'm sorry, Great Emperor, we cannot sign these documents."

"Do you understand that, if you don't sign them, you'll be exiled from the churches and the empire?" Constantine asked.

The three men nodded. "Yes, Great Emperor," Arias said. "I'm aware that my exile was planned long before the council began meeting. Secundus of Ptolemais and Theonus of Marmarica have chosen to join me in exile."

The Emperor stood. "Very well. Let it be known to all who are here that the three of you are expelled from the churches and exiled from the empire for a time that suits my pleasure. Tomorrow morning at dawn, you'll be escorted from Nicaea to Illyricum by my legionnaires. You may not return to the empire without my permission. Is that understood?"

"Yes, Great Emperor," the three men replied.

The Emperor turned and faced the Patriarchs and the bishops. "In addition, if any writing composed by Arias should be found, it shall be burned, so that not only will the wickedness of his teaching be obliterated, but nothing will be left even to remind anyone of him. And I hereby command that anyone discovered to have hidden any writing composed by Arias that wasn't immediately burned, his penalty shall be death by burning as soon as he's discovered in this offense."

Constantine turned back to face Arias. "Guards, take these men back to the church and see to it that they remain there until my legionnaires arrive in the morning to take them to Illyricum."

A squad of eight imperial guards formed up around Arias, Secundus, and Theonus. As they were escorted from the hall, Arias heard several of the bishops laughing.

"Congratulations, Flavius," Hosius said to the Emperor when they were alone a short while later. "You have your church, you have your religion, and you're rid of Arias all on the same day. All in all, I think this is the perfect way for the council meetings to end."

"It'll be good to get back to Byzantium," Constantine agreed. "I have an empire to rule, and you have to implement your grand designs for my church."

Hosius nodded. "Copies of the Creed, the Canons, your announcement about Christianity being the state religion of the empire, and your announcement about Arias' banishment and the purging of his writings, will all be ready to dispatch to the churches by the time we get back to Byzantium."

"How long will you stay, Hosius?" Constantine asked.

"Not long, Flavius. I need to get back to Hispania, but first I need to see Sylvester in Rome and tell him what happened here."

"I wish you could stay with me, old friend," Constantine said. "I miss your counsel and our conversations. You're one of the only men in the empire with whom I can just talk."

"I'll be where you need me to be, when you need me to be there, Flavius. You know that."

"Yes, I know. By the way, what will Athanasius do when he gets back to Alexandria?"

"He's been given Arias' church at Baucalis," Hosius replied. "He'll have his hands full stamping out Arianism there, but it'll be a worthy endeavor for him until it's time to succeed Alexander as bishop."

"You've done well, Hosius," Constantine said. "You've made me very happy and very proud."

"Thank you, Flavius. I live to serve you and the empire."

Hosius left to find Athanasius. *It's done. After years of planning and plotting, it's finally done. Christianity will be the official religion of the empire. No more persecution, no more having to hide and live in fear, and no more dissention between the churches. Everything that I've spent the last thirteen years trying to accomplish has been done. God's church will rule the world, along with the Emperor. When I stand before God to answer for my life, I'll point to the imperial church as proof of my fidelity to God. I've earned my place in paradise.*

Arias slept little that night. After hours of trying to rest, he got up and went into the sanctuary. Even though it still was several hours before sunrise, he was surprised to see a crowd waiting for him. His own acolytes and servant, the bishops who opposed the Divine Trinity and their priests and acolytes... all were there.

"What's this?" Arias asked.

"We didn't want you leaving without knowing how much we appreciate all that you've done for us and for the churches," Theognus said. "When our faith waned, you re-inspired us. When we thought all hope was lost, you gave us fresh hope. When we needed you to speak for us, your words touched us like the word of God. You've held us together, and now that you're leaving, it's the memory of your example that'll sustain us during the dark times ahead."

Arias was stunned at the praise Theognus gave him. "Thank you, my friend. But all I did was listen to and obey God as He directed my steps."

"That's more than what the Patriarchs did," Secundus said. "It's certainly more than what Hosius did."

"It's not about them," Arias pointed out. "It's about our Master and his commandments to us. They may have their new imperial church, but we have our Master's word and works to live up to and to sustain us. Don't let them change who you are, and don't let their new church change your commitment to The Way. We owe it to our Master and to his martyrs to preserve The Way during the persecutions from Rome."

"Well, don't be surprised if some of us end up in exile with you," Paulinus said. "Hosius and the others will be watching us very closely to see if we've truly joined them or if we were just pretending."

"If that's Gods will, then you'll be welcome," Arias said with a smile. "But you'll understand if I tell you that I hope I don't see any of you anytime soon."

Everyone laughed. *I'm glad that this isn't a sad occasion. It may look like we've lost everything, but we haven't actually lost anything. Our faith is still as firm as it was before. The Patriarchs can tell us what to preach, but they can't tell us what to believe. They can't change who we are any more than they can change God. Our triumph is not surrendering to them, even if it looks like we did. And when the world is ready for us once again, we'll be ready for the world.*

Shortly before dawn, a squad of legionnaires arrived and relieved the imperial guards who were posted around the church.

"I'm Centurion Gaius Antonius Messalla," the leader announced when he entered the church. "I'm here to escort the heretics Arias of Baucalis, Secundus of Ptolemais, and Theonus of Marmarica to Illyricum."

Arias turned to embrace his supporters. "God be with you, Arias," Theognus said.

"And God be with you all," Arias replied. Then he left the sanctuary to get his things from his chamber.

By the time that Arias join the legionnaires outside in the pre-dawn darkness, he was surprised at how many people were packed and waiting to leave. In addition to his own acolytes and servant, many of Secundus' and Theonus' priests and acolytes were going with them. In all, seventeen men were being escorted by the legionnaires into exile.

Arias approached his acolytes. "For the last time, please don't follow me."

"We're following you, Arias," Andrew said firmly. "We've followed you this far. Wherever you go next, we'll follow you there."

Arias surrendered. "Very well. If your minds are made up, I might as well be grateful for the company."

Arias' things were loaded onto the back of one of the camels, and soon he and the others were all mounted. The squad of twenty legionnaires formed up around them, and they rode away from the church as the first beams of the morning sun appeared on the horizon.

Theognus and the others who signed the Creed and the Canons waved to Arias as the small caravan left the church and made its way to the city's main gates. Once outside the city, the caravan turned north.

As the sun rose in the distance, Andrew asked, "Arias, why was all of this necessary? Why did God allow this to be done to his church?"

"It's not God's will that his churches be delivered to the anti-Christ, Andrew," Arias explained. "It's his will that we prove our faith by overcoming obstacles, challenges, and temptations that present themselves. The Patriarchs and the bishops were tempted, and they failed to demonstrate their faith by overcoming temptation. We accepted exile, rather than giving in to temptation, thereby refusing to be corrupted. We're doing God's will by not giving into the new theology that Hosius and the Emperor created."

Andrew looked troubled. "But shouldn't your prayers have given you an indication that something terrible was going to happen? How could things have gone so wrong if God is on our side?"

Arias put his arm on Andrew's shoulder. "This is not about sides, Andrew. My prayers were for guidance – to know God's will and to have the strength to carry it out. It was God's will that I defend The Way before the council, and it's God's will that I continue to practice The Way in exile. Praying doesn't mean that we'll win. Praying is what brings us closer to God's will. This battle is lost, but the war against the anti-Christ will continue until the final victory is achieved."

"But what about our congregation?" Barnabas interrupted. "They weren't tempted, and yet they'll be led astray through no fault of their own."

"It has happened a number of times throughout history," Arias replied. "The children of Israel lost their way – lost their nation – several times. They'd plead to God to save them, and once He did, they'd forget all about Him until the next time. But God was always there, just like The Way is always there. Christians may be lost now, but there will come a time when they'll return to the true worship of God. We must be patient and ready for when that happens so we can show them what the true worship of God is.

"So our job is to preserve The Way until Christians are ready for it again?" Euric asked.

"Exactly," Arias replied.

"Then our exile is not a punishment, it's a gift?" Andrew asked.

"You catch on quickly," Arias said. "By sending us away, the Emperor has made it safe for us to continue teaching, preaching, and practicing The Way. Those we left behind must do it in secret, but we can do it openly. In his desire to cast us out, he has failed to eradicate our faith from the world. We're now free to follow The Way and worship God in the true faith."

"So, we lost, but we *won*?" Barnabas asked.

"In a manner of speaking, yes. We couldn't save the churches from the anti-Christ this time, but the anti-Christ failed to destroy us. In time, we'll rise again and challenge the anti-Christ for the hearts and minds of Christians everywhere. If we faithfully follow The Way, then when that time comes, we'll cast the anti-Christ out of the churches and return Christians to the true worship."

"How will we be remembered?" Andrew asked.

"We won't be," Arias replied. "Our names will be stricken and reviled. But it's not important for us to be remembered. Who we are is not the issue. What we do is what matters. Our reward waits for us in heaven, not here on earth, and it'll be glorious. When we stand before God, he'll say to us: *'Well done, thou good and faithful servant'.*"

The End

EPILOGUE

Arias' enemies believed that the results of the First Council of Nicaea would end the Arian controversy once and for all. They were wrong. The Way continued being taught for centuries across Europe, Asia, and Africa. Arias and his supporters may have lost at Nicaea, but they succeeded in preserving The Way for future generations of Christians all around the world.

Neither the successful conclusion of the First Council of Nicaea nor the exile of Arias and his followers ended theological disagreements within the church. There were many additional conferences held over several decades until the basic tenets of the church were finally agreed upon. The Nicaean Creed was modified several times over the years. It even took until the late 6th or early 7th century for the Bishop of Rome to be accepted as the Pope – the supreme head of the church.

Once Arias had been exiled to Illyricum, the church wasted no time in altering Arias' words to discredit him and to make him sound like a heretic and blasphemer.

A few years after Arias' exile, Emperor Constantine relented and allowed Arias and his followers to return to the empire. Emperor Constantine ordered Alexander to give communion to Arias. Alexander prayed that Arias would die before the communion had to be given. However, it was Alexander who died in 327 AD.

Athanasius succeeded Alexander as Patriarch and Bishop of Alexandria, even though he wasn't old enough to be appointed as one of the Patriarchs of the church. Constantine ordered Athanasius to give communion to Arias, and Athanasius refused.

Hosius was summoned to Milan for a council of bishops, and he was ordered to condemn Athanasius for disobeying an Imperial command. Hosius refused.

The priests and bishops still secretly loyal to Arias took advantage of Athanasius and Hosius' disobedience to the Emperor. They began a campaign to have Athanasius exiled by making numerous accusations of impropriety against him. After a thorough investigation, Athanasius was exiled in 335 AD, although he was recalled a short while later.

In 336 AD, Emperor Constantine summoned Arias to Constantinople. As Arias walked to the Imperial Palace, he died suddenly and under mysterious circumstances. Some say that he was struck down by a sudden illness, and there were rumors that Arias was going to the palace to finally sign the Nicaean Creed when he died. Most believe that Arias was assassinated, although who ordered the assassination is unknown. Athanasius and Hosius quickly attributed Arias' death as his punishment from God for being a heretic and blasphemer.

After Constantine consolidated his power (following the defeat of Maximus, Licinius, and his other enemies), he devoted himself to promoting the welfare of the empire's provinces and the people. He also made provisions for the rule and administration of the empire after his death. He placed some of his nephews in charge of less important provinces, and he designated his three sons to be the future rulers of the empire.

In early 337 AD, the Persian King, Shâpûr, began encroaching into lands of the empire, and Constantine readied his legions for battle. As he was about to march out and fight the Persians, he became ill and died in May, 337 AD. Even though he was the secular head of the church for much of his reign, he was never baptized until his deathbed and only paid lip service to Christianity as the true religion.

Constantine II became Emperor upon the death of his father. Constantine II was an Arian sympathizer, and the efforts to end Arianism after the First Council of Nicaea failed for a time. Constantine II even went so far as to consecrate a Goth as an Arian bishop and to send him to minister among the Goths and Vandals.

Constantine II made several demands on the Church to allow Arian ideas back into the Church's theology. Hosius, who was out of favor with Constantine II by this time, wrote a letter of protest to the Emperor in 353 AD that condemned imperial meddling in Church affairs. Hosius was exiled in 355 AD to Sirmium in Pannonia (Serbia). He was nearly 100 years old when he finally relented and signed the decrees of the Third Council of Sirmium. He was allowed to return to his post in Hispania, and he died shortly thereafter at the age of 102.

Following the death of Constantine II and an attempt to return the Empire to the worship of the Roman Gods, Emperor Valens continued supporting the Arian position against the supporters of the Nicaean Creed. However, his successor, Emperor Theodosius I, ended the tolerance of Arian ideas within the empire. Through imperial decrees, the persecution of those holding to Arian beliefs, and a Second Ecumenical Council in 381 AD, he expanded the Nicaean Creed and managed to have Arias' beliefs condemned.

While the actions of Theodosius I succeeded in ending Arianism in the eastern parts of the empire, it did not succeed in ending Arianism in the western and northern parts of the empire. The success of the Arian bishop sent to the Goths and Vandals kept Arianism alive there until early in the 8th century. Arianism also continued to exist in North Africa, Spain, and portions of Italy until the 6th and 7th centuries.

The Church spent years persecuting Arians and altering Arias' words to strengthen the idea of Arias being a heretic. In the 12th century, Peter the Venerable declared that Muhammad was "the successor of Arias and the Precursor to the Anti-Christ," as a way to discredit Arias and his beliefs even further. In spite of the Church's attempts to discredit Arianism, it continued to exist.

Arias lost at Nicaea, but The Way lives on. There are still Christians today who are faithful Followers of The Way, and their works of healing through the teachings of Jesus are well-documented.

"Even so faith, if it hath not works, is dead, being alone.
Yea, a man may say, Thou hast faith, and I have works:
shew me thy faith without thy works, and I will shew thee

my faith by my works. But wilt thou know, O vain man, that faith without works is dead? Was not Abraham our father justified by works, when he had offered Isaac his son upon the altar? Seest thou how faith wrought with his works, and by works was faith made perfect? Ye see then how that by works a man is justified, and not by faith only. For as the body without the spirit is dead, so faith without works is dead also."

James 2: 17, 18, 20, 21, 22, 24, 26

About the Author

Award-winning author William Speir was born in Birmingham, Alabama in 1962, attended the University of Alabama, and graduated from the University of Alabama at Birmingham in 1984. He spent over 25 years in corporate America, serving as a management consultant, consulting practice leader, IT executive, and HR/Payroll executive for top tier consulting firms and Fortune 100 companies.

During William's corporate career, he published several articles on leadership and the human impact of organizational/technology change. His first experience with book publishing was with a series of ten textbooks he authored about field artillery in the 19th century. These textbooks were later consolidated into a single volume and re-published in 2015 as *Muzzle-Loading Artillery for Reenactors*.

In addition to his artillery manual, William has published 14 novels, including an 8-book action-adventure series (*The Knights of the Saltire Series*), four historical novels (*King's Ransom, The Saga of Asbjorn Thorleikson, Nicaea – The Rise of the Imperial Church*, and *Arthur, King*), one fantasy novel (*The Kingstone of Airmid*), and one science fiction novel (*The Olympium of Bacchus 12*).

William is a 5-time Royal Palm Literary Award winner: 2014 Second Place Unpublished Historical Fiction for *King's Ransom*, 2015 Second Place Unpublished Historical Fiction for *The Saga of Asbjorn Thorleikson*, 2017 Second Place Published Historical Fiction for *Arthur, King*, 2017 First Place Published Historical Fiction for *Nicaea – The Rise of the Imperial Church*, and 2017 First Place Published Science Fiction for *The Olympium of Bacchus 12*.

For more information about William Speir, please visit his website at WilliamSpeir.com.

Progressive Rising Phoenix Press is an independent publisher. We offer wholesale discounts and multiple binding options with no minimum purchases for schools, libraries, book clubs, and retail vendors. We also offer rewards for libraries, schools, independent book stores, and book clubs. Please visit our website and wholesale discount page at:

www.ProgressiveRisingPhoenix.com

Progressive Rising Phoenix Press is adding new titles from our award-winning authors on a regular basis and has books in the following genres: children's chapter books and picture books, middle grade, young adult, action adventure, mystery and suspense, contemporary fiction, romance, historical fiction, fantasy, science fiction, and non-fiction covering a variety of topics from military to inspirational to biographical. Visit our website to see our updated catalogue of titles.